SOLDIER

THE KOREAN CONTRACT

SOLDIER OF FORTUNE 2

THE KOREAN CONTRACT

Doug Armstrong

First published in Great Britain 1994
22 Books, Invicta House, Sir Thomas Longley Road,
Rochester, Kent

Copyright © 1994 by 22 Books

The moral right of the author has been asserted

A CIP catalogue record for this book is available from the
British Library

ISBN 1 898125 25 2

10 9 8 7 6 5 4 3 2 1

Typeset by Hewer Text Composition Services, Edinburgh
Printed in Great Britain by Cox and Wyman Limited, Reading

1

It was ironic, he thought, that he was about to die so near the graves of his ancestors. Of course he had been promised all sorts of things if he talked, but he knew, in his heart of hearts, that the only real fate awaiting him was death.

He wasn't afraid of it, but he hoped it would come quickly. He had already suffered enough at the hands of his captors. He had hoped that vengeance would be his, but it was not to be. As he hung on the damp wall, he remembered that one of his uncles had once called vengeance the highest of all honours, but it was an honour that would now fall to someone else. He had come to accept it.

There had been plenty of time for such thoughts during the night. It was strange how the most forgotten of things surfaced from the memory when you were about to die. Nothing profound, but little pictures from his boyhood visits to Sokch'o and the family tombs where he had been taken on festival days to make the offerings and say the prayers that he had long since scorned as so much wasted energy. Why did he have to remember them now? Was it his conscience, or was there really some unseen spirit, finally making a half-hearted attempt to console this lost and broken piece of humanity that was about to be crushed?

A smile creased his cracked and swollen lips and he shifted awkwardly in the shackles that chained him to the cellar wall. He raised his head and flinched at the bolts of sudden pain that shot through his body with the effort. He could tell that outside it was daybreak, for the slenderest crack of light penetrated under the heavy wooden door, despite the filthy blanket that had been nailed across it on the inside to deprive his senses and destabilize his mental equilibrium. Again he smiled.

Over the last three days, that crack of light had become almost a friend. None of the guards had noticed it because whenever they came into the cellar they first turned on the light from outside. Every time, he would first hear their footsteps approaching from across a gravel-covered yard, then the bolts of the outer door. Then there were some steps descending to a narrow corridor and lastly some more bolts and the heavy, ill-fitting key grinding in a lock. There must be a skylight of some sort in the outer chamber which had not been properly covered, and through this came his secret friend and ally, to comfort him and help him remind himself that whatever horrors were going on in the cellar, outside the day was coming and going as it always had.

Whenever he was being interrogated, he tried to distance his mind from his body and to focus on the world outside that was going about its business oblivious to the sufferings of this one tormented soul. Again, the teachings of his boyhood had come to his rescue. Separate the mind from the body. Look upon the broken flesh if you must, but view it as someone else's. Take your inner self elsewhere.

It had been impossible at the start and although he

had steeled every nerve and sinew, he had screamed despite his efforts at control. That had given them satisfaction, he had seen. It seemed to be an essential part of the process for the tall one: to inflict pain for its own sake and not merely to extract the information that they repeatedly said he must give them.

Then he had finally managed it. He had taken his mind away and floated across the surrounding hills, seeing the colours of the rich woodland and the hot springs, entered the houses of the hill farmers, walked invisible through the busy streets of Sokch'o and Yangyang, looking into the shops where people lived and breathed, talked and bartered, all oblivious to his presence in spirit and to the empty body being torn apart in the squalid secrecy of the nearby hills.

His captors hadn't noticed at first and had continued with the interrogation assuming that he was simply being stubborn. Of course it had been the tall one, the boss, who had first noticed the change in his prisoner's mind-set. The other two guards were as tough as oxen, but also as stupid. The tall one had then tried new techniques and each time, for a while, they worked. But once the separation of mind and body had been mastered, it became ever easier to effect.

Finally, giving up in exasperation, the tall one had subjected him to a merciless and uncontrolled beating that had left him in his present state, hanging in his chains, convinced that the end would not be long in coming. Unable to get the information they had wanted, they would now dispose of him quickly.

In a sudden realization that shocked him to his core, the prisoner understood that, mixed with the riot of terror and other emotions flooding through his brain, was a slender thread of gratitude. For somehow, over the period of his imprisonment, he had been put in touch with things that he had thought lost for all time. It was as if, in the extreme suffering inflicted by his tormentors, he had managed to link hands across the years with the family he had betrayed so long ago. But, more importantly, he had linked hands with the person he had once been and had thought dead. That person was not dead – simply waiting in some hidden place deep within himself to be contacted and given new life. Again the irony struck him that such new life should only come now, moments before his bodily death.

But at least the contact had been made. In his agony he had reached out and found them all there, waiting for him. His ancestors. Perhaps this was the only way to find them. Or rather, it was only at such moments of death that they drew near in readiness to gather another family spirit into their arms. The prayers and mantras he had mumbled through as a boy, usually bored and waiting for the ritual to end so he could go racing through the trees to play hide-and-seek with his brothers, gathered about him now and made a strange kind of sense.

Once more he raised his head to look across the darkness at the crack of light. He could hear footsteps coming across the yard, crunching on the gravel, and then the outer door being opened. There were several of them, the tall one in the lead as usual. They came down the steps, muttering to each other, and then the bolts were being pulled back and the key was turning in the lock. Suddenly the prisoner was blinded as the light was switched on and the guards burst into his room. He knew it was useless to pretend to be asleep – he had tried it before. So he simply looked from one to the other. And he knew that this was it. The two stupid

4

ones refused to meet his eyes. Only the tall one stared back. There was no hatred on his face, just complete indifference as if the whole terrible episode had, for him, been an exercise or a game. Unfortunately it was a game that he had lost and he didn't like losing. He wasn't used to it and the prisoner was about to pay dearly for his victory.

Francis Kwang didn't like to think of himself as an impatient man but as he stared out of the broad french windows that led from the modern but tastefully furnished open-plan ground floor of his country villa on to a large, sweeping, wooden balcony, he clenched and unclenched his fists, clasped behind his back. It was a sign that anyone who knew him would instantly recognize as a warning signal. From the bedroom at the top of a wrought-iron spiral staircase he could hear Lulu humming to herself; she had put on a Frank Sinatra record that she had obviously found while going through his cupboards, so, while old blue eyes was busy doing it *My Way*, Kwang was being kept from doing things to Lulu his way by that idiot 'Babs' Butler. What kind of name was that for a soldier? He snorted in derision at the thought of the white fleshy major attempting to do anything even remotely military.

From upstairs the humming stopped as Lulu changed the record, managing to bounce the needle across at least three other tracks in the process. In the delectable moments of peace before Tom Jones ground into another number, a woman's voice called down from the top of the banisters.

'Francis, aren't you coming upstairs?'

Kwang turned round and the forced smile was

startled into a genuine glow of pleasure when he saw that Lulu had already undressed and was wearing the nightgown he had bought her on his last trip into Seoul. Standing at the top of the stairs, she posed for him, twirling this way and that, pulling open the hem to reveal a tantalizing glimpse of her long, olive-coloured thigh.

'Do you like it, darling? It suits me, doesn't it?'

Kwang nodded. 'Yes, my dear. I'll be with you in a minute. Go and warm the bed for me. That's my kitten.'

With a pout of disappointment Lulu flounced out of sight but a moment later was humming her inane tune again. She was like a rabbit, Kwang thought. One minute her entire attention was focused on something as if her life depended on it, and the next she had completely forgotten what it was and was pursuing some altogether different and vapid thought. Still, that had its advantages. Conversation, such as it was, was effortless. But then he hadn't acquired her for her conversation.

Looking once more out of the expanse of window, he cast his eyes over the stunning vista before him. At this time of year the tree-covered hills were a beautiful patchwork of greens and golds. Rising into jagged peaks, they were clad to the summits with pines, spruce and birch, and all manner of bushes and shrubs. From down in the deep valleys wisps of smoke rose from the few farmsteads and monasteries that lay between his villa and the coast many miles to the east. Looking to the north, he noted how they rose ever higher until they seemed to melt into the sky. But in that direction lay the border and the ridiculously termed demilitarized zone, the DMZ, or 'D M Zee' as the Americans called it. It was one of the most militarized areas on the planet but with a double-speak worthy of Orwell, it was referred to with clinical detachment as the DMZ.

Kwang sighed. Ever since the Korean peninsula had been partitioned along the 38th Parallel at the end of the war in 1953, the heavily armed truce had frozen the two states in unrelenting but impotent hostility. Backed by their foreign allies throughout the decades of the Cold War, neither side was strong enough to overcome the other, nor indeed would they have been allowed by those same allies to try.

But with the collapse of the old Soviet Union and with China embroiled in the uncertainties of reform, all of that was changing. The old pieces of the political jigsaw were inexorably shifting and soon the greatest of prizes would once again be up for grabs.

Glancing for the hundredth time at his Cartier watch, Kwang was about to give way to a combination of impatience and mounting lust when the phone rang. In two strides he was bending over the glass-topped coffee-table.

'Yes?'

'Mr Kwang?' The voice on the other end of the line was instantly recognizable. Coiled like a snake about to strike, Kwang forced himself to relax, sinking on to the white sofa and crossing his legs with effemi-nate grace.

'You've kept me waiting again. I hope it isn't always going to be like this, Major Butler.'

'Babs. Everyone calls me Babs,' said the voice a little uncertainly, and then, remembering the threatening tone of the renowned Francis Kwang: 'No, of course not. It's taken me quite a while to get what you wanted, that's all.'

Kwang revelled in the hint of submission, feeling sufficiently appeased to allow himself to relent.

'So tell me, Babs, have you got what I want?'

'Yes. The team's almost complete.'

'Almost? I don't think you realize the urgency of what we're attempting here.'

There was a flutter at the other end of the line before the voice replied: 'I do, believe me. But these aren't the easiest men to get hold of. You don't find them in the Yellow Pages, you know.' And then, regretting the stab at humour, it went on: 'I mean, they . . . Look, Mr Kwang, the team's virtually together. There's just one other guy I can't get hold of.'

'What do you mean?'

'I mean, I'm waiting for his reply.'

'Then get someone else instead.'

For the first time in the conversation the voice of Babs Butler took on the ring of authority, at home on his own ground at last.

'There is no one else. At least not of the same quality as this guy. You said you wanted the best in the business, and that's what I'm getting you. But it takes time, a bit of negotiating here, some encouragement there . . .'

'Spare me the advertisement, Major Butler, if you please.'

With the nub of their conversation complete, Kwang felt his concentration wandering. He had waited all morning for his chauffeur to return from the airport with Lulu and now she was here again he was being prevented from getting his money's worth by this mumbling idiot of a Westerner. The man was being paid an obscene amount of money simply to hire a bunch of marginally capable thugs. But oh no, he had to inflate himself to the status of professional. A connoisseur. It was really quite pathetic.

Lulu, on the other hand, was a real professional. Ever since Kwang had met her in the cocktail lounge of the Hyatt Regency in Seoul, he had been besotted by her. Her look of sweet innocence had captivated him instantly but he had quickly been enlightened as to the standard of her hidden talents. Since then he had flown her across to his villa in the Sorak-san National Park numerous times, and on each occasion she had never failed to surprise him with her variety and guile.

The voice on the phone droned on and on and was in the middle of something about someone flying in from Australia or South Africa when Kwang's patience snapped.

'Just tell me one thing. Will they be at the camp and ready in time? Yes or no?'

'Erm . . .'

'Yes or no?'

'Ye . . . es.'

'Right then. I'll see you there as planned.'

Kwang was about to hang up when the voice hurriedly stammered something down the line.

'What was that?' Kwang snapped.

'My money, Mr Kwang.'

Kwang sighed in exasperation. This current project had occupied him for several months already and his concerns about it centred on matters of far greater import than mere finance. The stakes were possibly the highest he had ever gambled for and to lose would mean . . .

But his mind automatically veered on to a safer track. Failure was out of the question. He wasn't altogether an unreasonable man and he appreciated that not everyone was fortunate enough to be called upon to shape history and the fate of nations. In a voice that could be mistaken for kind, he replied: 'I suggest you check your account again, Major Butler. You might have a very pleasant surprise.'

When he had replaced the receiver, Kwang felt the need to wash his hands. This part of the business was so sordid and vulgar. He crossed the fur rug to the bar and ran the tap until the water lost its mountain-spring iciness and steamed pleasantly. Then, cracking several cubes of ice from their tray in the freezer, he poured himself a generous Scotch and watched it swirl around the smooth blocks in pale-golden luxury. He gently shook the tumbler from side to side, listening to the chink of the ice and, holding it up to the light, watched the patterns shimmering through the perfectly cut glass.

This was the way to begin, he thought. A slow alerting of the senses to the pleasures to come. The music from upstairs had stopped and he knew that Lulu would have heard his conversation end and would be preparing herself to receive him. He wondered how she would surprise him this time.

Sipping the whisky, he was about to make his way to the bedroom when he remembered something. He pushed a small button and spoke into the intercom.

'Yi, could you come up to the house for a moment.'

He had almost forgotten. That wouldn't do at all. The operation was now far too advanced to allow anything to go wrong, not even if Lulu was waiting for her lover. It was already beyond the point of no return. The countdown had started and over the coming days he would have to keep his wits about him. Even while making love.

There was a knock at the door and when Kwang pressed the security button it opened to reveal a fit, lean man in his early thirties. Comfortably over six foot tall, Yi Soong walked like a cat, perfectly balanced, the natural spring of each step disguised in part by military bearing ingrained during his years as an officer in the Republic of Korea special forces. His trim waist and broad shoulders spoke of strength and agility, but it was somehow from his gait and very core that the sense of immense physical power emanated.

'Still no luck?'

Yi Soong's shake of the head was barely perceptible.

'Hm.' Kwang hadn't really believed that they would get anything out of the infiltrator. They were always the toughest individuals to crack, selected, as much as anything, for their ability specifically to resist interrogation.

'It's not good for the men to see, sir. They might start to fear the mettle of the enemy.'

There was a surprising quality about Yi's voice, a sophistication that was masked by his imposing appearance. Kwang had always known that Yi had a first-class brain beneath his close-cropped, jet-black hair. In fact he was an awesome character altogether and Kwang was grateful, not for the first time, that Yi was in his employment. He thought a moment longer.

'Finish him.'

Yi nodded again.

'Rid us of every trace that he ever existed. We can't afford the slightest risk of compromise.'

He gazed out of the window and took another sip of his drink. When he looked back at the door it was closed. Yi had gone without a sound.

Kwang shuddered. Tipping back the glass, he drained it in one gulp, closing his eyes and holding his head back, luxuriating in the twin sensations of the liquid, at once ice-cold and pure fire. Mounting the steps to his bedroom, he pushed open the door and gazed at Lulu. She had removed her nightgown and fallen asleep on the bed. He went and sat down beside her, gently stroking her smooth, unblemished skin, soft and warm. She moaned in her light sleep and, half-waking, rolled on to her back with eyes still closed.

As his hand moved over her stomach and up on to her breasts, Kwang felt them harden beneath his palm. Circling the nipples with his fingers, he felt Lulu wriggle with delight. With eyes still closed she reached up to his neck and pulled his mouth down to hers, opening her lips as they met.

When Babs Butler put down the phone from his conversation with Francis Kwang, he too poured himself a stiff whisky, but for very different reasons.

'The bastard,' he said to himself, his palms moist with nervous perspiration. 'That slant-eyed, gook-fucking bastard.'

He could tell from the Korean's evident impatience that his whore was probably loafing in the background. Babs had seen her when he had been graced with an audience with the great Kwang the other week. He was reluctant to admit that there was a high degree of envy rolled up in his resentment. She was a stunner, one of those gorgeous little Asian tarts that Babs had come to love seeking out on his visits to the brothels in the It'aewan district where the American GIs hung out.

She was called Lulu or something, but who cared about her name? The price-tag was the problem. Kwang had doubtless found her in some high-class joint and for now she was his and his alone. But sooner or later she would end up where girls like her all ended up in Seoul, flogging her raddled wares to some spotty teenaged Yank doing his stint in the army to pay his way through college. By then Kwang would be deep in the knickers of his next young thing, and probably even richer and more powerful than he was now. It made you want to spit.

Babs took a gulp of whisky, refilled his grimy beaker and sank down into a frayed armchair, the centrepiece and only significant furnishing of his sitting-room. He allowed himself the luxury of wallowing for a further five minutes in colourful daydreams of lurid and impossible sexual exploits with Lulu, sinking ever deeper into the shapeless armchair and staring into the middle distance through dull, half-closed eyes.

Starting into full consciousness, he blinked, wiped his mouth with the back of one hand and reached across to a bulging file on the side table. Leafing through the pages, he made a mental tally of the team so far. For once in his life he was proud of himself. Kwang had asked him to recruit the best and he really believed that he had. As he skipped from page to page Babs counted them off, grinning with self-satisfaction.

'Jee-zus,' he said. 'He's going to get the Magnificent fucking Seven and the Dirty Dozen rolled into one!'

He leaned back in his chair and stretched towards the ceiling feeling his joints crack in surprise at the effort.

'The Ghostbusting sodding A-Team!'

13

Chuckling at his own wit, he pulled himself out of the chair and waddled over to the whisky bottle. He had done it. He had really and truly, bloody done it! When the first discreet enquiries had been made some weeks ago by Kwang's henchman, Babs had marvelled that a guy like that should need a guy like him. Sure, Babs had been good in his day. He had been in the Congo with Mike Hoare, hadn't he? In fact, there was hardly a colonial war or brush-fire campaign that he hadn't seen in one capacity or another. But it had been a while since he had last bloodied his hands. Babs Butler had been an agent for some time, a middleman and go-between, setting up deals and putting together teams for various hirers.

Surveying the miserable suite of rooms that he called home, he found himself wondering where all his earnings had gone. None of it ever seemed to stick. Only shit did that.

Then, one evening when he had been half-cut in a bar near the Wonhyo Bridge, this evil sodding monster with a smile to chill a vindaloo had approached him with a proposal that had set his head spinning. There had followed the meeting with Kwang and . . . Babs your uncle!'

Of course he hadn't a clue what Francis bloody Kwang was up to or what he wanted with the biggest band of cutthroats since Henry Morgan sailed the seven seas. But why should he bother? Kwang had promised him good money and Babs knew he could deliver. The team was due to assemble next Monday. Babs had laid on a little surprise reception for them before they all moved up to a secret training camp near the border where they would be equipped and briefed on the mission. Kwang had said that his own aide would then take charge; Yi the monster was apparently going to lead the expedition himself.

'So, he's not just a pretty face,' Babs had been rash enough to say. By that time his meeting with Kwang had been nearly at an end and Babs had enjoyed several large tumblers of remarkably fine Scotch. Even so, through the haze of his blurring vision he had seen a sweet smile spread across Kwang's face as he repeated Babs's comment to the monster who had been hovering in the background like the earth-bound spirit of some dead relative.

The monster had glided forward without seeming to use his legs and, placing a hand on either arm of Babs's chair, had bent over him, grinning broadly, revealing a perfect set of glistening white teeth that reminded Babs of a Dracula movie he had seen, although this titbit of information he thought it best to keep to himself.

'My name is Yi Soong,' the monster had said with surprising friendliness.

'And what do your friends call you?' Babs had replied, offering him a pudgy hand and hoping that he'd get it back intact. The monster was obviously puzzled by the question, answering it obliquely.

'You can call me Mr Yi,' he had said after a moment's pause, his grin freezing into something much less pleasant.

Babs's hand had hung limply unacknowledged in the air for a second or two before he had replaced it on the reassuring familiarity of his glass. He had smiled meekly at the time, thinking to himself, Well, fuck you, Mr Yi. I'll call you Odd Job if I want.

Remembering the meeting, he chuckled to himself. Almost everything was ready. Looking at his watch he decided to lash out on a decent meal in It'aewan, so pulling on a shapeless jacket and thumbing through his wallet to check his resources, he bounced out of the apartment, locking the door as an afterthought. He didn't have anything worth stealing, but it would be best to keep the file secure.

Once out in the street he took a deep breath of the fumes. The traffic was particularly heavy at that time of day and, having decided to take the subway, Babs pushed through the crowds to the nearest station, bought a ticket and fought his way on to an escalator. Once a month the government held civil-defence drills and for anything up to half an hour the entire city would grind to a halt. Cars were abandoned where they stood and people would pack into the basement shopping arcades and subways, anywhere under cover and out of sight of the notional threat of North Korean aircraft. As they were only a few minutes' flying time from the border, it was essential that the drills were efficient and disciplined. Disciplined? Standing on the escalator and looking around him Babs thought that the people of Seoul made the Germans look like a bunch of pissed Millwall supporters. It never ceased to amaze him how, within seconds of the first siren, the streets would be utterly deserted. But then they would have to be if ever the North really did decide to attack. In that event, the good Lord himself would be hard pushed to deliver the city. The last time it happened, in 1950, Seoul had been fought over at least twice and been flattened in the process. Hardly two bricks had been left standing on top of each other; the next time, who could tell? The North might even play the final card and use nuclear weapons. If they had them, that is.

*　　*　　*

Yi had enjoyed his morning workout. It was always so much more enjoyable having a real person to practise on. But then in some respects the prisoner was a disappointment. He had barely uttered a sound and Yi was ashamed to find himself even respecting the man. He seemed to have deep inner reserves that Yi hoped he also possessed.

After leaving Francis Kwang, Yi had decided it was such a beautiful day that he would go for a run before carrying out the directive. He was no simple henchman and enjoyed considerable leeway in the execution of his orders. So, after changing into a trim-fitting tracksuit and trainers, he had strapped on ankle and wrist weights and jogged out of the compound towards the unmade path that led across an area cleared of undergrowth, through a tall barbed-wire fence topped with razor wire, and off down the wooded hillside.

The air was wonderfully fresh and crisp. He fully appreciated his boss's preference for the countryside over the city. Seoul was full of American servicemen and Western or Japanese tourists. The heart of the city had been prostituted to the foreigners, but it wouldn't be for ever.

Having reached the foot of the hill, Yi pushed on up the far side of the valley, selecting a narrow trail that wound through the trees and crossed a stream of crystal-clear water. At the top of the far crest he stopped and looked back over the two miles he had come. The villa was well concealed and could hardly be seen until you were almost upon it. Only the pointed wooden roof could be detected protruding from the green and golden treetops. Yi sought out a branch at exactly the right height, jumped up to grab it and did fifty rapid pull-ups, changing his grip from under to over, halfway through.

Then, down on the forest floor coated with pine needles, he burned through a hundred press-ups and two hundred sit-ups before jumping to his feet and setting off on the return jog back to the villa. It would soon be time for the next international Taekwondo championship and Yi very much hoped that he would be able to compete as usual. But the mission obviously took top priority and if that meant that his competing days were over, then so be it. The need for absolute secrecy might well prevent him taking such a prominent role in the games again, but he had had his day: six times national champion, and world champion twice. His skills these days had a more practical bent. There was a huge difference between facing an opponent across the bare wooden boards of the arena and tackling a sworn enemy, possibly armed, in some backstreet at night.

But he had taken to it like a natural. His time in the ROK special forces had been the first step; there it was not unusual for men to be killed in training. But after that he had met Francis Kwang and nothing had been the same again. It was as if his whole life had been a preparation for this: from his long hours as a serious-minded youth in the training gyms, to his military service, officer selection and special forces work, then his triumph in numerous tournaments and at last the approach by Kwang, one of the top figures in the South Korean intelligence service.

Yi entered the compound and loosened up with some stretching exercises, before steadying his breathing as he had been taught to do long ago by his instructors. Then, with joints and muscles loose and supple, and feeling powerful enough to uproot a tree and snap it in two, he adopted a low fighting stance and went through a few basic punches and kicks.

A door opened on the other side of the yard and one of the guards coughed politely. Yi ignored him for a full two minutes before bringing his exercises to a close.

'What is it?'

The guard bowed from the waist and with a jerk of the head towards the open door behind him, asked: 'What are we to do with him?'

'You are to do absolutely nothing with him. Not yet.' But as an afterthought he asked: 'Have the pigs been fed yet?'

'No.'

'Good. They'll be getting a little extra protein in their diet today.'

The guard looked puzzled for a moment until the light dawned and a thin smile spread across his pock-marked cheeks.

'OK,' Yi said. 'Let's do it.'

Unbuckling his weights, Yi grinned with pleasure at the wonderful sudden lightness of his limbs. He looked full into the sun as if daring it to take him on, and with a final glance around the compound, he followed the guard down into the cellar.

After days of interrogation he was suddenly bored with the prisoner and the whole business of the infiltration into the network. Who cared what he had discovered? In all likelihood he had been found out before he had time to do any real damage. The mercenaries were arriving in a few days, the camp was prepared, and he, Yi Soong, was at the height of his powers.

Placing himself in front of the pathetic creature chained to the wall, he beckoned the two guards aside. Then, after sinking once again into the fighting stance, he waited until, with a great effort, the prisoner raised his head, before speaking softly to him.

In the house overhead, Kwang supported his upper body on clenched fists, his neck muscles hard and glistening, gasping as his pelvis drove forward in urgent spasms. Lulu twisted beneath him on the bed, her tanned legs locked at the ankles in the small of his back, forcing him down and in. She bucked, ever faster, ever softer, then froze, a shriek escaping from her gritted teeth as her nails dug into the taut shoulders of Kwang, who was transfixed on his own summit, suddenly motionless save for the subsiding pulse of his hips, ebbing like a quiet sea.

The motion, when it came, was swift and beautiful in its fluidity and power but terrible in its effect. Yi Soong seemed to draw on some invisible reserve of untold strength, spinning into a reverse back-kick of lightning speed and ferocity.

As his heel made perfect contact with the centre of the prisoner's chest, the dark cellar resounded with the sickening crack, and before the guards had realized what had happened, gaping in mesmerized fascination as if watching a cobra with its prey, the sternum had shattered, puncturing the exploding heart with jagged ribs.

2

Without appearing to, Terry Williams was carefully gauging his opponent. Some new kid who had been watching too many Chuck Norris videos, no doubt replaying particular fight sequences again and again, freeze-framing them to practise later in front of his bedroom mirror when his mum had given him his tea and buggered off to watch *Eastenders*.

The image was so depressing he felt like laughing out loud. Yes, here it came, a bloody great clumsy step forward in preparation for an attack, so obvious to even an untrained eye, he wondered if he had time to slip out for a cup of tea before the kick was landed. What made it worse was the expression on the youth's face, a sort of grimace that might suit Steven Seagal in *Marked for Death*, but smeared across the gob of this pimply git, it made Terry want to throw up.

In it came, the kid's rear leg rising with painful slowness off the floor and coming round at waist height with a final effort to crank it up at the last moment and hit Terry in the face. He was even having a stab at a *kiai*, the shout that was supposed to come from the gut, but in the kid's case was uttered feebly from his throat, sounding more like a newt being stepped on.

Trying hard to disguise his impatience, Terry

brushed away the approaching limb, grabbing the trouser leg as he did so. A look of alarm appeared on the kid's face, replaced a second later by shock as Terry executed an *ashi-barai* footsweep, knocking his opponent's supporting leg from under him and taking him down to the floor. Being a decent bloke at heart, Terry let him down lightly, keeping a firm grip on his clothing. The finishing move would have been a drop-punch to the face, shattering the bone and, if done with full force, fatal. But instead, with one effortless heave, Terry yanked the kid to his feet again and slapped him on the shoulder.

'That *mawashi-geri* is coming along nicely, Matthew. Keep at it.'

With his self-esteem salvaged in front of his mates, the kid blushed and swaggered back to his place on the dojo floor among the other kneeling students. Tossing back greasy locks, he rolled his shoulders as he walked. Get a shift on, Popeye, Terry thought. Run home to mummy for your spinach.

'Right. Let's have you, Barry.'

The training sessions always finished like this. At the end of formal practice, the *kata* and some free-fighting, Terry would take on a few selected students to give them a chance of going all out. In answer to Terry's command, a youth in his late teens sprang to his feet and leapt into the arena. Taking up his position opposite Terry, he bowed from the waist, but kept his eyes alert and fixed on his instructor. Good, Terry thought. Stay alert, stay alive.

'*Hajime!*' With the command to begin, the youth danced backwards to the edge of the arena and moved round to the left, circling, looking for an opening in Terry's guard. Good! Terry was pleased to see the youth's style, his awareness of his opponent, his measurement of the distance between them and his use of the different hand positions.

Terry tried a couple of exploratory moves forward and on each occasion the youth responded as Terry would have hoped, always moving, always changing his position and stance. To remain static was to offer yourself up as a target. What was more, whenever he moved he shifted his weight carefully, maintaining his balance at all times, ready for any attack that Terry might try to throw at him.

OK, Terry thought, come to daddy. After circling a few more times and trying several unoriginal attacking moves, he purposely froze on the spot, breathing heavily as if winded. He allowed his eyes to wander to the clock on the wall behind his opponent. The youth, who also knew it was there, fell for the ploy, hook, line and sinker. In a flash he had closed the gap and was lunging at Terry's face, dropping his centre of balance at the last moment, turning his attack into a feint and using his other fist for the real attack to the solar plexus.

Terry saw it coming but even so the kid was fast and he only just managed to step back in time, dropping his right hand and deflecting the blow with the heel of his right palm in a downwards block. Then, with the youth's momentum still carrying him forward into the space where his target should have been, Terry sidestepped and executed a left punch to the temples. He felt the youth was good enough to take a little pain, so he delivered the blow, albeit at greatly reduced power.

'Good!' he said as the youth sprawled on the floorboards. 'You'll get me yet.'

When the class had been dismissed and the last of them had changed and gone home, Terry turned off the overhead lights and went to his office by the gym's entrance and the notice-boards. It was dark outside and rain swept across the car park. Coming off the Bristol Channel, it drenched the bleak Swansea streets and petered out somewhere over the Black Mountains. He had pulled a tracksuit over his karate *gi* and stepped into a pair of flip-flops. He kept a kettle in the large bottom drawer of his desk, and after making himself a cup of black instant coffee, he sat back and blew on the steam before sipping the strong, dark liquid.

A light flickered in the night outside and he made a mental note to fix the sign over the doorway.

'Karate Dojo – Terry Williams, Fourth Dan. Children's classes every Saturday,' it read.

Yes, there was many a toddler in Swansea simply dying for someone to kick sand in their eyes. Go on punk, make my day.

Terry smiled. He'd be lucky if he could afford this month's rent, let alone buy a new strip light for the sign. The trouble was that kids just didn't have the self-discipline nowadays. He knew he sounded like a dull old fart, but he didn't care; just let anyone say it to his face. Oddly enough, he enjoyed taking the children's class the most. At least they never pretended it was anything but a game. The older kids were the worst. All they wanted to learn were the fancy moves, the stylish spinning and jumping kicks and all that shit. No one ever used that crap in competition, or if you did, you only did it once.

He leafed through some papers in the plastic 'Pending' tray. Most were bills. Since he'd lost his job and had been obliged to rely on the earnings of his karate dojo, things had gone from bad to pig-awful.

Then, out of the blue, he had received the letter from Babs Butler. Terry cursed him for getting in touch again. It wasn't so much that he had specifically told Babs after the last time that he was retiring from that line of business; more that the devious fat bastard should catch him at such a low point when he was vulnerable to a good offer. And the offer was certainly good, suspiciously so.

Terry had never been to Korea and the idea of seeing the Far East again was a big attraction. He had been based in Hong Kong some years back when in the British Army, and had got as far as Okinawa, where he had spent several months training under Master Nishime Higashi, one of the greatest karate masters in the world.

The rest of his army career had been spent among the featureless towns and training areas of the north German plain, preparing for a war that no one ever really believed would come. Disillusioned to the point of despair, he had chucked in his hand and after a period of trying to hold down a job in Civvy Street, had answered an advert in a flashy magazine. Before he knew what was happening, he found himself bouncing along a dust track in central Africa in the back of a Nissan pick-up truck, being fired at by guerrillas with an RPG 7 rocket-launcher.

But all that was several years ago now, and like the world itself, he had changed or, more to the point, grown up. When he was younger he was able to excuse his participation in other people's wars by saying that they would be fighting each other whether he was there or not. Later, however, he grew tired of the sight, sound and smell of death and went home to Wales wanting no more part of it.

He had even married and now had two kids of his own, but it hadn't lasted and his wife had taken the kids with her. He knew that he wasn't the easiest bloke in the world to live with but he bitterly regretted the separation. He kept telling himself that he would patch it up somehow, make it up to his wife and kids, but in his present state, when he couldn't even afford a new strip light for the dojo sign, he was hardly much of a prospect.

Balancing back in his chair sipping his coffee, he jumped when the phone rang. He knew before he picked up the receiver who it would be and, sure enough, a moment later he was listening to the familiar voice again, the sentences punctuated with the unnerving gaps of a long-distance call from the other side of the planet.

'Terry? Is that Terry Williams?'

He didn't answer. Let the bugger guess.

'Have you considered my offer?'

'Yes.'

'I don't like to press you, but I need an answer.'

Terry remembered hearing that everything before the word 'but' is a lie.

'Yes.'

'You'll come, then?'

'Who's putting up the money?'

There was a chuckle at the other end of the line and Terry could imagine the loose, thin lips slobbering into the mouthpiece.

'An old hand like you knows better than to ask questions like that.'

'I just want to be sure that the money's up front, not like that Peruvian fiasco.'

'It's there, trust me.'

'I really would be fucked if I did that.'

The same chuckle repeated itself. 'Look, come over and see for yourself. I'll send you a return ticket and if you don't like the set-up when you get out here, you're free to leave at any time. Can't say fairer than that.'

Terry let Butler stew for a while. What the hell? The rain was lashing against the window, the flickering light had gone out altogether, and he felt suddenly very alone.

'OK, Babs. You've got me.'

'Terrific. I've put together a great team, you'll see. How's Liz?'

'We've split up.'

'Oh, I'm sorry. But at least you're a free man again.'

Before Babs condemned himself with any more 'buts', Terry brought the conversation to a close. Afterwards he sat in the dark for a long time and then did something he hadn't done in a while. He stopped at The Bull on the way back to his bedsit and got horribly drunk.

Pushing himself up the hill into the teeth of the blizzard, Andy Buchan cursed himself to keep going. The pack on his back was almost as big as he was but it was mainly his exhaustion and the biting wind that doubled him over as he laboured up the slope, each step draining his dwindling reserves of energy.

The moment he had heard the weather forecast announce that heavy snow and high winds were expected in the Grampians over the next three days, he had packed his bergen and taken the bus north out of Glasgow. All the way along the banks of Loch Lomond and right on until it finally laboured into the Cairngorms, he stared morosely out of the misting window. The bus was nearly full of tourists and some stupid English bastards had tried to start a sing-song with a selection that even Kenneth McKellar would have spurned. Well, maybe not. But it put Andy in a vile mood anyway.

Not that that was difficult. His temper had been his downfall on many occasions and he had never really bothered to try to master it. For a while the Paras had provided a fitting home for his anger. Selection had been a piece of piss, especially the 'milling', when you had to go all out for the other bugger and do as much damage as you could before the whistle. He'd loved that. The best thing was to get put against an officer. In P Company there was no rank among the candidates and the officers always thought that when it came to milling they were supposed to box. They could handle the assault courses and the tabs but milling was something else. Getting the shit punched out of them by a squaddie was not what they had gone through Sandhurst for.

Sure enough, Andy had been paired with a six-foot artillery captain. He could see the bloke smiling as he sized up the grubby little Glaswegian the PTIs were about to feed to him. Dashed fine of you, he'd probably thought; I promise I'll go easy on the fellow. The silly bugger even had a toothbrush moustache and some of the lads had christened him Aldershot Adolf.

Andy had come out spitting like a scalded cat stroked the wrong way, arms and feet flailing. His opponent had blinked in consternation and attempted a combined jab and hook, by which time Andy was in under his guard and kneeing him in the balls like there was no tomorrow. For the captain there wasn't. He was casualty-evacuated off the course the same afternoon and Andy was threatened with being RTU'd if he tried that again. But he was buggered if he'd return to his unit. The chief PTI gave him a sly wink when he came out of the OC's office.

'Don't worry, lad,' he said. 'It's stuff like that took Goose Green.'

That was just about the only compliment anyone had ever paid Andy and he didn't know how to react. He remembered feeling appallingly shy and embarrassed, and felt like laying one on the PTI himself for being nice to him.

After that he had enjoyed the only stable period in his life and over the next five years had done as many courses as he could, compensating in some way for the truancy that had wrecked his education. Most of them were physical: combat survival, mountaineering, Arctic warfare. He had tried an unarmed-combat course but came away with the conviction that it was purely for wankers. If you had to drop a bloke, simply nut him. Why ponce about with fancy footwork and hand techniques? The instructors had probably never been in a real fight. When it came to a rumble the outcome would depend on guts – that and nothing else.

Eventually he had been recommended for SAS selection and had pushed himself to the limit of his physical ability. He had sailed through all the 'tabs' and endurance tests and everything had been going fine until, yes, his temper got in the way. One of the instructors had cracked a joke at his expense and Andy had seen red. It had taken four of them to get him off the tosser. But that had been that. After returning to his regiment he had gone rapidly downhill. Everyone seemed to pick on him after that and it wasn't long before he decked a subaltern. Then it had been a spell in Colchester and out of the forces.

He didn't even try getting an ordinary job but went straight out and bought a paper to find out where there was a war on, then dropped into his local branch of Thomas Cook, bought a ticket and was off. If Thomas Cook do it, do it. His latest escapade had been in Bosnia with a Muslim militia, but when a bunch of mujahidin had turned up from Afghanistan, they had taken exception to being called rag-heads, even though Andy had meant it as a joke. They had ended up threatening to kill him, whereupon his Bosnian commander had politely notified him that his services were no longer required.

Coming over the crest of the hill, he was almost knocked off his feet by the force of the wind. He sank to his knees and clawed his way forward, the hurtling snow stinging his cheeks and eyes. Pulling on a pair of goggles, he begun to surge ahead, rising once more to his feet as soon as he was over the top and heading down towards the next valley, invisible behind an impenetrable white mask.

His heart thrilled at the challenge. He was out on the edge, the only place where he could feel alive. He felt it every time he approached the brink of death in combat, but here at home this was the closest he could get. Denied an enemy, he pitted himself against the elements; he became his own enemy. And Andy Buchan needed an enemy. It was what kept him going, what convinced him he was alive. He despised a lot of things but most of all he despised anyone who only wanted a cushy life, a soft option. They were the pits and he would die before he became like them. That was why he had leapt at the chance of going East. Major Butler had spelled out the terms as if Andy was some kind of moron. Well, screw him. He would play Babs's little game if it got him what he wanted. And right now he wanted the Korean contract more than anything else.

Reaching the foot of the hill, Andy pushed back his goggles and looked across the valley floor. For a few brief moments the wind dropped and the snow cleared, revealing the lie of the land ahead. The hills had disappeared and instead he found himself facing a snowscape of farmland and distant cottages. A mile away a snowplough was clearing a road down which people would soon be gingerly driving, complaining about the weather and the local council's lack of preparation. Andy Buchan had made it through. He had broken the back of the mountains.

Clearing his throat, he spat savagely in the snow and pulled his goggles down again. He tightened the straps of his bergen, turned and looked at his footsteps in the snow, already disappearing under a renewed fall, and as the wind lashed at him with raging force, he started up the mountainside the way he had come.

Danny Grey Wolf knew there was going to be trouble the moment he saw the row of bikes outside Dog's Diner on the edge of town. For a moment he thought about going elsewhere, but only for a moment. After cutting the engine of his pick-up, he stepped out into the night, the deep treads of his Chippewa boots crunching on the wet gravel of the car park. Driving north from Tacoma to Seattle, he had pulled in off the highway for a drink and some food and there wasn't another place as good as Dog's until you got into town. A Montana man, Danny looked upon cities as places for passing through. Do what you've got to do and get out. If you stayed, you were lost, especially if you were an Indian.

He had seen the Indian drunks down near the waterfront of Puget Sound: sad old men, mostly Nisquali, Yakima and Chinook, with long, black, matted hair, beer guts hanging over shapeless jeans and eyes dulled by the white man's liquor. Danny had last been there to trade in his hunting rifle for a new Winchester. The shelves had been full of automatics, pistols, assault rifles of every kind: M16s, Colt Commandos, Ingrams. How could anyone be surprised that the country was in the state it was? Sure, the right to keep and bear arms was enshrined in the Constitution, but didn't anyone realize that the frontier days had been over since before the turn of the century? What the hell.

He walked along the row of bikes, taking in the *Easy Rider* handlebars, the tassels, the chrome. Eat your heart out, Dennis Hopper. He could almost smell the unwashed hair and picture the overweight, bearded, out-of-condition slobs that would own these surrogate penises. Shaking his head, Danny Grey Wolf sunk his hands in his pockets and slunk into the diner. Right every time, he thought a moment later.

To an observer, the tall, powerful, square-jawed man who entered the diner simply minded his own business, went to the bar and relaxed on a stool. But anyone who had worked with Danny Grey Wolf before would know that within two seconds of opening the door he had evaluated the whole situation, noted every individual present, and correctly divined from which quarter the first trouble was likely to come and in what form.

The man behind the bar looked up. 'Oh shit.'

Knowing Danny as well as he did, Dog cursed his luck that he should come in just now. The bikers would have been going in a few minutes, but with Danny's arrival the writing was on the wall. He had often dropped in when he had been based at Fort Lewis with the Rangers. There were only two Ranger battalions in the whole US Army, one in Georgia and the other here in Washington State, Dog's backyard. The competition was fierce to get into such a small élite and Danny had been one of the top instructors, at least until four years ago. Dog had only heard that Danny had been obliged to leave in a hurry, but he could guess why. His furniture had been reduced to matchwood on more than one occasion.

'Hi there, Dog. Been a long time.'

Dog slid along the bar. 'Shame it wasn't longer.'

'Hey, what kind of a welcome's that? What's the special?'

'Same as ever.'

'Better give me one of those then, fries on the side and a coffee.'

'Coming up,' Dog said, and trying to disguise his one concern as if it was an afterthought, added: 'Be good tonight, Danny. Please, for my sake.'

Danny smiled warmly. He liked old Dog and besides, he was in a good mood. He had received his air ticket that morning and tomorrow would be flying back to his old stamping grounds in It'aewan. God, it was so long since he had been based up on the border alongside the ROKs. There were a few old friends he would have to look up. A few old mamasans too.

He reached up and swept off his baseball cap. There was a hoot from the far corner.

'Well, if it ain't the last of the fucking Mohicans!'

Danny ran his fingers across his scalp. His head was shaved clean except for a two-inch-high ridge of jet-black hair running down the centre from front to back. In the middle of pouring the coffee Dog glanced round, screwing up his face as he saw the approach of the inevitable, swearing as he spilt the scalding coffee on his fingers.

Danny ignored the bikers and thanked Dog when he had the mug between his large hands. It was warm and he relished every sip. He had driven a long way and still had quite a few miles to go before he reached the motel. Farther along the bar another Indian had already drunk himself into a stupor. His eyes were glazed, and tears ran down the deep wrinkles of his face, dropping in pools that mixed with the stale beer.

There was muttering and giggles from the corner and two of the bikers got up from their table and rolled across past the pool table and up to the bar. Flanking the old man, they looked in disgust at his dishevelled hair and grimy coat. He was wearing a battered old hat with an eagle feather stuck in the band.

'You're one sorry son of a bitch. D'you hear me, Hawkeye?'

The old man's head wobbled as he tried to focus on the nearest of the bikers, then snapped back as the other one kicked his stool from under him, sending him to the floor with a crash.

Dog came hurrying over. 'Easy, boys, I don't want any trouble.'

But their real target all along had been the new

arrival, who carried on sipping his coffee. The nearest biker planted his hands on his hips.

'Ain't you goin' to help the old fucker? He's one of yours, ain't he?'

Danny looked down at the old man, now being helped to his feet by Dog.

'Why should I? He's a Nisquali. You've done me a favour. Dog, give these men a beer on me.'

The biker's face reddened. 'Hear that, boys? This Injun's going to share a drink with us.'

From their corner table the other bikers sauntered over to the bar. Danny looked across at Dog and shrugged apologetically.

'Listen, boys,' he tried once more, 'let's all cool down. You go back to your table and I'll move on.'

Shock and surprise registered on Dog's face. He had never seen Danny smile as sweetly before. Nor, for that matter, had he ever seen Danny walk away from a fight. There must be something big on. But by now the bikers could smell blood; and the four of them were spread in a semicircle around Danny.

Danny slowly swivelled round on his stool to face them, his elbows leaning back on the bar, relaxed and casual.

'Do I take it we've got a problem here?' he asked.

'No, Redskin. You've got the fucking problem.'

With that, Danny's stool was kicked out from under him. Landing face down on the floor, he used the spring in his upper arm muscles to absorb the shock of the fall, grunting loudly as if winded. I can do without this, he kept thinking. I can really do without this. Not tonight, not on my last night in the country. Perhaps they've made their point. If I let them have just a little bit more . . .

Encouraged by the ease with which he had put the big Indian down, the biker moved in close to kick Danny in the ribs. Seeing it coming, Danny tilted on to his side and allowed the kick to land in the heavy folds of his woollen jacket. But he was starting to get angry. The bikers had so far been enjoying their stop-over at the diner. They had each had several beers, the best hamburger and fries in Washington State – according to Dog's sign outside – and they had beaten the shit out of two Indians. But when Danny rolled on to his side to take the kick, their luck ran out.

Some years ago Dog had hung a big mirror on the ceiling over the bar, angled down so that whenever a drunk slipped off his stool, Dog could check he was all right without having to come out from behind the counter. But now the man on the floor was Danny Grey Wolf. Still groaning, Danny inadvertently caught sight of himself in Dog's mirror.

'Fuck it,' he muttered. He didn't mind his jacket and trousers being dirtied but what really pissed him off was the spectacle of four white men standing over a Blackfoot Sioux whose forefathers had fought under Crazy Horse at Little Big Horn.

Seeing there was no need for caution, the other bikers had closed in.

'Give it to him, Frank,' one of them goaded.

'Yeah, take his fucking scalp off.'

Rolling on to his back, Danny glared up at the nearest biker, who was about to kick him again. Releasing the full power of one heavily muscled leg, Danny propelled the sole of his boot into the biker's testicles, lifting the man clean off the ground as the underside of the boot made contact. As his attacker toppled forward with a squeal like a stuck pig, Danny caught him by the shoulders and adding the man's forward momentum to the power of his own substantial neck muscles, shattered the biker's nose with his forehead.

Before the others realized that the odds had drastically changed, Danny shoved the semi-conscious biker to one side and drawing up both knees to his chest, sprang to his feet in a single movement. Going straight into a forward roll, he dived through the gap he had created and spun to face the three remaining bikers, whose surprise was already turning to red-hot anger.

The next to come at him was the biggest of the gang, but his size in no way compensated for his lack of speed. Swinging wildly, his fist sailed through the empty space where, a second earlier, Danny's calm, expressionless face had been. Ducking below the punch, Danny brought his balled fist up hard into the man's gut, driving behind it with the full weight of his body and kicking the biker's legs out from under him at the same time. As the man went down like a giant redwood, Danny pushed him from behind so that his chin met the bar on the way, smashing his lower teeth and snapping his neck back with a sickening crack.

Seeing the turn of events, the other two had made a snatch for weapons. One had grabbed a cue from the pool table, the other had taken a lock-knife from his pocket and flicked open the seven-inch blade. Facing them across the writhing bodies of their companions, Danny judged it was time to even the odds. Without taking his eyes off the two bikers, he reached behind him, lifted the tail of his jacket and pulled out a tomahawk.

'Holy shit!' one of the bikers muttered, lunging at Danny's throat with the sharp end of the pool cue. But Danny was already sidestepping and with a single swing of his tomahawk severed the cue and then, changing his grip on the handle with a spin of the wrist, whiplashed the flat of the blade first into the biker's nose and mouth, then into his windpipe.

By now the man with the knife should have been scared, but he wasn't, and Danny instantly changed his tactics to match. Let him come to you, Danny-boy, he thought. See what he's got to offer first. Don't spoil it now. He might look like a fat asshole, but a knife's a knife, whoever's on the other side of it.

The two men circled each other and Danny noted that the biker was surprisingly agile. Twice he feinted with the knife but Danny kept moving back, judging his opponent's proficiency before committing himself to a counter-attack. Then, as the biker lunged again, Danny knocked the blade aside with his tomahawk and lashed viciously at the man's forearm, slicing through the black leather and denim, severing flesh and the tendons underneath. The man winced and leapt backwards. In a wild effort to save himself, he heaved a kick at Danny's groin, but the Indian swung his tomahawk again, this time directing the razor-sharp blade downwards on to the biker's shin. There was a dull thud as it found its mark and for a second it lodged in the bone, then sprang loose as Danny yanked it out and the man went down into a foetal position, hugging his wounded arm and leg.

With the last of the bikers out of commission, Danny walked over to the bar, paused and drained his coffee mug. Dog stared at the bodies.

'I suppose you're going to fuck off now and leave me to make the peace with these assholes?'

Danny grinned at him. 'I've got a plane to catch. You know how it is.'

'Sure I do. Has anyone ever told you you're one mean son of a bitch?'

'Only my friends.'

Danny grabbed his cap off the bar and stuffed it in his pocket.

'Be seeing you, Dog. Take it easy.'

He wiped the blade of his tomahawk on the sleeve of his jacket and was sauntering towards the door when a shout split the air.

'Danny! Look out!'

The deafening roar of a gunshot filled the diner and a bullet cracked past Danny's head, splintering the edge of the door frame. The biker who had pulled the knife was still lying on the far side of the room where Danny had left him, blood pouring from his arm and leg. But with his good hand he was levelling a snub-nosed Magnum at Danny and already steadying his aim for the second shot.

In one fluid movement, Danny spun and dropped, his right arm reaching back over his head, pausing for one frozen moment as he locked eyes with his attacker. Then, with the power of a steel spring, he unleashed his terrible weapon, the blade and handle tumbling end over end towards the biker. It struck with deadly accuracy, finding its target and splitting the man's forehead clean open. With a single grunt, he sank back against the wall, eyes fixed on the ceiling, dead.

Danny slowly got to his feet and walked across to the biker. Dog stared at the figure sprawled on the floor of his diner with a tomahawk sticking out of his head.

'If you're thinking of checking for a pulse, I wouldn't bother.'

Danny sighed. 'I could have done without this.'

'I reckon he could, and all,' Dog added wryly.

Retrieving his weapon, Danny wiped the blade again and made to leave.

'Can you give me a couple of hours before you call the cops?'

'You know I can't do that, Danny,' Dog replied. 'You'd best get going.'

Danny nodded. Why did it always seem to end like this? He eased himself into his pick-up, gunned the motor and pulled out on to the highway. Looking at his watch, he made some quick calculations. He had hoped to relax at the motel in front of the TV, but he could forget that now. Best move on. That seemed to be the story of his life. Always moving on.

3

The rush-hour traffic in Washington DC clogged the air with a thick pall of smoke that made Alex Leitner wish he was back at his desk, but ever since Bill Clinton had taken office it had become the norm for senior executives in both government and business to skip lunch, zip themselves into outrageously expensive designer track suits and be seen jogging in the park instead. Being seen was the crucial part. No one did it to get fit. Who the hell needed to be fit in this day and age? What was the point of screwing the ozone layer with carbon monoxide if you then went and used your legs?

'Hi there, Jack!' he panted as he passed a fellow fifty-five-year-old jogger. 'When the going gets tough, the tough get going.'

'Fuck . . . off,' the senior foreign affairs adviser wheezed.

Another one bites the dust, Alex thought. If this goes on I'll get that promotion after all. Every other sucker will have dropped dead. But in his saner moments he knew that promotion was no longer on the cards for him. His boss had seen to that. Before the arrival of Eliot Masterson, the CIA's Washington office had been staffed with OK guys, but Masterson had changed that seconds after walking through the door. He was one of those characters who was going to rule the world, or so he thought. If ex-CIA boss George Bush could make President, why couldn't Eliot Masterson? Alex hated his kind and all he stood for.

Coming to the end of the park, he slowed to a walk, even though a casual observer would have been hard pushed to see the difference. It was the arms that gave it away: when he was jogging they bounced up and down, his clenched fists level with his hollow chest, but when he walked they just hung down uselessly.

He had managed to park his car near the main gate, and he collapsed into the driving seat, his sodden pants squelching on the blue imitation leather. He had taken longer than expected today and would have to hurry if he was going to be back at his desk by two. Still, he had been seen by a couple of big shots, the first of whom had even told him to screw himself – a sure sign that Alex was liked. It was all good networking.

A short while later, when he was towelling himself after a shower, he found himself thinking about the satellite photographs that had arrived on his desk the week before. It had only taken him a few seconds to realize the significance of what he was looking at. As an intelligence photographic interpreter, he had been working closely with the Korean desk for some months and felt he knew every square yard of the Communist North as if it was his home town.

The first cursory glance had been enough to set the alarm bells ringing in his head as he saw the evidence on the small squares of paper laid out in front of him. It was considerably less sophisticated than a Soviet rocket site, yet the ramps and rails were plain to see and could mean only one thing, that the North Korean nuclear programme was nearing completion.

The bomb might not yet exist, but they were making damn sure that as soon as it did, they would have the facilities in place to launch it.

Naturally Alex had filed an immediate report to Eliot Masterson, the head of department, for onward passage up the line, but it was strange that he hadn't yet been summoned to the full briefing that usually followed any such new discovery. He had sounded out Masterson's secretary, but she had given him the brush-off.

'Ours not to reason how,' she had told him.

'Ours not to reason why.'

'What?'

'I said, it's "Ours not to reason why",' he had repeated as if talking to an idiot, which he felt was probably the case. She had giggled and left it at that. Well, now that a week had gone by he was damn well going to ask the reason why. He had made an appointment and intended to get an answer.

Straightening his tie, Alex was shown into Eliot Masterson's office and left standing in the middle of the carpet while his boss finished reading a letter. OK, you bastard, Alex thought, I've got the message. I'm dirt under your feet. Now get on with it.

Eventually Masterson raised his head and feigned surprise to find one of his subordinates standing there.

'Why, Alex, forgive me. I was engrossed.'

Like a glutton with his lunch, Alex thought.

'What's the problem?'

'No problem,' Alex replied, remembering the golden rule: never admit there's a problem, even if King Kong is on the loose and a rocket full of Martians has just landed on the White House lawn. 'I was just wondering whether you had had time to look over the report I sent in last week about the North Korean nuclear programme. It seems they've been busy.'

'Haven't we all, Alex. Yes, I read it thoroughly and found it deeply interesting. A fine piece of analysis. Well done.'

'And?'

'And what?'

'When are you going to need me to brief the chiefs?'

'I think you can leave that to me. As a matter of fact I don't think it'll be necessary.'

Alex was thunderstruck. The North Koreans were possibly within weeks of acquiring a nuclear weapon and this asshole didn't seem in the slightest concerned.

'If you'll excuse me, sir, if the government in Pyongyang gets its hands on . . .'

Masterson leaned across his desk, the colour draining from his cheeks, and interrupted him brusquely.

'Alex, you've made your point. I think the matter's quite safe in my hands, don't you?'

Alex looked back into the chilling, pale-grey eyes that bored into him. Whatever this bastard was, he wasn't incompetent. Everyone knew that Eliot Masterson was a fast-stream high-flier who was going places. It was just a pity he had stopped off here on the way. But if he said he had things in hand, then who was Alex Leitner, a passed-over loser, to contradict him?

Without another word Alex left the office. It would be Friday soon and then he would be free for two whole days to do what he wanted. He had promised to take his son fishing. They would probably drive down to the Potomac at Chesapeake Bay, or maybe go up to Annapolis. Stephen loved it there and desperately wanted to pass the entrance exams for the Naval Academy next autumn. They would watch the cadets go by in their crisp new uniforms and joke about Alex coming to pick him up at the end of term in his derelict Chevy. Those were the real things, the things that mattered.

But then, with a son in the Navy, the last thing Alex wanted was another war. His own father had fought in Korea the last time round and although Alex had only been a scrawny twelve-year-old, he remembered as if it was yesterday the arrival of the telegram from the Marine Corps and his mother's scream, which had echoed through the house moments later. The last thing he wanted was another Korean war.

As soon as Alex had left his office, Masterson swivelled round in his chair, put his feet up on the window-sill and stared out bitterly at the city skyline. Why should he bother about Leitner? The guy was a burnt-out shell whereas he was the man of tomorrow and it wouldn't be long before tomorrow dawned and he found himself one of the most powerful men in Washington, and therefore in the world.

The sound of the traffic was muffled by the thick reinforced glass of the windows. It was a murky day, partly because of the smog but partly because the grim wastes of the Atlantic were so near. He would far rather have been in California, sunbathing by a pool with the red-roofed villas of Santa Barbara spreading out below instead of this dismal mediocrity. Still, this was the seat of power and to Eliot Masterson power was as essential as oxygen. Later perhaps, he would land some prize political fish like the California governorship as another step on his path to glory, but for now he would have to endure the grey smog of Washington and the pedantic narrow-mindedness of clerks such as Alex Leitner.

He reminded Masterson of the idiots in the UN inspection teams who had been trying for months to gain access to North Korea in order to inspect its nuclear facilities. Did they really expect the world's last hard-line Communist regime to give them a conducted tour of its most highly guarded secrets? Couldn't they see that so long as the government of President Kim Il Sung thought it had one card left to play it would sit it out, happy in its dangerous isolation?

Masterson got up from his desk and walked across to a sideboard where a pot of coffee steamed below a large oil painting of General Cornwallis surrendering to George Washington at Yorktown. He poured himself a cup and stood contemplating the picture for a moment, stirring the coffee with a solid-silver spoon. He had come to this new post as a result of rapid promotion and was set on proving himself one way or another. Let the UN fool themselves if they wished; let them believe that fanatics are open to persuasion and reasonable argument from reasonable men. He knew otherwise. There was only one way to deal with a bunch of maniacs like the North Koreans, even if it involved gambling with the highest of stakes. Unless you were prepared to accept a high risk, you couldn't expect to receive the high gains that came with it.

Back at his desk he pressed the intercom button.

'Julie, I'm not to be disturbed until further notice.'

'OK, Mr Masterson.'

Picking up a handset from the bank of phones, he flicked back a small panel and stabbed at the buttons underneath, before settling back in his chair to await the arrival of his radio signal on the other side of the world. He toyed with the spoon, fascinated by the whirlpool he was able to create and control with a turn of his wrist.

'Hi there, it's me. We'd better turn turkey.'

He reached back to the panel, punched in a code and waited for a small green light to appear, along with the gobbling sound of a scrambled voice at the other end.

'Are you hearing me OK? Terrific.'

It's not so much like a turkey, Masterson thought; more like the guy's got his head underwater. Even so, the words were clear enough and the speaker was easily recognizable as Francis Kwang.

Diving through the thick undergrowth, the two Korean boys flung themselves down the embankment, sending a cascade of loose stones tumbling down the slope faster even than their own bruised and aching bodies. Behind them, shouts and screams echoed angrily through the forest and the harsh white beams of torches criss-crossed in the overhead branches as the guards drew closer.

Little Chiao sobbed as he ran, fighting with all his pathetic might to suppress the terror that had seized him the moment they had vaulted from the trucks as they slowed to take yet another hairpin bend on the painfully slow climb away from the labour camp. Glancing sideways at him, Liang wondered if it had been a mistake to bring the younger boy. By himself he might even have got away unnoticed and then, by the time the idiot guards had done a head count, he would have covered a reasonable distance and would be well on his way to the border and to the freedom that he had heard his father speak of so often.

But since Little Chiao's own brother had been murdered he had attached himself to Liang for the protection that was vital to survival in the brutal environment of the camp. Against his better judgement, Liang had brought him. Then, just as they were easing towards the tail of the truck, Little Chiao had slipped on the wet boards and gone down on his face. Liang should have covered it up by pretending that he was simply helping his friend back to his seat, but journeys outside the compound were rare and he was desperate to try his luck. It hadn't lasted very long. The guard had been sitting up behind the cab and by hammering on the roof had managed to bring the whole convoy to a halt in the space of a hundred yards. Why was Liang cursed with such bad luck?

Suddenly one of the torches locked on to them. The screams rose to a frenzy and a second later the guards opened up with their Kalashnikovs, sending a wild hail of bullets crackling through the forest. All around them branches splintered and whistled. Little Chiao cried out and for a moment Liang thought he had been hit, but catching sight of his friend's terrified face in the torchlight, he realized the shout had been a warning. Liang turned back a moment too late, missed his footing and pitched head first over the drop and into the darkness.

He must have passed out for a few seconds because the next thing he knew was the feeling of an arm around his neck, holding him above the freezing water of the river. He tried to speak but a small hand was clamped over his mouth and he twisted round to see Little Chiao grimacing and pointing upwards. Torch beams still swept the undergrowth but seemed farther away now. There were bursts of gunfire as the guards fired into the dense bushes and anywhere that might conceal the two runaways.

It was a cloudless night and the moon cast a silvery glow on the water's surface. In the ghostly light Little Chiao's wide eyes were as huge as saucers and Liang felt a sudden flood of gratitude for his friend, who had probably saved his life. He was just about to risk a hushed thank you, when he heard a new sound, still far off but, unlike the bursts of gunfire, getting closer. Dogs.

A sob burst from Little Chiao before he could help himself. Then he put his mouth close to Liang's ear and said: 'What are we going to do now? The dogs will find us and you know what they'll do.'

Liang knew only too well. Barely a month had passed since the whole camp had been paraded to witness the punishment of a youth who had been recaptured only hours after escaping from a work detail. They were made to form up in a hollow square and then, as they watched in horror, the fugitive's hands were tied behind his back, he was led into the middle and the dogs were set on him. Liang thought the youth was still alive when the dogs were pulled off some minutes later and the body was dragged away, but it would have made no difference. The medical facilities at the camp were reserved for the guards; prisoners were forced to make use of whatever herbs they could smuggle in from outside, and for the sort of wounds that the youth had sustained there wasn't a medicine in the whole of North Korea that would have helped.

'We must stay in the water,' he hissed. 'Follow me.'

And then, without believing it himself, he added: 'We'll be all right, I promise you.'

Pushing away from the bank, Liang allowed the current to take him. With his left hand he gently swam with the river while his right fist kept a firm hold on Little Chiao. In the centre of the river the current was powerful and it took all of Liang's strength to keep his head above the surface. Trailing behind him, the younger boy paddled furiously, spluttering and gulping for air.

As the current took them faster and faster, it was strangely comforting, as if an invisible force was whisking them to safety. Liang even found himself wondering at the events of the whole extraordinary day. The trucks had arrived without warning soon after their breakfast of rice and watery tea. There had been twelve of the big Chinese vehicles and he had quickly seen that all but four of them were already full. In one of the trucks a man had peeled back the canvas side and was peering out. He was an old man with white hair and Liang had also been able to see that the other people in the truck were a mixture of men and women, old and young; there was even a baby which a woman was holding to her breast. But then the man had been spotted and the guards had screamed at him to sit down as they rushed to refasten the flap.

About forty of the boys from Liang's youth labour camp had been selected and told to board the trucks. Liang had overheard two of the guards talking. One of them had asked if he should order the boys to pack their few personal items, but the other had just laughed in response. Liang had thought about this as he had climbed aboard but his mind had soon been sent spinning in a new direction as he peered occasionally through a rip in the canvas and contemplated his escape. It had been rumoured that some of them were soon to be moved to a new camp and the bundles of new clothing that they found in the truck convinced them that this was now happening. Liang knew that any new camp would be just as heavily guarded as the last one, maybe even more so, and that as the son of a well-known political prisoner he could never expect to be released. Escape was his only chance of freedom.

Floating downstream, Liang was suddenly jolted by the realization that the current was taking them towards the sound of the barking dogs. In a panic he swung himself around and tried to kick against the river, but it was useless. He and Little Chiao were now firmly in its grasp. The next moment they heard voices from the bank behind a screen of trees.

'I don't care. The trucks have got to be at Wonsan by dawn.'

'But we were specifically told to deliver a set number, divided up by age and sex.'

'I don't give a stuff. If the Commandant doesn't take delivery by midday at the latest you'll be floating face down in the river yourself.'

Liang couldn't see the speakers but as he tried to ease his way towards some drifting branches for better concealment, a shout from behind pierced the night.

'There they are, the little fuckers! Get the dogs over here!'

A burst of fire from a sub-machine-gun rattled across the water, the bullets stinging into the river in tiny trails of spray.

Yanking Little Chiao by the hand, Liang dragged him back towards the middle of the river, where the current was strongest, and kicked with all his might, shouting: 'Swim! Swim for all you're worth!'

Twenty yards away, on the nearer bank, a handler thrust through the bushes, a brace of huge black dogs tugging at their leash, berserk and almost roaring with the excitement of the hunt. Then another guard appeared, aimed his Kalashnikov and emptied a full thirty-round magazine into the water at Liang and Little Chiao.

Liang's ears were ringing with the noise of the bullets, the water and the terrified screams of Little Chiao.

'It's no use, Lan-Lan! It's no use! They've got us!' And as if to confirm it, another spray of bullets whined all around them.

Exhausted by the river and half-deafened, Liang felt the last of his strength draining from him. He turned to look at his young friend one last time, smiled weakly, tightly clasped his hand, and dived.

Thirty thousand feet over the Bay of Bengal, Terry Williams was trying to decide whether to have the lamb dish or the chicken chasseur. He couldn't remember if the chasseur was the one in the red wine sauce. He had had it once at a restaurant in Cardiff and liked it, but looking across the aisle at the passengers who had already been served, he settled for the lamb and sat back ready to order.

His seat was right at the front of economy class, and peering through the dark-blue curtain he could see that the business-class passengers were well into their meal and being served with champagne in real glasses. That was just typical of Babs bloody Butler. A man could risk his life for truth and justice and a better world, but Babs would still send him a sodding economy ticket. Terry had never travelled business class in his life and every time he flew he made a promise that one day he would treat himself to it. First class was another world altogether and he scarcely bothered to contemplate it.

Once in his army days, he had been flying back from Germany with a captain from his own regiment. There had been some mix-up over the allocation of seat numbers and Terry's had been double-booked. The officer had sat there grinning, saying that Terry would have to fly in the baggage compartment, when the steward had come along to sort it out. There had been some spare seats in business class, but instead of upgrading Terry's ticket, they moved the captain forward and gave Terry his economy seat. The bastard had gloated about it for weeks. Still, Terry had got his own back at the next Christmas party when the officers came to the sergeants' mess for drinks. He had roped several of his mates in on the plan. They had laced the captain's drinks, got him pissed as a rat, stripped him stark bollock naked in the toilets and sent him wandering off through the barracks. The officer's wife had not been amused, particularly by the photos in the next edition of the regimental magazine.

With his meal finally in front of him, Terry set to work, fighting to hold his elbows down in the confined space. He would have a word or two to say to Babs when he arrived.

Just before the meal had arrived, Terry had made a trip to the toilets at the back of the jumbo. Scanning the sea of faces on the way, he had recognized the vicious little Scot. Andy something, he thought. They had worked for the same side in Angola. What a bloody mess that had been! Training the UNITA guerrillas of Jonas Savimbi had not only paid badly, but the end result had not been up to much. Even when most of the Cubans had left, Terry's team had still been unable to better the opposition. He had seen the writing on the wall and got out soon afterwards when the war deteriorated into just another intertribal feud, with the innocents caught up in the middle as usual.

The Scot, on the other hand, had had a terrific war. Terry remembered some of the stories circulating about him, most of them no doubt originating from the twisted little bugger's own relentless gob. How he had foiled an enemy ambush, how he had captured a position single-handed, how he had cleared a path through a minefield with his commando knife while the engineers looked on from the sidelines. But not all of it was bullshit. Terry had seen him in action in the bush near Mussende. A bunch of South Africans had got themselves pinned down and the Scot had led his team on a wide flanking move that caught the enemy by complete surprise. Terry's platoon had been held in reserve on a hillock on the Umpolo road and had enjoyed the grandstand view as the Scot went screaming in from the side, rolling up the enemy position and winning the day.

The South Africans had given the Scot first pick of the captured weapons, which Terry thought was jolly decent of them, seeing as they would all have been butchered if he and Andy hadn't shown up. There had been a real mixture of stuff, piles and piles of it. Russian AK74s, the brand spanking new 5.45mm assault rifle, RPK light machine-guns, some Chinese Type 56s – their own version of the older Russian AK47 – and the thing that had been doing most of the damage: an AGS 17 grenade-launcher that had a very nasty habit of accurately lobbing 30mm grenades over half a kilometre.

But what had appalled Terry was the Scot's treatment of the enemy wounded. He had mumbled something about not having the rations to feed extra mouths and had gone through the scrub finishing them off with a captured Chinese Type 59 9mm pistol. Terry had not arrived on the scene until the killing was over and had been incensed, but the South Africans had sided with the Scot and the UNITA guerrillas didn't seem to know what the fuss was about, so there hadn't been anything Terry could do.

Except leave, which he did soon afterwards. Since then he had only taken part in specific missions. Brush-fire tribal wars were too open-ended and brutal for his liking. Some mates had tried to persuade him to go with them to Bosnia, but things had been going fairly well with the dojo at the time and he and Liz had been trying hard to make a go of their marriage once again. So, while some of the lads had packed up and gone off to what was now cryptically called 'the former Yugoslavia', he and Liz had left the kids with her mum and gone for a weekend in Snowdonia. It had hardly been a great success; Terry wanted to shin up the mountains while Liz insisted on spending hours in the bloody visitor centres. They had made love twice, but the first time the walls of their room in the bed and breakfast had been paper-thin and they could hear the couple on the other side attempting to do the same, and the second time Liz kept talking about the cost of a cream tea they had eaten that afternoon. It had all ended up in a huge row and another split.

When Terry had finished his meal and searched

every little envelope and plastic container to make sure he had eaten everything, the air hostess collected his tray and pulled back the blue curtain leading into business class to give Terry a clear view of the overhead screen.

'Your seat's too far forward to see the screen in the economy section, sir, but it's exactly the same movie in business class,' the hostess said.

'Are you sure I won't contaminate them, love?'

The hostess laughed and walked away, smiling stiffly as if she had just trodden in corgi shit at a Buckingham Palace garden party.

After plugging his headphones into the armrest, Terry turned the dial to the correct channel and settled back to enjoy the film, which he had been dying to see. After the preliminary advertisements reassuring everyone that they had made the best possible selection in their choice of airline, the titles rolled, the action began, and Terry discovered that the soundtrack being broadcast to his economy seat was out of sync with the pictures on the business-class screen. As the heroine opened her mouth to speak, a deep male voice boomed in a Germanic accent: 'Screw you, asshole.'

Fighting to control his temper, Terry took a couple of deep breaths and took off his headphones, dreaming blissful images of Babs Butler tortured by the Spanish Inquisition.

As the plane droned high over central China, Terry tipped his head back, closed his eyes, steadied his breath, and went through the basic hand techniques. Resting lightly on his knees, his hands became a series of deadly weapons, one after the other, each pair of weapons perfectly suited to a particular lethal task. The basic fist *seiken*, the knife hand *shuto*, the palm heel *shotei*, *haito* the ridge hand, *boshiken* the thumb fist, *yubi hasami* the finger pinch, *washi de* the eagle hand, *kuma de* the bear's paw, *keiko ken* the phoenix-eye fist, on and on. And then the whole list was repeated. The techniques had been ingrained through years of training and relentless self-discipline until they were part of his very being.

Startled by a hand pulling gently at his sleeve, Terry opened his eyes to see a little girl leaning across from her seat on the other side of the aisle, grinning at him.

'I can do that too,' she said, interweaving her fingers. 'Look. Here's the church and here's the steeple. Open the door and here's all the people!'

Terry smiled at her waggling fingers.

'Come on, you try it,' the girl persisted, and a moment later Terry's favourite *nukite* finger-thrust, capable of crushing a man's windpipe, had dissolved into a chapel full of pious Welshmen.

Kneeling astride Babs Butler's naked thighs, the woman moved rhythmically, driving forward in sharp lunges, grinding her buttocks downwards, forcing him deeper into her. Grasping her by the hips, Babs rocked back and forth, reaching up to caress her breasts, the wine-dark nipples taut and quivering. He circled one with his thumb until she threw back her head and moaned, her long, black hair cascading down her arched back, thrusting her breasts sharply forward into his coaxing palms.

Nearing the end, the woman doubled forward, dropping her head and bucking furiously, racing, flattening her stomach against his. Their bodies glistened with sweat and as Babs thrust savagely into her, he clasped at her buttocks, thighs, shoulders, frantic in the final moments as lights exploded behind his eyes and he shot into her moments before she cried out, shuddered and collapsed across his chest, panting hard.

Opening his eyes, Babs looked up at the fan circling lazily on the ceiling, then lifting the woman's head, stroked back her hair, kissed her and held her face between his hands.

'Michelle, you're getting bags under your eyes. Too much shagging's not good for you.'

The woman bared a broad set of white teeth, her almond eyes narrowing at him like a cat's.

'Babs will be good to me. You take care of me, no?'

'Sure I will. When Babs got plenty money, he give you very special present.'

Michelle's face lit up. Babs nodded.

'Just you wait and see.'

She reached down between his legs and took him lightly in her hand.

'This present?'

'No. Other special present.'

A look of puzzlement crossed Michelle's face. 'I no understand. We go holiday?'

'How would you like long, long holiday?' Babs asked, watching her changing expression with delight.

'You mean we go away? Leavey Seoul?'

'Yes,' he nodded. 'We leavey Seoul. For good. You, me. Like real couple.'

Unable to contain her joy, Michelle threw herself on Babs and hugged him tightly until he could hardly breathe. Easing out of her arms, Babs slid out from underneath, swung his legs off the bed and reached for a cigarette. He stared down at his soft, flabby stomach, where no sign remained of the muscles that had once coated it. His legs were still strong but he winded quickly. There was no denying it: he was way out of condition. What was more, he knew that he would never again be properly fit. His life from now on would be a steady decline through a series of illnesses to eventual and inevitable dissolution. What a bitch, he thought.

Michelle had sprung off the bed and was sitting naked in front of a mirror combing her hair. Babs looked at her back and long, brown legs. She too had seen better days, but he still felt a thrill whenever he saw the genuine delight in her eyes when she opened the door and saw him standing there. He knew that she really liked him. 'Loved' would be too strong a word perhaps, but then again, why not? Stranger things had happened. Watching her brisk movements and listening to her shrill humming, he resolved to stick to his word this time. He really would come for her. They would be a couple and make something of themselves with whatever time they had left.

She caught sight of him in the mirror and smiled warmly.

'Babs, you good man. You know that?'

He smirked. 'Don't you believe it.'

Wrapping himself in a sarong, Babs walked over to the window and peered through the slats. It was raining outside and the coloured neon lights blurred in the puddles as people splashed through them. The thought of stepping out into the bustling crowds depressed him. He went over to the stool and sat beside Michelle, taking one breast in his hand and kissing the nipple.

She closed her eyes with pleasure but gently pushed him away.

'No time now, Babsy. No time.'

There never was, he thought, getting to his feet with a heavy sigh and shuffling to where his dishevelled clothes littered a corner of the spartan room. He would rather go now while there was still the illusion of love, before the tentative knock at the door, reminding them both that they lived in a harsh world and that her next client would soon be stumbling up the poorly lit stairs, drunk on his own brand of dreams.

4

Looking around the large private dining-room of the Golden Carp restaurant, Babs Butler smiled at the sixteen mercenaries assembled before him.

'Welcome to Seoul, gentlemen. I think I'm right in saying that you all know me, or at least know of me, so I won't bother with a lengthy introduction.'

Sprawled in a chair at the back, a large Australian shouted: 'Thank buggeroo for that.' A couple of men laughed, but most sat stony-faced. Babs nodded good-naturedly.

'Thank you, Ken. Remind me to fuck up your account number when I sort out the bank drafts.'

'There'll be a draught between your eyes if you do, mate.'

'Be that as it may,' Babs continued, 'I welcome you all to Seoul and to what I'm sure will be a profitable and successful enterprise. Now, for obvious reasons I am going to keep this short. You're all here to do a job and you'll be fully briefed on the task in a few days. But for now there are just a couple of points I want you to take in. Firstly, security. It won't come as any surprise to you that you're being sent somewhere where you really oughtn't to be.'

A ripple of cynical laughter spread around the tables.

'That being so, there are going to be a lot of people trying to make sure firstly that you don't get there, and secondly that you don't make it back. I hardly need emphasize that you'll stand a better chance of fucking up their plans if you all keep your traps shut. So tonight, when you're pie-eyed and in the voluptuous arms of your latest conquest, don't start mouthing off about what a big-shot mercenary you are and how you're going to do this and that to so and so. Get the message?'

'Yes, Mr Butler, sir,' came the chorus from the floor.

'Good. My next point is an admin one. I've put you in different hotels around the city, all part of my fiendishly clever plan to avoid drawing attention to ourselves. Don't whinge that Fred's in a better hotel than you are, because if you were all at the Hyatt or the bloody Savoy, it'd be rubble by the time we moved on.'

'That's all very well,' piped a South African, 'but why the hell do I get the bloody YMCA?'

'Hey, mun. Got the bleddy YMCA, hev you?' the Australian hooted in imitation.

The South African turned round, glowering darkly, and said: 'That's ripe coming from a bloody sheep-shagger like you, man.'

'. . . a bleddy ship-shegger like you, mun,' echoed the Australian.

'I'm glad to see you all getting on so well,' Babs continued quickly. 'Now, before this ends in tears, to conclude my admin points, you've been split up for a reason and I would be grateful if you would keep it that way. So, even if you recognize a mate that you haven't seen since butchering babies ten years ago, say hello now, but when you leave this room, go your separate ways.'

He paused to take a sip of whisky. 'Lastly, you are all to rendezvous at the address on the card I will shortly give to each of you, at the day and time stated. Transport will pick you up at the spot and take you to our next meeting place. Anyone who's late or decides to sleep in and misses the RV is on his own and his contract's terminated. Is that clear?'

Heads nodded.

'Sorry, gentlemen, I can't tell if that's an affirmative or if you're falling asleep.'

'Yes, Mr Butler, sir!' came the unanimous answer.

'Lovely. What happy campers we all are! By way of an appetite-whetter, I will simply say that after being picked up you will be transported to a training camp where you will be equipped and do some warm-up and familiarization training.'

'Bloody 'ell,' a cockney voice called out. 'They came in search of paradise and found . . . Babsy.'

'Not quite,' Babs continued once the laughter had died down. 'I'll be at the camp but sadly I won't be accompanying you on the mission.'

'Who's in charge, then?' someone shouted.

'A gentleman you've yet to have the pleasure of meeting,' Babs answered with some satisfaction. Yi Soong will shut the buggers up, he thought. We'll see how verbose that Aussie git is by the time Yi's finished with him.

'Are there any questions?'

One or two of the men asked about the method of payment and someone else started probing for details of the mission. When he had answered the pay queries and deflected the operational question,

Babs stood up and clapped his hands theatrically.

'Right then, you've been a wonderful audience and I love you all! Tonight is for merriment, so I've arranged a little treat for you. Maestro, play!'

With that, the double doors behind him swung open and a line of girls in Korean national dress danced into the room, followed by drummers and a line of waiters balancing trays of food.

As the girls twirled and spun in time to the music, the Australian groaned loudly. 'Christ, I didn't come all the way from Oz for a fucking cultural show.'

But before anyone else could agree with him, the girls loosened the ribbons that fastened their flowing pink dresses, which gently slid from their shoulders until they were dancing naked. An enormous cheer went up, and as beers and dishes heaped with food were distributed to all the tables, Babs sat slumped in a chair, mopping his brow with an unusually clean handkerchief and watching with pride the team he had assembled, a selection of some of the most dangerous men in the world.

When Terry Williams saw the dancers slip out of their dresses he knew it was time to go. At first he had thought he was in for an entertaining evening and had been on the verge of congratulating Babs on his planning. But as he looked at the expression on Andy the Scot's face, leering at the closest of the girls, he realized that Butler was still the same old Babs. Why can't he realize that we're not all a bunch of animals, he thought. Some of us have got principles even if they are a bit flexible at times.

Declining an offer from one of the girls to dance, and

negotiating his way around the tables from which his fellow mercenaries were being pulled on to the floor in what seemed to be turning into an orgy, Terry weaved across to Babs.

'Why, Dojo!' Babs shrieked, opening his arms wide as if welcoming the prodigal son. 'Long time no see.'

Terry winced at his old nickname. Hearing it on Babs's lips conjured up images from the past, not all of which were pleasant to remember. They had seen a few wars together and been in a number of tight corners. The nickname had been coined by a Londoner, himself a karate instructor. He had once overheard Terry saying how much he would like to open his own karate dojo, and for no particular reason the name had stuck, long after the Londoner had died in an African ditch from a stomach wound and Babs and Terry had moved on to other countries and other wars.

As Babs was obviously not about to be parted from his chair, Terry crouched beside him.

'Listen, Babs, this isn't really my scene,' he said, indicating the girls and the mercenaries, most of whom were already well on their way to being horribly drunk. 'I think I'll slope off and take in some of the sights.'

'Same old Dojo, I'm glad to see. As you please. You'll miss a great show. I've got a few other surprises in store for the lads.'

Terry had a fair idea what they might be. He also noted with distaste the way Babs said 'the lads'. It reminded him of the sort of officer in his old regiment who employed the term in the belief that it would somehow make him one of the lads. It never had and it never would. Looking at Babs's floor show, Terry couldn't help feeling like a citizen of ancient Rome, fêted with games and vulgar morsels by an emperor trying hard to conceal an underlying contempt for his populace.

He forced a smile that Babs, his senses blunted by two double whiskies, took to be genuine warmth. Making his way to the door, Terry went out into the corridor, down a flight of steps and out into the street. He had picked up a street map from the dressing-table in his hotel room, so once he had got his bearings and pinpointed the restaurant in the Seoulin-dong nightclub district, he decided to walk a few blocks north and have a look at the Kyongbok Palace.

Strolling through the crowded streets, he soaked up the battery of sights, sounds and smells. He always relished the first impressions of a country, and did his best to open his senses wide and take it all in without prejudice or expectations. In many ways Seoul reminded him of Hong Kong. On the surface, it was one of those modern prosperous Asian cities that were springing up all around the Pacific rim and which were tipped to be the dominant trading centres in the next century. Terry could well believe it. There was a vibrancy and sense of urgency and direction that had long vanished from the streets of London, Paris and Berlin; everywhere he saw people getting on with life. They didn't have time to moan about what was owed to them or about how terrible it was that the government wasn't doing more to help them solve their own personal problems. Perhaps it was because over the centuries they had grown accustomed to survival under a series of tyrants. To them, democratic government was an unknown concept, and by the time it arrived their tradition of survival and of driving ahead using their own wits and determination was ingrained.

As he scanned the high-rise buildings, the packed

markets and shops, and the streets clogged with the latest Japanese cars, Terry found it hard to believe that forty years ago the city had been rubble. After crossing Samchong-no Street, he entered the park surrounding the Kyongbok Palace and gardens. There appeared to be no one in the gardens at this late hour, which made it all the more enjoyable as far as Terry was concerned. As he strolled along the tree-lined pathways he could make out the rise and roll of the surrounding hilltops. His route wound through old-style pavilions, statues of Buddhist deities, and ornamental ponds, and eventually led him to the foot of steps that climbed through a series of levels up to the imposing five-tiered roof of the National Museum. He stared up at it and whistled. Nothing like this in Swansea, he thought. Brushing past some rhododendron bushes, he moved towards the steps.

The speed with which his reflexes operated never ceased to amaze Terry. After years of training they had acquired a life of their own; it was rather like having an ever-watchful bodyguard on hand at all times, almost a separate person who was ready to spring to his defence when required. So it was now.

Although he was hardly conscious of the knife and the dark shape of a man looming behind it, even as it was being thrust towards his side Terry's body was moving to face the attack, his right arm scything down, his hand open in a *shotei otoshi uke* palm-heel block. His head whipped round, eyes seeking out his opponent and locking on to him with the speed and precision of a missile. In a fraction of a second, Terry Williams had switched from being an inquisitive Western tourist, easy prey for a mugger, to the lethal fighting machine that had earned him the nickname of 'Dojo'.

Driving into the attacker's wrist, Terry's block pushed the knife harmlessly aside as if it was a toy. Calculations spun through his brain as he did so, evaluating the enemy and the situation, deciding on his own response. There was no question of pulling his counter-punch; the attacker's intention was as clear as if it had been written on the blade itself. As Terry's reflex defensive block flowed into an automatic counter-attack, his thigh and leg muscles locked in place, fixing him to the ground as solid as a launching platform, and his left fist powered away at lightning speed, the twin knuckles of the index and middle finger clenching into the *daikento*, the concentrated area of bone into which Terry focused his entire strength and life-force. As it met the space immediately below the attacker's nose, Terry's *kiai* shattered the night and the mugger was flung backwards like an unwanted doll.

Before the body had hit the ground, Terry was turning, executing a *mawashi-uke* double block as he did so. The standard precautionary measure paid off as he found himself facing two more men, both short and powerful, the nearest of whom was already delivering a ferocious front kick that might have caught Terry in the small of the back, shattering his spine. Instead, the Welshman's right forearm swept it up and with a forward drive from the hips, he tipped the man off balance, dropping him to the ground.

Terry had no time for a drop-punch to finish off the third mugger. However, having seen how he dealt with the two previous attacks, the man faltered and held back, preferring to size up this unusual tourist before trying for an opening. That was his big mistake. Switching from defence to attack, Terry went into action. His blood was up and he was out to fix the bastards who had spoiled what might otherwise have been a pleasant stroll.

Gliding forward with swift, measured steps, Terry feinted at the retreating mugger with a blinding series of punches and kicks, dazzling him with the display until it was impossible to guess from which quarter the real attack would come. When it did it was a roundhouse kick from an unexpected direction, and as the ball of Terry's foot slammed into the man's jaw he crumpled in the dirt, his eyes rolling in his head and shutting out the image of the Welsh tornado.

Fully aware that the second man would by now be on his feet again, Terry went into a forward roll, turned and lunged forward at the point where he judged the man would now be. Instead he was barely able to avoid launching himself at a tall, thickset man with a Mohican haircut.

'What the . . .?' Terry shouted as he pulled his punch an inch short of the man's face. The man grinned and Terry noticed that he was holding a tomahawk. The second mugger was lying silent and unmoving on the floor at his feet.

'Oh shit,' Terry groaned.

'It's OK,' the Indian quickly reassured him, 'he's just getting some shut-eye.' And by way of explanation he smacked the flat of his tomahawk blade on his other palm.

'That's a relief,' Terry said, smiling. 'I thought you'd bloody scalped him.'

The Indian kicked at the man's jacket with the toe of his boot and a pistol slid out on to the pathway.

'This one had a sting in his tail, I heard the noise and saw him pulling the pistol from his pocket while you were busy rearranging his buddy's face.' He gestured to the nearby body. 'Nice footwork.'

Terry shrugged, then remembering the first attacker, went to look among the rhododendrons.

'I'm afraid that one got away,' the Indian called over, checking the other muggers for signs of life. Terry scratched his head.

'Oh dear. Must be losing my touch.'

'I don't think he'd agree. I caught a glimpse of him and his nose seemed turned inside out.'

Wondering what to do with the two unconscious men, they decided to heed Babs's warning about drawing attention to themselves. Instead of calling the police, they dragged the muggers back to the main road, stripped them naked and used their clothing to tie them securely to a lamppost.

'Let them talk their way out of that when the next patrol car passes by,' said Terry with a wicked grin.

Checking that they hadn't been seen, they jogged across the road and headed off down Taepyong-no Street, back towards the hotel district, several blocks away. As they parted, Terry held out his hand. 'Terry Williams. Thank you for what you did back there.'

The Indian grinned. 'I'm glad you're on my side. The name's Danny. Danny Grey Wolf.'

Terry whistled. 'Not many folks in Swansea with a name like that. Well, Danny, this could be the start of a beautiful friendship.'

The camp consisted of a cluster of wooden huts in the bottom of a steep, forested valley. An assault course had been built along one side of the camp, and along the other white-painted stones marked out a rifle range some six hundred yards long. A firing point was similarly marked every hundred yards to enable firers to practise with different weapons from a variety of known ranges.

Andy Buchan felt immediately at home the moment he set eyes on the huts as his truck rumbled over the crest and began its descent to the training camp.

'Now that's what I call a hotel,' he bragged. Ken, the Australian, spat over the side.

'Listen to him. Fucking beam me up, Scotty. I don't know what planet you're from, mate, but down here we call that a shit-hole.' He leaned across and thrust his face towards Andy's.

'Repeat after me: shit-hole.'

Andy reddened and the men on either side of him had to hold him in his seat as Ken laughed and said: 'Only kidding, mate. Nothing personal.'

To Andy Buchan any slight was deeply personal. He would remember the Australian and sort him out. He always did, sooner or later. Consoled by the thought of future revenge, he slumped back on the bench and grinned.

'Sure, mate. Nothing personal.'

With the mercenaries concentrated at the training camp, Babs put them through a couple of days of simple warm-up exercises before Yi Soong arrived to take over the real training. A daily routine was quickly established whereby the men were woken early and pushed over the assault course three or four times before a light breakfast. During the rest of the morning they practised on the firing range.

The basic personal weapons issued to the men were the American M16 and the Colt Commando, both using interchangeable 5.56mm ammunition. In addition there were four of the tried-and-tested British general-purpose machine-guns, a seemingly endless supply of M72 single-shot disposable rocket-launchers, boxes of grenades, M79 and M203 grenade-launchers, an M202 Fireflash, and two American 60mm light mortars complete with a range of ammunition, high-explosive, white-phosphorus smoke bombs, and para-illuminating shells.

Andy Buchan was in his element, pitting himself against the assault course and then, after breakfast, being handed an array of the best weaponry in the world and ammunition to match, and told to blaze away on the range. He passed each day like a schoolboy on the loose in a toy shop; until the third day and the arrival of the new commander, Yi Soong.

The moment he set eyes on the tall, broad-shouldered Korean ex-special forces officer, Andy Buchan felt an intense dislike that was, in a matter of hours, to distil into hatred. For his part, Yi Soong was scrupulously polite, tactful and almost too solicitous of the welfare of his men. He seemed displeased that Babs had them running over the assault course, and immediately ensured that they finish each day's training two hours earlier. He arranged for a truckload of beer from Seoul and set up a canteen where everyone was entitled to four free cans of San Miguel before they had to start paying.

'This is more like it,' Ken said one evening. Andy was silent, staring into his mug. Ken prodded him lightly, having learnt that it was best to tackle the little Scot with caution.

'What's the matter, Scotty? Don't you like his face?'

'No. He's a smooth bastard and I'd like to stick one on him.'

Ken chuckled, popping open another can. 'I wouldn't try it if I was you, mate. You might not like his face, but there's one big fucker underneath it. Inscrutable fucking Orientals, that's what I say.' He belched. 'Don't trust 'em if you like, but there's nothing wrong with their money.'

The next day Terry Williams and Danny Grey Wolf were cleaning their rifles after a session on the range. Since their encounter in the park they had become friends and whenever a team effort was required for any of the tasks they naturally drifted together. Andy Buchan had tried to join in but neither of the other two men seemed particularly keen to encourage him.

They had stripped down the rifles and were scraping the carbon off the breech-blocks before oiling them, when Yi Soong came up and started to chat. He asked where they came from and about their military qualifications and battle experience.

'I can expect you boys to keep me on my toes then,' he quipped. 'It sounds as if you should be in charge.'

Terry smiled. 'Double my money and I'll consider it.'

Yi Soong wagged a finger at him. 'You'd put me out of a job. By the way, I hear you're pretty good with your hands?'

'You'd better believe it,' Danny grunted, snapping the butt of his rifle back in place and ramming home the locking pin. 'Damn near killed three guys who jumped him in Seoul. Luckily I came along and saved them.'

'Is that so?' Yi Soong said, smiling easily. 'You and I should do some sparring some time.'

Terry shook his head. 'Not me. I've seen you Taekwondo boys in action before. We've only got stumpy little legs in Wales, you see. Haven't got the reach.'

'That's too bad. Maybe one day.'

'Maybe,' Terry agreed doubtfully.

Yi Soong laughed and slapped him on the back a little harder than necessary. As he strolled away with a cheery wave Danny eyed his friend.

'I'd watch him, if I were you. I think Mr Yi likes to be the biggest fish in the pond.'

'Yeah,' Terry said thoughtfully. 'I was thinking more of the biggest turd in the bowl.'

The next evening the whole camp gathered for a briefing. As they trooped into the main dining-room the men found that the chairs had been rearranged in rows and a large bed sheet had been hung on the wall at the front. Babs was fussing about getting everyone seated and when this was done, Yi Soong appeared, strode straight to the front and pulled down the sheet to reveal a large map of Korea with the border indicated by a thick red line and the main towns on both sides marked by coloured pins. Yi stood aside and watched his audience for a while before speaking.

'Gentlemen, the time has come to explain to you the reason why we are all here. As some of you will know, the North has been attempting to build a nuclear weapon for quite some time. This is no big secret. The UN has been trying to persuade them to open their facilities for inspection.'

A ripple of laughter ran through the room. Yi smiled.

'Exactly. I am glad that you all seem to agree with me. It is a futile approach. Worse than that, it strengthens the North because they see the West as both weak and gullible, and by the West I include my own South Korea. They will never allow the UN access, and if they do they will show them factories making baby food or condoms. Which brings me to one Professor Lim Choy.'

He pressed a button on the remote control of a slide projector and the face of a stern, bespectacled, middle-aged man grimaced down at them from a screen.

'Professor Lim is, quite simply, the most brilliant man in North Korea.'

'Is that like the wisest man in Ireland?' someone called out, following it with a convincing impression of a mental defective. Yi smiled politely.

'Not exactly. He is the head of the North Korean nuclear weapons programme. Without him, even at this stage in the development process, the whole edifice tumbles. The wheels stop turning and, with luck, the North suffers a delay from which they will not recover.'

By now the room was completely silent. Terry raised his hand.

'Excuse me, I might be being thick, but surely any delay will be just that, only a delay.'

Yi nodded and said: 'That is correct, but it is all that we will need.'

'For what?'

Yi shrugged as if the answer was obvious. 'For our own bomb to be ready, of course.'

There was a subdued muttering until Yi waved his hands for silence.

'Let me reassure you, South Korea is not going to start any nuclear war. We are going to prevent one. It's simply what you in Europe have been doing for the last forty years. A balance of terror, if you like.

Don't hit me or I'll hit you back, you say to your enemy.'

He waited until his words had sunk in before continuing.

'You and I, gentlemen, are going to rescue Professor Lim. Or to put it another way, we are going to enable him to defect. So you see, for those of you with scruples, it is a rescue mission. For the others' – he shrugged – 'the money is even now being transferred to your accounts.'

During the ensuing outbreak of chatter Yi unrolled another map and a large diagram, and pinned them both to the wall. When the room was again silent he picked up a long pointer and indicated the diagram, which showed a compound.

'This is where we will find Professor Lim. It is a government holiday resort for the use of the top members of the politburo only. President Kim Il Sung himself uses it.' He grinned. 'Maybe we'll even find him in residence when we drop in for tea.'

There was a nervous laughter from the men, all of whom now leaned forward to absorb every detail of the forthcoming operation. As the significance and the risks involved burned into the minds of the mercenaries, each in his own way focused his full attention on the task ahead.

'The resort is south of Wonsan, here,' Yi said, pointing to the map. 'The insertion phase will be by sea and under cover of darkness. Once ashore we will march inland, lie up throughout the hours of daylight, carry out a covert close recce, finalize plans and assault the following night as soon as it is dark. If our secrecy is compromised we can expect some stiff resistance from the guards but I hope to accomplish entry to the compound undetected. Professor Lim will be ready and waiting; the RV and time have been arranged by one of our agents. We will then exfiltrate, get back to the coast and be away long before first light.'

Proud with himself, Yi Soong stood back with folded arms. He ran his eyes over the assembled mercenaries, anticipating the volley of questions that was sure to come.

'And before you all start shouting, I will now explain the details of the plan.'

In response to another press of the buttons the slide projector covered the screen with a mass of timings and grid references.

Two hours later Yi Soong knocked on the door of the office and waited for permission to enter. Seated in the red plastic chair behind the desk, Francis Kwang was talking with Babs Butler. Ignoring Babs, Yi reported that the briefing was complete and that rehearsals for the infiltration of the compound would begin the following morning.

'We'll use this camp as a model to practise on. It's far from perfect but it'll do. I want to run them through some set procedures that we'll use at the objective.'

'Of course,' Kwang agreed, full of admiration for his subordinate and right-hand man. 'A dry run will be invaluable.'

'Oh, not just one. I intend to get them working together as if they were one of my old special forces groups.'

Kwang nodded, then turning to Babs, suggested politely that the men might have some final queries about administration that he may be able to answer. Taking the hint, Babs left the office. Once he had heard the outside door close, Kwang turned back to Yi.

'And will they all do?'

'Major Butler has produced exactly the team we knew he would.'

Kwang tipped back his head and laughed. 'You mean, the toughest bunch of killers ever to walk the earth.'

Yi joined in, mimicking Babs's voice: 'Of course. The top men in their field, every one.'

Suddenly serious, Kwang examined his fingernails. 'Good. Well then, there's nothing more to be said.' He picked up the slide of Professor Lim and held it up to the light.

'Good night, Professor Lim Choy. This time next week you'll be enjoying the freedom of Seoul.'

In the back of his limousine, Kwang helped himself to a drink from the cabinet. Yi had done a good job, but then he always did. Kwang had slipped in and out of the camp unnoticed, but while he had been waiting in the back office, he had studied the assembled mercenaries through one of the security cameras that had been installed for the purpose. He had seen pretty much what he had expected: a sad collection of losers. Still, he thought as he stirred the ice in his gin, they were good enough for the task in hand. He had read through a selection of their dossiers and had found several who sounded very interesting. In other circumstances he might even have been willing to offer some of them more permanent work with his organization. It was something to bear in mind.

His car sped through the night along the east–west Yongdong Expressway, whisking him back to Seoul, where he had some last-minute business to attend to. Ideally he would have liked to return straight to his villa, where Lulu was waiting for him, but she would just have to wait. If he found himself at a loose end in Seoul he could easily look up someone else. There was never any shortage of women ready to do anything for a man like Francis Kwang. It was true what they say: power is the best aphrodisiac.

Watching the cars and trucks speed by, Kwang marvelled at the life of the ordinary man. What on earth motivated such people? He found it impossible to imagine a life without intrigue. He had acquired most of the things that he had ever desired. He had power, wealth, a beautiful mistress; he was in good health, and he was feared. Fame was less important. Indeed, in his line of work it was highly undesirable. He took a far greater satisfaction in being anonymous, walking through the busy streets of Seoul, driving like this along the expressways, as if he was just another good and law-abiding citizen. The delight came in the secret knowledge that he, Francis Kwang, was far from average and ordinary. He could look through anyone with the sweetest smile masking his contempt, knowing in his heart that he could topple governments. Let the politicians strut like peacocks, mouth their bold words like fish behind thick glass. He was the real kingmaker. He was the mover of mountains.

As he passed a sign indicating that Seoul was fifty kilometres away, Kwang eased back in the leather seat. Yes, he would give Linda a call when he got in.

5

In the final days at the training camp, the sixteen mercenaries were divided up into four teams of four. Yi Soong did the selection, basing his decisions on observations made throughout the training period. He had noted which groups of men gravitated together and by the time of his final preparations, the teams had virtually formed themselves. Everyone was happy with the choice, recognizing that it would be the most efficient way of operating.

As always, there were one or two loners. Rather than stick them together in a group of their own, Yi divided them between the teams who would be best able to absorb them. Since the fight in the Seoul park, Terry and Danny had stuck together throughout the warm-up course. As Kén had antagonized everyone except Terry, who seemed extremely slow to anger, and Danny, who didn't care, Yi grouped the three of them together and completed the team with Andy Buchan.

'Fuck a stoat,' Ken said loudly when he heard the news. 'Why do we have to get lumbered with Bonnie Prince Charlie?'

'Well, why not?' Terry said good-naturedly, noticing Andy's warning scowl and anxious to avoid a dangerous rift before the operation had even begun. 'We've already got Robert the Bruce.'

'Ha!' Andy bellowed. 'You tell him, Dojo.'

Although he kept himself to himself, Andy liked the look of Terry's team. The Welshman was a smooth operator, as Andy had seen before in Africa. OK, so what if he was a soft touch when it came to sorting out the prisoners: he remembered the run-in they had had, with Dojo screaming and him standing over the bodies, pistol in hand.

'It's a dirty job, but someone's got to do it,' Andy had said. Dojo hadn't liked that. For a moment Andy had thought he would have to shoot him too, but then the South Africans had turned up and cooled him down. Nevertheless, the Scot had felt a grudging respect for the Welshman. He recognized that it had taken guts to put a stop to the killing, even if Dojo was wrong to try.

He had also been impressed by the big Indian. Danny Grey Wolf was obviously a natural – anyone could see that. Andy hadn't liked to admit it to himself, but he had longed to join their team. It was a shame about the loud-mouthed Aussie but nothing was perfect.

Yi had announced that he would make up a fifth team with three fellow Koreans. They had arrived at the camp only the day before departure and a couple of the men voiced concerns that the newcomers had missed out on all the preliminary training.

'Let me worry about that,' Yi had answered. 'They're in my team and if I'm happy to trust them with my life I don't think it should bother you.'

'More to the point,' Terry had said quietly to Danny afterwards, 'why isn't Yi prepared to commit himself to a team made up of our boys?'

But he never got his answer because the next

morning four large trucks pulled into the camp and the operation began. After loading all the weapons, stores and ammunition, the convoy set off for the coast, arriving in darkness at a small fishing village north of Konsang. As the trucks drew up beside the walls of what appeared to be a schoolhouse, they were met by a man who waved them to a halt with a torch and then led them down to the waterfront. At the end of a long, narrow pier a large fishing boat lay at anchor. The captain leaned from a window on the bridge, looking at the trucks with only mild interest, while below him the crew scuttled about their tasks, making space for the mercenaries.

'Why did I ever break my golden rule: never travel by sea?'

Hanging his head over the side of the fishing boat, Jules Merkoen, the South African, was in a bad way, his voice muffled by the waves breaking over the prow and slicing along the rusty, green-painted sides in foaming crests. With a violent convulsion he retched and vomited again, his knuckles white from grasping the railings.

'Here you are, mate,' Ken said, handing him a packet. 'I saved you an egg-and-cress sandwich.'

'Oh shit . . .' Jules heaved again, ending with a fit of coughing as his empty stomach rebelled.

Elsewhere in the boat every member of the little force was busy. Weapons were being stripped, cleaned and checked for the hundredth time; ammunition was being packed and repacked in pouches and bergens in the search for the most efficient method of distributing the weight; and webbing was being adjusted to sit securely but comfortably on the wearer, allowing him freedom of movement, but not fitting so loosely as to rattle and give him away.

Danny was sitting on the deck, leaning against one of the five inflatable dinghies, one for each of the teams. He had spread a cloth over his lap and was oiling the pieces of his M16.

'You'll wear them out,' Terry said, dropping down beside him. 'Here, have some coffee.'

He gripped the plastic mug between his knees, unscrewed the cap of the vacuum flask and poured as carefully as he could against the pitching of the boat.

'Bit rough, isn't it?' he said passing the mug to Danny.

'Thanks.'

Danny took a swig of coffee, paused to let it cool in his mouth before swallowing, took a second swig and handed the mug back.

'Did you make that yourself?'

'Do you like it?' Terry asked eagerly.

'Tastes like shit.'

'Now there's gratitude for you. I slave all day over a hot stove and that's all the thanks I get.'

From the other side of the inflatable Ken called over: 'Shut the fuck up. I'm trying to get some kip. You sound like an old married couple.'

Since leaving the jetty, Yi and the captain had insisted on a complete black-out. Not a single light showed from anywhere in the boat; only the stars shone on the water, glinting on the tossed waves and dimly lighting the distant horizon. At one point another vessel was sighted far away to the north-east and the skipper swung his fishing boat towards the shore in case it was a North Korean gunboat on patrol and he needed to seek the shelter of the inlets and coves.

Ken swore under his breath. 'Just our luck to get caught in the middle of this bloody lot. We're sitting ducks out here in a tub like this.'

Danny Grey Wolf peered long and hard through his binoculars and when he eventually lowered them, he looked puzzled.

'What's up, Danny?'

Without looking at Terry he examined the horizon again, scanning from side to side.

'Nothing, I hope. It's gone now anyway.'

'What was it?'

'An Osa missile-attack boat.'

Ken whistled. 'Thank God it missed us.'

Danny nodded slowly. 'Yeah. Stroke of luck, wasn't it.'

In the early hours the fishing boat turned towards the shore again, only this time going to within half a mile of the beach. The captain hissed from the bridge.

'What's that fat bugger on about?' Andy said, scowling.

Danny listened carefully, then translated. 'He says he can't go in any closer. It looks like this is our stop.'

'Your Korean might come in useful,' Terry said.

Danny shook his head. He had picked up a rough understanding of the language when he had been based just south of the border.

'If it does it probably means something's gone wrong.'

At Yi's command, the inflatables were dropped over the side and two men from each team climbed down into them. While one handled the dinghy, keeping it close alongside the boat, the other stowed the kit that the remaining members of each team handed down to him. Throughout the operation Yi stood calmly on the other side of the boat, occasionally checking his watch, then looking up at the horizon for any sign of the returning gunboat.

'Cool customer, isn't he?' Jules said, heaving a box of bombs overboard for the 60mm mortars.

Terry looked across at Yi. He had to admit that whatever they thought of their commander as a human being, it was rapidly becoming clear that he was a highly professional soldier. His training at the camp and the detailed rehearsals had demonstrated a thorough grasp of low-level tactics, while his superb physical fitness was beyond question. During a break in one of the range practices Yi had laid on a little Taekwondo demonstration, executing various fancy spinning and jumping kicks. As usual he had tried to coax Terry into a sparring match, but Terry had joked his way out of it. He had a gut feeling that he and Mr Yi might one day do more than simply spar together, so while he took careful note of the Korean's style and favourite techniques, he took care to give away nothing of his own considerable ability.

When the dinghies were loaded and the last of the men had clambered over the side, Yi signalled to the skipper and swung himself down into his own dinghy with his three fellow-countrymen. As the five inflatables bobbed in the water the fishing boat turned away ponderously and headed out to sea, leaning into the waves towards the south and home.

Each inflatable was fitted with a small outboard motor, easing the short trip to the shore and giving each of the teams greater control over their tiny craft in the heavy sea. When they were about two hundred yards from the shoreline, Yi held up his arm as the signal for the dinghies to swing out into an extended line, so that when they hit the beach a minute or two later they did so in line abreast, disgorging their teams of heavily armed mercenaries simultaneously.

Leaping over the sides, two men from each team raced ashore, sprinted across the bare stretch of sand and dived into the sparse tufts of grass at the foot of a wall of dunes. Scanning the beach and searching inland with the aid of night-vision goggles, they prepared to give covering fire to their mates if necessary. Meanwhile the other half of each team manhandled the dinghies across the sand and pulled them in among the dunes, where a thick tangle of mangrove provided sufficient cover to hide the boats from any patrolling aircraft that might fly over the beach in daylight.

While some of the men hacked at the mangrove and camouflaged the dinghies, others went back over the beach, sweeping away their tracks until all sign of their arrival had been eradicated.

Finally, when he was satisfied that everything had been done according to the plan, Yi called together the other four team leaders.

'All OK?' he asked.

They nodded.

'Let's go, then. Same order of march as in rehearsal. I'll take the lead, then you Dave, followed by Dominic's team, Jules, and you Terry to bring up the rear. Any questions? Then move.'

As he doubled back to where Danny, Ken and Andy waited by the mangrove, Terry felt a thrill of excitement course through his veins. It happened every time he approached combat. Later on would come the ruthless self-control and cool nerve that had made him one of the best in the business, but for now he allowed himself the adrenalin. It was what kept him coming back.

Waiting until the other teams had headed out through the dunes, Terry hand-signalled his men into position, himself leading, followed by Ken, then Andy, with Danny bringing up the rear. If anyone was able to detect a tail it was the big Indian. Terry had witnessed Danny Grey Wolf's tracking skills on the warm-up course and he seemed to have a sixth sense when it came to bush work.

The track leading inland from the beach soon started to climb and it wasn't long before the men were sweating under the weight of their heavy bergens and webbing.

'Jesus,' Ken muttered, 'we must have brought enough kit to start a fucking war.'

'If we fuck this up that's exactly what we could end up with,' Terry answered, plodding resolutely forward, head down, his breathing steady and deep.

Having crested the first ridge, they went down into a valley, leaving the track and striking out across rough, scrub-covered country. By now the moon had risen and Yi was careful to keep the line of march below the skyline lest they be silhouetted against the velvet-black sky for any chance security patrols to see.

Clumps of pine trees dotted the hillside and as the column began to climb again, Terry knew from his previous study of the maps that they were scaling the last of the ridges before the final descent towards the resort, the objective that had brought them together from the four corners of the earth.

With the first hint of a glow beneath the eastern horizon, they rounded a summit and dropped sharply across two hundred yards of open gorse before Yi signalled a halt, put out sentries and summoned the team leaders.

'OK, this will be the lying-up position. We'll be staying here throughout today. Adopt the triangular harbour formation as we rehearsed. Dave, you take twelve o'clock. No lights, no fires, no cigarettes, not even after first light. Nothing. Is that understood?'

This is just like a bloody exercise, Terry thought. If it goes on like this it'll be money for old rope.

'Terry, you'll come with me on the close recce later this morning,' said Yi. 'Cam up and get Danny to come too. I want to select our exact route in for the infiltration.'

'Right you are,' Terry answered, regretting his complacency.

'Jules, work out sentry stags and anyone not on duty is to sleep. Tomorrow's a busy day,' Yi continued, looking at the blackened faces of the men crouching around him. 'So far so good, gentlemen. Let's hope we've caught the Commies napping.'

He smiled broadly and sent his team leaders away to organize their rotas. Watching from the shadows, only Andy, the cynical loner, noticed how the smile disappeared a little too quickly from Yi's face the moment the last back was turned. But then Andy had never liked the bastard anyway.

Slumped in a deck chair, Alex Leitner gazed across the choppy waters of Chesapeake Bay. There must be some kind of race on, he thought, judging by the number of brightly coloured sails that bobbed and whizzed back and forth in front of where he and his son sat fishing. Windsurfers darted across the water like skimming pebbles, hands holding fast to the boom, backsides sticking dangerously over the edge.

He nudged his son. 'Can you imagine your old man doing that?'

Stephen laughed. 'Nope,' he said, and a moment later he shouted and grabbed the rod as the line was tugged sharply downwards.

'You've got something, Pop! Here, you play him. Careful now.'

Struggling out of his chair, Alex was almost sorry. Now he'd have to get his hands all wet and slimy on some poor creature that was swimming along minding its own business, thinking it had just found a nice little snack to take home for the kids.

It was only a short mental step from a slimy fish to Eliot Masterson. After the unsatisfactory interview with his boss, Alex had tried to put the photographs and the report from his mind, but it wasn't easy. The habits of a lifetime in intelligence work were not easily bypassed and ever since Masterson's cursory dismissal of the affair Alex had been deeply troubled. Against his better judgement he had been making a few discreet enquiries but so far had found nothing unusual in his boss's past.

Masterson had graduated from Harvard with just about the finest degree known to man, had been recruited by the CIA while doing a doctorate in Far Eastern Affairs, and since joining the organization he had sky-rocketed, keeping his nose so clean it almost squeaked. Still, Alex wasn't done with him yet.

He laid the cod on the bank and worked the hook from its lip. Stephen had run over to the car and was rummaging in the boot for a basket to put it in. They had taken the old route past Annapolis and cracked the usual jokes. Alex had enjoyed the day.

Holding the fish in his hand, he turned round to check that Stephen wasn't looking then tossed it back into the water. In a flash of silver it was gone. Alex's hands hung limply between his knees. What kind of an agent was he? He didn't even have the heart to kill a goddam fish.

When Stephen came back he looked at the empty space on the grass where the fish had been, then at his father.

'Shit, Dad. You didn't throw it back again?'

'The one that got away?' Alex shrugged.

'But they all do!'

Alex peered out across the windswept waves. The leading windsurfer had just overbalanced and toppled head first off his board, the sail crashing down on top of him.

'Not all of them,' he said.

Hugging the ground, Terry nudged his way through the undergrowth. In his day he had been one of the best stalkers in the British Army, passing his sniper course with flying colours. He had had to carry out a one-mile stalk across a bare-arsed stretch of Salisbury Plain, with the Directing Staff watching for him with binoculars. He had not only completed it successfully, but had then put a single shot through the centre of the target's chest at eight hundred yards and withdrawn, still undetected.

He regretted not having brought his custom-made

gillie's suit with him, but had improvised just after first light by shredding a spare combat jacket and then rapidly stitching strips of camouflaged cloth, branches and undergrowth into the fabric. He had been particularly careful to crawl a little way forward with his binos and study the ground that he would have to cross, selecting his route and gauging the right combination of colours he would need if he was to stand a good chance of remaining undetected.

Yi, Danny and another of the Koreans had done likewise, and the four of them had set out at mid-morning, moving as quickly as possible over the first leg of the journey, crawling only to cover gaps in the undergrowth. But as they neared the resort itself, they found themselves having to crawl more and more often until by the time they were within six hundred yards of the outer fences, they were wriggling on their stomachs at a painfully slow pace.

'This is as close as I dare go for now,' Yi whispered in Terry's ear. 'We'll have a good look from here and then circle around to see if there are any better approaches. I also want to select an emergency exit point in case we have to get out in a hurry.'

Terry hand-signalled Danny to crawl forward beside them, and while the Korean guard stood watch the three of them studied the compound buildings, fences and guard posts.

Having made a sketch map for use in the planning meeting that would be held in the afternoon, Terry was surprised to find the layout was just like that of any large Mediterranean hotel, only with a few security fences and watch-towers. He could see a pool with a couple of people floating lazily in the clear water; others were sunbathing while the guards kept a discreet distance from the holidaymakers. So the Communists, for all their talk about equality, are just like the rest, Terry thought as he sketched in a guard position that he had just spotted. It's one rule for the rich and one for the poor. Those fat cats round the pool are full of bullshit about the proletariat, but when they're on holiday, God help any worker who strays too close. Still, that would work to the mercenaries' advantage. If the guards were ordered to keep away from the VIPs, then they wouldn't be around when Terry and the other teams infiltrated after dark.

He looked across at Danny, who was obviously thinking the same, and they exchanged grins.

'Candy from a baby,' said Terry.

When they had gained all the information they could from their present position, they crawled around to the west with slow, agonizing precision, Yi leading, the other Korean following behind, guarding the rear. Once established in another observation post, they refined the sketch, adding in details that had not been visible from the other part of the hill, gradually building up a detailed plan of the resort.

There were five main buildings in the complex, all substantial accommodation blocks, with balconies and terraces where the recce party could see powerful North Koreans dozing in the sun or reading the newspapers that only they would have access to. There were three swimming pools in all, and an open-air restaurant that reminded Terry that he was starving.

'Have you seen enough?' he asked Yi, who was scribbling in a notebook. He looked up and smiled.

'More than enough. Let's get back.'

If anything, the return journey took longer than the

outward stalk, as every member of the recce party fought against the desire to switch off and rush. They were all experienced enough to know that many a close recce had been compromised at the withdrawal stage, when team members' guard went down because they thought it was as good as in the bag.

It was only when they were back within the relative safety of the lying-up position that Yi spoke again and they relaxed, slipping out of their sweat-soaked jackets and shirts. Ken thrust his water bottle into Terry's hand.

'Nice going, mate. Give some to Tonto as well,' he said, pointing at Danny. The Indian looked up slowly and for a moment Terry felt his stomach muscles tighten. The last thing they needed before an action was a bloody split in the team. It was bad enough already coping with Andy's moods.

Danny got to his feet and stood over Ken. Slowly he took the bottle and took a swig.

'Thank you, Kimosabe,' he said quietly.

Terry felt the tension drain from him in a flood of relief. Ken laughed and clapped Danny on the back. They were happy. It had been a good recce, the operation was going according to plan and with luck they would all soon be back in Seoul and considerably richer.

Francis Kwang really didn't see why he had to explain his behaviour to anyone, least of all to a call-girl. But he had and it disconcerted him. It had started when Lulu discovered a piece of paper with Linda's name and telephone number on it, and it had finished with several of his Chinese vases shattered on the sitting-room floor of his villa. Having spent her wrath in the only way she knew how, Lulu had padded upstairs and collapsed on the bed in a flood of tears, leaving Kwang wrestling with a range of emotions that he was uncomfortable to discover in himself.

He had considered the reflex action that he had used before with other women, of having her put in a cab by one of the guards, roughed up a bit, driven back to Seoul and dumped in It'aewan. But halfway to the phone he had stopped. The thought of not seeing her again suddenly struck him as unpleasant, inconceivable even. With a chill feeling that was partly dread and partly excitement, he realized that he had allowed Lulu to become special to him. So, taking a bottle of Veuve Clicquot from the icebox, he had gone quietly upstairs and attempted to appear contrite.

Since that unforgettable night, the balance of power in their relationship had undergone a radical shift and Kwang knew that Lulu knew it. It was intolerable. She was as happy as a child and moved about the villa with a new ease as if she was truly the mistress of the place. But she was also wise enough not to push her luck. She had discovered an Achilles heel in her lover, but unlike the Greek hero, Lulu could not be sure that Kwang's weak point would remain vulnerable for ever. The result was a deepening of their relationship as both partners felt their way forward as if in a pitch-black room, hands outstretched, but moving inexorably closer together from their opposing sides.

Tonight of all nights, Kwang wanted to keep a clear head, but he had returned to the villa to find that Lulu herself had prepared dinner, having dismissed the cook and dimmed the lights.

Instead of the Sinatra record that she loved, she had put on one of Kwang's favourite Pavarotti CDs. The food by candlelight had been surprisingly good and although he had tried to stick to just one glass of red wine, Lulu had refilled it without him noticing, so that by the time she produced a dessert made with fresh lychees, cream and an unidentifiable liqueur, he could feel himself expanding from his customary reserve into an extremely pleasant torpor.

Lulu slipped round the side of the table and stood behind Kwang's chair, draping herself over his shoulders like a fur stole, warm and soft. Kissing him at first on the cheeks, she ran her fingers through his hair, pulling his head gently back and pressing her lips to his. As he opened his mouth Kwang felt her silky-smooth tongue flick the tip of his, and her hands caress his chest, seeking the buttons of his shirt.

'Lulu,' he whispered, pulling away from her and looking in her eyes. 'Can we do this later? There are things I have to do.'

But she smiled as if she hadn't heard and pulling open his shirt, slid around him and straddled his lap.

'Lulu, please,' Kwang moaned, feeling the heat rising through him. Against his will he found his hands sliding down her legs, stroking the little hollows behind her knees, then rising again, pushing her dress up over her thighs. Lulu was kissing his ears, her hands unfastening the front of her dress and a moment later he caught the sweet scent of her breasts and tipped his face forward into them.

Somewhere in the villa a clock chimed. Now would be the time, he told himself, fighting to order his brain before Lulu's irresistible onslaught. But her weapons were such as had no counter, and as she felt the palms of his hands slide under her buttocks, and as she wriggled and brought him into her, she heard him gasp and knew that she had mastered the most powerful man in South Korea.

After crawling up the last slope below the compound fence, Terry elbowed slowly through the undergrowth and peered over the top. The base of the fence was a mere ten yards in front of him, across an open strip of close-cropped grass. Christ, he thought, this is a piece of piss. A bloody holiday home for important invalids. Not a guard in sight and, as far as he could tell, no dogs either.

He signalled to the other members of his team, who were waiting below, and crawled across the narrow lawn until he reached the bottom strand of barbed wire. According to Yi, their intelligence had reported that the fence was not electrified but as Terry was the one who had to cut it, he tested it first. The report was correct. Unable to suppress a feeling of disgust at the appalling security of the camp, he spat in the dirt and prepared to cut the wire as Danny wrapped pieces of sacking around the point of the cut to muffle the noise.

When Terry had cut a hole big enough for a man to crawl through, he rolled aside and Ken and Andy slithered through and doubled across to the outside wall of the nearest accommodation block. Then Danny and Terry themselves crawled through and signalled for the other teams to close up. Jogging out of the darkness, the remaining twelve mercenaries and the four Koreans came up the slope and through the wire while Terry's team provided close protection on the inside.

Kneeling beside Terry, Yi glanced up at the lights,

shaking his head in disgust when Terry scoffed at the lack of video cameras or trip-wires. They had entered at a point that Terry had found, a complete blind spot, out of direct line of sight of any of the watch-towers.

'Fuck 'em,' Yi hissed. 'Whoever designed this show will be facing a firing squad tomorrow.'

Under the plan that Yi had drawn up after the recce, he and his team would enter the accommodation block that was known to house Professor Lim Choy. The Professor had arranged an RV, Yi said, and they would wait there for only two minutes. If the Professor didn't show, they were to withdraw immediately. While they were gone, the other four teams were to move to a garden and pool area that would be deserted at that time of night, and await Yi's return. In the event that his team was compromised, the mercenaries were to withdraw to an emergency RV halfway back to the lying-up position and wait there for five minutes in case Yi and his Koreans were able to escape. If not, they were free to return to the dinghies and the pick-up point.

When Yi and his team had gone, Terry led the others round the edge of the building, steeled and ready to silence any guard they encountered. Danny had slung his M16 and carried his tomahawk in the throwing position. Terry preferred to use his hands, and grinned back at Ken, who had picked up a feather and stuck it behind his ear.

'Christ alive, it's like Dances with bloody Wolves,' he whispered as he came alongside Terry, waiting for Danny to clear the next corner. There was a dull thud and they raced forward to see Danny lowering the body of a guard to the floor, a savage gash at the base of his skull where the tomahawk had severed the spinal column.

'Nice work,' Terry whispered. But Danny was frowning.

'What's up?'

Danny turned the guard's face to the light and studied it.

'He's only a fucking kid, Terry.'

Ken patted him on the shoulder. 'He can still pull a trigger, mate.'

'That's not what I meant. It doesn't add up, raw kids guarding a resort used by the President himself.' He stooped and picked up the Kalashnikov.

'No security cameras, no noise of partying. Fuck it, Terry, this is supposed to be a holiday camp where these bastards let their hair down. Why wasn't there anyone in the restaurant when we saw it on the recce? It was midday; it should have been packed. And that patrol boat veering off like that. It just doesn't add up.'

He sprung open the cocking handle of the assault rifle and tilted the chamber towards the light. The magazine was empty.

'Shit,' Ken murmured, as one of Jules's team jogged up to them out of breath and said: 'Dojo, Jules said you'd better come and have a look.'

'What is it?' Terry said, feeling the hair rise on the back of his neck.

'Just come and have a look.'

Leaving Andy and Ken to cover their backs, Terry and Danny followed the mercenary to one of the pool areas. Jules had also come across one of the guards and silenced him. But like the one Danny had killed, he was no more than a teenager and his magazine was empty.

'What's going on?' Terry asked.

'That's not all. Look at this,' said Jules.

The South African and Terry came out on to a lawn where deckchairs were laid out ready for sunbathers. Although it was late at night, several of the chairs were occupied, men and women in brightly coloured trunks and swimsuits lazing in the darkness, some with papers over their faces as if fast asleep, others tilted on their sides, eyes closed.

Despite his training and despite his years of combat, Terry felt a wave of sickness sweep through him, followed by a chill iciness that gripped his chest. As he took in the distended bellies, swollen and bloated with the build-up of gases, and the limbs mottled and stiff in death, his body reacted first, as it always did in extreme danger. He spun on his heel, raising his voice from the whisper of the past hours to the full pitch of a battle cry.

'Ambush!'

6

'Headlights coming up the main road, Dojo. Looks like a convoy of troop carriers.'

'Strength?'

'At least two companies. About a mile away.'

Terry cursed. Why the hell hadn't he smelt it? It had all been far too easy. The coastal insertion, the approach march and recce, no perimeter patrols, cameras, trip-wires or dogs. They had walked straight into a trap.

Even under his cam cream, Terry could see that Jules had gone pale. 'What the hell's going on, Dojo?'

'No time for that now. Let's get the fuck out of here.'

A couple of the men called out for Yi.

'That bastard'll be miles away by now,' Andy said bitterly.

'What do you mean?' Ken growled.

'Who do you think set us up?'

Terry felt the pieces slowly starting to fit. 'Let's see if he's still around. Danny, Ken and Andy, come with me. Jules and Dominic, you and your men cover the main entrance. Force the gooks to debus from the trucks and slow them down. Dave, give them your mortar and ammo and get your team back to cover the entry point.'

Dave Bedford looked doubtful. 'You're not going out that way, are you?' he asked.

'No fucking way; they'll have ambushed our route by now, hoping to catch us making a run for it. But make sure they don't come in the same way we did. I'll check for Yi, then recce a new exit point on the opposite side.'

'Right.'

Terry spoke quickly, trying to sound calm and in control, masking the thoughts and fears tumbling through his brain. He realized they were probably in the tightest corner any of them had ever been in and that they were going to need all their skills and co-operation to escape. Deep inside a hostile country, their mission had been compromised and if they weren't already surrounded, then they soon would be, just as soon as the troop carriers arrived.

'Listen in, lads,' Terry shouted as the teams sorted themselves out, swapped kit and mortars, and filled their pockets with spare magazines and grenades. 'From now on, any Koreans you see, blast them,' he ordered. 'And that goes for Yi too. If they think we're going to be a pushover they've picked a fight with the wrong bunch. OK, move!'

The teams jogged away from the pool area and disappeared to their various tasks. With a final check on the grenades attached to his webbing, Terry led the way towards the accommodation block that Yi had indicated. A central staircase climbed up through the four levels, with a balcony on each floor dividing to both left and right. Rows of doors led from the carpeted corridor into the plush holiday suites.

Moving in pairs, the team leapfrogged forwards in a series of short tactical bounds, Terry and Danny going first and then covering Ken and Andy when they moved. Dropping into a kneeling position and aiming his Colt Commando, Terry shouted for Andy to move.

'Go!'

Opposite him Danny was pressed into an alcove, his M16 covering the other direction, tensed and ready to fire at the slightest sign of movement. Darting between them, Ken and Andy burst up the last flight of stairs, dived for cover and a moment later Ken's voice echoed down the stairwell.

'All clear!'

Bounding up three steps at a time, Terry and Danny split left and right at the top, dropping again into an aiming position, their eyes sweeping the corridor on either side, taking in every detail and evaluating possible targets.

Locating the nearest door, Terry hand-signalled Danny to cover him, and cradling his assault rifle for a forward roll, shouldered his way straight through it, dived across the carpet and came up ready to fire. The room was empty, but Terry's nostrils were filled with a stench that made him retch. On the hotel lawn he hadn't noticed the smell of the bodies, but here in the confined space of a bedroom it was overpowering.

'Jesus Christ,' Danny muttered, coming in after him. 'Where the hell's that coming from?'

Terry went carefully over to the bed and flicked back the sheet with the tip of his rifle. Staring up at the ceiling with glazed lifeless eyes, a man and a woman lay in each other's arms. Between them a baby clung to its mother's breast, from which it would never again draw life. Even through the mass of blood that soaked the mattress, Terry could see that it had been shot, like its parents.

A shout came from the adjoining room and they ran in to find Ken and Andy staring at a similar spectacle, only this time the man was fully dressed and propped in an armchair while the woman lay in a half-filled bath, the water pink and stagnant.

Ken held his hand over his nose. 'I wonder if they'll get a refund?'

'Shut it, Ken,' Andy snapped.

'Do you think there's a mini-bar?'

'I said shut it!'

Terry laid a hand on Andy's shoulder. 'Easy. Come on, lads. Let's get out of here.'

Having made their way to the end of the corridor, they found more corpses in the other rooms but no sign of Yi or his team.

'He'll be under the wire by now,' Danny said. 'Waiting to guide in his friends.'

Terry nodded. 'We'd better find an exit quick or we'll end up like these poor buggers, whoever they were.'

'One thing's for certain,' Danny said, 'They're no government honchos. Look at their hands.'

He bent down beside the body of a white-haired old man and pointed to the calluses covering his palms.

'And there's no luggage. They've all been dressed in bright holiday clothes but where are the cases?'

'Yeah, and no toothbrushes or razors in the bathrooms,' Ken said. 'Nothing. What the fuck happened to them?'

Terry led the way back down the corridor. 'I don't know and right now I don't care,' he muttered.

Halfway to the perimeter fence, the noise of a mortar

firing shook the ground, followed a few seconds later by the crump of the distant explosion as Jules and his men opened fire on the North Korean troop carriers.

Jules had waited until the leading truck had slowed to negotiate a hairpin bend on its descent to the resort before signalling the mortar team to open fire. Judging the range as best they could, they had set the elevation and then sited for direction along the barrel towards the target, waiting for a signal from Jules for exactly the right moment to slide a dark-green HE bomb down the short black tube.

As the cartridge in the base of the tail fin hit the firing pin and detonated, launching the bomb on its arcing flight towards the unwary troops, the team were already preparing to adjust the elevation and bearing.

Scanning the road through his binos, Jules waited for the fall of shot. A moment later there was a bright flash followed by the thump of the exploding shell.

'Nice shooting, lads,' he called across to the others. But the round had landed a hundred yards from the intended target, spraying its fragments of splintered metal harmlessly into the darkness as the truck lumbered on. Stretching his arm towards the target, Jules squinted along it, using the knuckles of his clenched fist to measure the distance from the round's point of impact to the place where the truck would next be forced to slow for another bend. In this way he estimated the degree of adjustment necessary.

'Go right two clicks, up one click,' he shouted. 'Repeat.'

As the two men adjusted the mortar, Dominic allocated arcs of fire to the rest of the men, concentrating on the machine-guns, which would do most of the long-range killing. The M16s would come into their own when the battle got to closer quarters.

'Hold your fire until they debus. Get the fuckers when they're milling around in the headlights. Once they're into cover we've lost them.'

Planting the bipods of their GPMGs firmly in the grass, the gunners tucked the butts into shoulder and cheek, aligned the sights and shuffled into comfortable positions to steady their aim. Meanwhile each gun's number two laid a belt of ammunition across the breech, slammed shut the top cover and clipped fresh belts on to the end ready for a prolonged fire-fight. With a series of metallic rasps, the gunners cranked back the cocking handles, slid the first rounds into place, and huddled down to wait.

Again the mortar fired, its 60mm HE bomb climbing almost vertically into the night sky, high above the valley, turning lazily at the summit of its trajectory, then accelerating down towards the convoy of trucks. The driver of the lead vehicle had stepped heavily on the brake and was fighting with the gear stick when the bomb drove into the gravel beside his cab, exploding in a blinding flash of light, showering the truck with white-hot splinters of shell case that pierced the fuel tanks, igniting them in sky-rocketing clouds of flame.

A cheer went up from the two teams of mercenaries at the main entrance and with the range determined, the mortar went fully into action, bracketing the convoy with a shower of HE bombs. As the first truck exploded, those following behind screeched to a halt in the dancing light of the flaming wreckage, helplessly nose to tail as the officers screamed to regain control of the panicking drivers, leaping from their cabs for the cover of the roadside. Ordered to debus, the soldiers tumbled from the back of the trucks on to the tarmac, but in doing so entered the killing ground of the GPMGs.

'Fire!'

Dominic's voice carried above the noise of the pounding mortar and each of the gunners squeezed his trigger, tightening the metal butt-plate into his shoulder as the guns juddered into life. A stream of empty brass cases spilled on to the ground as lines of tracer snaked gracefully away from the compound, their arcs shallower than the mortar's but even more lethal. Sweeping back and forth, the streams of copper-coated 7.62mm machine-gun bullets chewed through the canvas, wood and metal of the stationary trucks, tearing flesh and splintering bone.

When the soldiers dived for cover in the grass verges, the continuing rain of mortar bombs sought them out. To add to the confusion, Jules ordered the mortar team to intersperse the HE rounds with white-phosphorus smoke bombs. Detonating in livid balls of orange flame, the smoke added to the chaos while the phosphorus particles stuck to flesh and material, burning with merciless efficiency.

With the column successfully halted some eight hundred yards from the main entrance, Jules and Dominic brought the fire of their teams under tight control to conserve their limited stocks of ammunition.

'Steady, lads. Keep it topped up but don't let them recover. Rifle group, hold your fire. Wait for them to close to three hundred yards and then fire on my command.'

The tiniest movement in the bushes brought Dave

Bedford to full alert. He and his three men had been listening enviously to the ferocious fire-fight at the main gate, their trigger fingers itching, anxious to get stuck in and release the tension that had built up over the last hours.

Taking cover to the flank of their original entry point, Dave had selected a pool of darkness for his team's position, in welcome contrast to the flood of spotlight beams illuminating the breach in the wire on which their weapons were trained.

The first man to emerge from the undergrowth moved cautiously with the wide-awake tenseness of an animal, sniffing the air for danger.

'Not good enough,' Dave muttered to himself, bringing his M16 into his shoulder and silently thumb-flicking the safety-catch on the pistol grip to automatic.

'So the road was a diversion, was it? Draw our fire, reveal our strength, then hit us in the rear with the big boys. Well, it didn't fucking work, mate. We're too bloody good for the likes of you.'

Behind the first man, a second and then a third and a fourth emerged into the full glare of the light and approached the foot of the slope below the wire fence. Dave hand-signalled his man with the M203 grenade-launcher to prepare to fire into the cover from which the enemy had come. He guessed that this new threat would be of at least platoon strength. Good old Dojo. Trust him to know what to do, even in a monumental fuck-up like this. Lots of other blokes would have bolted for the boats, straight back the way they had come. Not Dojo. He had been around too long for such basic mistakes. One route in, a different route out. Never follow a track, always blaze a new trail; that way you were harder to ambush.

When an eight-man section were out in the open and the lead scout was nosing up to the wire, Dave squeezed off the first round, the signal for his whole team to open fire in controlled four to five-round bursts. But while two of his men took on the enemy point section, he and the M203 fired in depth, directing their 5.56mm M16 rounds and the deadly 40mm grenades from the M203 into the cover where Dave knew the platoon commander would be watching and waiting, tensed and ready for the all-clear signal from his point-section commander.

Not this time, mate, Dave thought. This time you play it our way.

Scythed down where they stood, the point section crumpled, the ground at their feet dancing with impacting bullets while the undergrowth behind them jumped and crackled, shredded by the jets of high-velocity bullets and the grenades' jagged fragments.

As Dave had anticipated, the Korean officer staggered out of the bush and tumbled into the dust, his face a pulp of ripped flesh and bone. But these were not the simple regular troops that had been used as a decoy on the road; they were a special forces detachment from an élite North Korean parachute division, every bit the equal of the mercenaries behind the wire. Unlike the chaotic leadership on the main road, the platoon sergeant instantly took command and rallied his men for a frontal assault.

But fanatical courage was no match for the ice-cold steadiness of Dave's fire control. Unmoved by the sight and screaming ferocity of the attacking paratroopers, the four men of Dave's team swivelled on their bellies to face the new threat, each man picking his target with cool deliberation, aiming and firing, working inwards from the outer ends of the charging line. Soon only a handful of North Koreans were left, stumbling up the slope, where they were met at point-blank range by the two Browning pump shotguns that Dave's team carried for close-quarters jungle work.

As the bodies rolled back down the slope, Dave's team took advantage of the lull to tear off half-expended magazines and clip on fresh ones.

'Change your fire positions!' Dave called, rolling to his left and seeking a new angle from which to cover the clearing. Already he had spotted a dark line of figures winding down the hillside, and estimated their strength to be at least another two companies of paratroopers. They would take a bit more stopping. They would have seen the reception their scout platoon had been given, and forewarned was forearmed.

Turning to one of his riflemen, Dave whispered: 'Reckon you've got enough time to set out some Claymores?'

Even in the darkness he could see the answering grin.

Out on the main road, the officers had managed to regain some semblance of control and were now pushing towards the resort compound. Although they were attempting to move using the tactic of fire and manoeuvre by platoons, the troops had been unsettled by the ferocity of the mercenaries' resistance and by the deadly accuracy of the mortar and machine-gun fire. With one company strung out in an extended assault line on either side of the road, their own return fire was desultory by comparison. Striding at the back, the officers brandished their 9mm Type 59 Chinese pistols more at the soldiers themselves than at the enemy mercenaries.

As soon as he had heard the noise of battle from Dave's team, Jules had ordered the mortar out of action in case their scarce ammunition would be needed on another flank. But the GPMGs continued their steady chatter, hosing the oncoming ranks that were nearing the three-hundred-yard line, coming nicely into the battle range of the M16s.

'Come on, Jules,' Dominic shouted. 'We're going to sleep over here.'

Muffling his South African drawl with the best English accent he could manage, Jules called across: 'OK, old boy. Rifle group, carry on.'

'Fire!' Dominic yelled, and the concentrated bursts from four M16s skimmed over the scrub, seeking out the infantry, who were just enjoying the first sense of relief that the mortar had fallen silent.

After leaving the accommodation block, Terry and his team went quickly back through the pool and restaurant area towards the far side of the compound. Moving in pairs, they still used short tactical bounds to cover the ground, ever aware that Yi and his three Koreans might be somewhere in the vicinity and convinced by now that it was Yi who had double-crossed them.

Terry's main concern now was to locate a new exit point from the compound. He had expected the noise of firing from the main gate and had only detached Dave's team to the breach in the wire as a standard precaution. However, it was obvious from the weight of fire that Dave was now engaging a considerable force there and Terry's worst fears were proving correct. The North Koreans already had their two main exit routes covered and were moving quickly to encircle them completely. He knew that he could trust Dave, Jules, Dominic and their men to impose a good delay on the enemy and to make them pay dearly for every yard of ground, but there was a limit to what a small force could do against overwhelming odds with far greater supplies of ammunition, even if that small force was made up of the best mercenaries in the world.

Beyond the restaurant, the ground fell away through an area of gardens, the bushes becoming increasingly dense until at the foot of the slope, where they met the wire outer fence, the undergrowth was almost impenetrable. Using their machetes, Terry's team hacked a way through to the wire. Then, cutting the strands one by one, they peeled back the loose ends to make a hole big enough for a man in battle gear to get through.

'Andy and Ken, stay here,' Terry said. 'Danny and I will get the others to break clean and move back. One of you keep an eye on the garden in case our old friend Yi turns up; the other one watch the outside. The Koreans may try another angle of attack if Dave's giving them too much trouble at the breach.'

But the situation at the breach had deteriorated rapidly. The depth companies of Korean paratroopers had learned from their comrades' mistakes and were not going to take the mercenaries so lightly. Instead of putting in another direct assault across open ground, they had detached two platoons as a diversion while the main force worked its way around the side in an effort to outflank Dave's team. Approaching stealthily through the forest, the two platoons came to the edge of Dave's killing ground but refused to enter it. Instead they put down a withering fire, drawing the four mercenaries into a battle of attrition that the latter couldn't hope to win. If they tried to withdraw, the Koreans edged forward, threatening to come through the breach, but so long as they remained locked in the ferocious fire-fight Dave was painfully aware of the threat developing to his flank. He could see figures moving far off to the left but the moment he tried to detach half his team to deal with it, the Korean platoons to his front pushed forward again. He was locked fast in a pincer and knew that the Koreans would squeeze it ever tighter until the two points met and destroyed him and his men.

Racking his brain for a solution, Dave knew that he couldn't break clean and withdraw until the two teams at the main gate had pulled back. If he bugged out now the Koreans would flood in and Jules and Dominic would be cut off. Somehow he had to hold his line.

'Are the Claymores set?' he shouted back over his shoulder.

'Yes, boss.'

'Fix a grenade necklace fifty yards behind them and set it to a trip-wire.'

'Wilco.'

If anything, the main-gate position was under even heavier pressure. The assaulting infantry companies had faltered the moment the M16s had opened up and one or two of the younger soldiers had even turned to run. But the officers had reacted with clinical efficiency, shooting them down in full view of the rest of the troops and threatening to do the same to anyone else who thought they could sit out the attack hiding in a ditch.

Trapped between the mercenaries and their own officers, the infantry had pressed on, realizing that their only hope of salvation was to eliminate the intruders in the resort compound as quickly as possible. With a renewed determination born of desperation, the Korean soldiers surged forward into the hail of fire, learning their manoeuvre skills the hard way, living or dying according to their use of the sparse cover available.

'These bastards don't give up, do they?' Jules yelled.

'You're not kidding. We'll have to withdraw in contact by teams,' Dominic shouted in reply, slamming a new thirty-round magazine on to his M16. 'I'll set up an intermediate fire position by the first accommodation block. You move back through me on my command and when they reach the gate I'll hit them with the Fireflash. That should give us enough breathing space to break clean and fuck off out of here.'

Dominic had just fired a couple of rounds from his new magazine when his team took its first casualty. Vince Paulis was wriggling across an open patch of ground to a new fire position when a burst from a Kalashnikov caught him full in the face and chest. His body jerked with the impacting rounds and lay still.

'Vince is down!' cried his mate Jimmy Hughes, who had been paired with Vince in the warm-up training in the south. He edged across and checked the carotid artery for a pulse. Finding nothing, he rolled the body over and stripped the pouches of ammunition and grenades, stuffing them into his own.

At that moment Terry and Danny rounded the corner. Seeing the foremost Koreans rush forward in the lull Vince's death had created, they brought their own assault weapons into the aim and blazed off a full magazine each. Terry pulled the hard-plastic butt of his Colt Commando into his shoulder and felt the recoil judder through his entire body like an electric shock. Beside him Danny's M16 poured out a stream of empty cases, the red-hot brass tinkling on the paving stones.

'Pull back!' Terry shouted across to Jules.

'About bloody time, man.'

'Danny'll lead the way. I'll blister on to Dominic's team. Move!'

By now Dominic had got the surviving members of his team into their intermediate position fifty yards back and had set up two Claymore mines to cover the main gate. In preparation for the first stage of their withdrawal, every man in Jules's team emptied a full magazine into the enemy, spraying every piece of bush and scrub where the assaulting Korean infantry might be taking cover. Then, throwing a grenade each, they waited for the detonating blasts and the screams of the wounded, before turning and bolting for the cover of the first accommodation block, reloading as they ran back through Dominic's team.

'We'll go firm between blocks two and three,' Jules shouted as he jogged past, following Danny and disappearing round the corner.

'OK, Dojo,' Dominic said, 'let's show them what this little beastie can do.'

Opening his pack, he took out a two-foot-high rectangular green box resembling a huge biscuit tin, unclipped and folded open the front flap and with a stiff tug telescoped out the back end to double the overall length.

'Give us a hand, Dojo.'

Terry hoisted the huge box on to Dominic's shoulder.

'What setting?'

'Let's give the fuckers the full house,' Dominic replied, flicking out the sight.

'Right you are. Don't expect to use your ears again.'

Unable to hold his position any longer, Dave had just started to pull back when he took two casualties in quick succession. First to go down was Mike Timmis, shot in the throat by a single round from a Kalashnikov. But the 7.62mm bullet not only tore through the cartilage but shattered his neck, killing him stone dead. Then, when the survivors were almost at the cover of their first fall-back position, Kevin Hughes screamed and clutched his leg where a grenade fragment had ripped into the flesh and lodged itself, still white-hot from the explosion.

'Help him back!' Dave shouted. Grabbing the wounded man's shoulder straps in one powerful hand and dragging him backwards, Alan Steers clasped his M16 in the other and blazed away at the Koreans at the edge of the trees.

Pulling the pin on two grenades, Dave lobbed them over the wire and into the nearest trees, waited for the explosions and then bolted for cover. The paratroopers who had attempted to outflank him had disappeared and Dave was worried that they were about to give him a nasty surprise. But for now he was powerless to do anything about it: his hands were full with the platoons to his front. They were already inching up the slope, pressing him hard and would soon be through the wire and on to him. He had to get back to the Claymores.

Diving over a low wall, he almost landed on Alan, who was frantically knotting a field dressing on Kevin's leg.

'Where're the fucking clappers?' Dave shouted, scrabbling around for the Claymore firing triggers.

'On the wall.'

Peering round the wall, Dave waited until at least a full eight-man section had come through the wire. He would have loved to have caught more of them, but the first men would soon be pushing out from the breach and leaving his Claymore killing ground. Grasping a clapper in either hand, he squeezed them shut, shooting the electrical pulse on its split-second journey down the hair-thin wires towards the detonators plugged into the top of the mines. With an ear-splitting roar, the 680gm of plastic explosive in each mine exploded, rocketing a jet of ball bearings towards the Korean section. The directional mines had been sited by an expert and as the seven hundred steel balls from each Claymore tore into the flesh and bone of the Korean point section, not a single man escaped alive.

But the ambush had created little more than a breathing space. The depth sections were already closing up, knowing that the Claymore was a one-shot weapon and prepared to gamble that the mercenary commander had expended his limited supply.

'Look!' Alan shouted, pointing to the far side of the compound a couple of hundred yards away. 'Jules is pulling back. Let's get the fuck out of here.'

Dave was getting to his feet when a series of explosions rocked the compound and from the direction of the main gate a mushroom cloud of flame and smoke erupted into the night sky.

'Jesus Christ,' Kevin gasped. 'They've gone nuclear!'

'No, mate. The Koreans have just had a taste of the Fireflash.'

The 60mm anti-armour rocket of the M72 was a lethal enough weapon, adaptable for use against bunkers and dug-in machine-gun emplacements. The big biscuit tin of the M202 contained four of them in a block, capable at the flick of a switch of being fired singly or in a ripple of all four, one after the other, the firing option that Terry had selected. However, unlike the HE of the M72, the four rockets of the M202 Fireflash were each packed with napalm.

When the Korean officers had seen the men of Jules's team pulling back they realized that the time had come to urge their troops forward into the final stages of the attack. With threats and screams, they pistol-whipped their men out of cover and drove them towards the gates of the compound.

Leaving Dominic free to handle the Fireflash, Terry had taken command of his team, ordering them to hold their fire and lure the enemy into the trap. Watching the first of the Korean soldiers reach the gate, they ducked out of sight as he sprayed the courtyard with bullets, smashed the locks and burst the gates open.

'Hold your fire,' Terry hissed at his men as their fingers tightened the triggers of their automatics to second pressure.

'Steady . . . steady . . . Fire!'

A shock wave rocked Dominic on his feet as the first

of the Fireflash rockets exploded from his shoulder, spouting a jet of flame into the massed ranks of the terrified infantry. As the second and then the third rockets shot away from the launcher, Terry and the rifle group fired from the hip, raking the gateway with a hail of high-velocity bullets. Slamming into the killing ground, the last of the rockets sent a spiralling torrent of flame skywards and the gateway vanished in a seething orange ball.

Tossing aside the empty M202 case, Dominic took up the two Claymore clappers and detonated the mines, pumping the open gateway with a searing mass of steel ball-bearings that cut short the screams of the human torches and tore into their fleeing comrades who had broken and run. Shooting the fugitives at random, the Korean officers were themselves overwhelmed, cut down by their own men, who were desperate to escape from the tornado of the gateway where the mercenaries stood firm, awaiting the next onslaught, the barrels of their weapons smoking like sated dragons.

'Move now!' Terry shouted, pitching his voice to carry above the noise of battle.

Leapfrogging back in pairs, the team jogged through the resort complex until they reached Jules's men, who were lying in wait, weapons in the aim, ready to give covering fire and take over the battle at a moment's notice.

'No probs,' Dominic called jauntily as he hopped over a low hedge, following Terry back to the exit point where Andy and Ken were waiting. 'We've broken clean. They've had enough.'

But as he landed on the grass Dominic was flung forwards as if hit by a sledgehammer between the shoulder blades. A voice seemed to be screaming in his ear, but it was coming from very far away. He wondered why everything had suddenly gone so quiet and peaceful. They had given the North Koreans a licking at the gate, but he was baffled by this complete silence. Then he was being rolled on to his back and looking up at the stars. Terry was staring at him, stern and serious, both hands pumping at his chest. But now Terry was fading too, and as Dominic's lifeblood seeped from the gaping wound in his back he was left to spend the last seconds of his short life alone, while Terry and Jules and every member of the team desperately scanned the surrounding buildings for the sniper.

7

An eerie screech rebounded off the compound walls and was followed a moment later by the rasping voice of a PA system.

'Well done, gentlemen, well done. But I'm afraid your little game's over.'

'Yi,' said Danny, catching the same recognition and cold hatred in Terry's eyes.

'Lay down your weapons and surrender. You've had a good run for your money. You will be treated as prisoners of war with more honour than you deserve. You have my word on it.'

'Fuck you!' Jules shouted, firing a burst at a speaker attached to one of the accommodation blocks. But the voice went on relentlessly, echoing throughout the resort and into the surrounding countryside.

'Even now you are being cut off. Surrender and you will live. Fight on, and you will die.'

'Not before a lot more of you bastards!'

The speakers chuckled, there was the crack of another single shot and the mercenary cried out, toppling on to his side, clutching his arm. In response the mercenaries fired at random, blazing at windows, shadows, into doorways and across rooftops.

Terry glanced from Dominic to the wounded mercenary. 'There's more than one sniper.'

Danny checked the angles of fire. 'I'd guess there'll be at least one more. Yi on the mike and those three fuckers from his team – all trained snipers. We really fell for that one.'

'We're smack in the middle of their killing ground. If they've got night-sights they can pick us off one by one.'

'Then why don't they?' Danny asked.

'I don't know. They haven't used mortars or artillery either. For some reason they want at least some of us alive, but I'm not about to stick around to find out why.'

Hand-signalling to Jules and the remainder of Dominic's team to get ready to move, Terry shouted out to Yi.

'What are your terms?'

'None. Surrender unconditionally or die. I would have thought even a dull-brained *karateka* like you could understand that.'

Holding his temper in check, Terry checked his assault rifle, slipped two white-phosphorus smoke grenades from his webbing, then signalled to Danny and Jules to do the same.

'OK. Give us a moment to think it over.'

Grasping both grenades in one hand, he gripped the two pins in his teeth and yanked them out. Next to him, Danny did the same and across the pathway Jules nodded that he was ready.

'You're not playing for time, I hope,' Yi's disembodied voice echoed. 'It would be very silly of you to think that I'm bluffing.'

'Throw!' Terry screamed. In one convulsive motion he lobbed his grenades over the wall, Danny throwing his to the left and Jules his to the right. Exploding in a cascade of brilliant flashes, the six grenades created an instant semicircular screen of dense white smoke.

'Move!' The breath was hardly out of his lungs before the mercenaries sprang into action, following Danny who zigzagged back through the pool area towards the restaurant.

'Go! Go! Go!' Terry screamed, emptying a full magazine from his Colt Commando into the smoke to deter any follow-up. He was about to turn and follow when across to the left he caught sight of Dave and Alan helping a wounded man between them.

'Shit,' he muttered. The smoke was already thinning and he had used his last WP grenade.

'Run!' he screamed, and slamming another magazine on to his assault rifle, fired single aimed shots into selected windows and doorways that might be sniper firing positions. But there were too many even for a whole platoon to cover and as the smoke began to clear, first one shot and then another rang out. There was a scream and Kevin toppled forward into a swimming pool. He floated to the surface a moment later, to turn in slow circles, as a film of blood spread across the water, further rounds pocking the rippled surface, nosing towards the dead body like piranhas.

Terry provided wild covering fire as Dave sprinted towards him, weaving and ducking, a rain of sniper bullets kicking up showers of fragmented plaster and concrete around him.

'Jee-zus!' he screamed as he streaked past and on towards the restaurant.

With him in the clear, the snipers turned their attention to Terry. However, with Jules and the rest of the men now safely through the wire, Danny had returned with Ken and Andy and together they put down a withering fire into the compound. Tearing straight through the middle, Terry moved faster than he had ever moved in his life. On reaching the outer ring of scrub at the top of the slope above the new exit point, bullets thudding into the soft grass and cracking in the air, he dived over the edge and plummeted down into the thick bushes. A moment later, Danny, Ken and Andy followed in a hail of arms and legs.

Picking themselves up, they pushed through the gap in the undergrowth they had cut earlier and wriggled under the wire to be met by Dave, Jules and the others, hastily organized for all-round defence.

Terry checked his assault rifle and did a head count. Four dead, and almost everyone else had at least one light injury, ranging from multiple cuts and scratches to puncture wounds from grenade fragments. Dave was the first to speak.

'There's a company of paratroopers unaccounted for, maybe two. They sent a couple of platoons to probe at the old entry point but the rest cut round us. They could be between us and the beach.'

'You can bet on it,' Terry said, his mind racing. Well, if they expected him to walk into an ambush, they would be sadly disappointed. But as he was about to speak, Jules cut in.

'If we do a wide hook we can outflank them and still reach the boats by daybreak.'

Terry stared at him dumbfounded. 'What boats? You don't think they'd allow us to waltz along the beach, jump in the dinghies and sail away, do you? They'll have destroyed or booby-trapped them by now.'

'How do you know? And anyway, who said you're in charge?'

Terry felt himself go taut inside but fought to keep control. 'Listen, Jules, we're all in this together. We've been double-crossed and must count the beach hiding-place as compromised as well.'

'Well, what do you suggest?'

Terry was aware that every pair of eyes was on him. He hadn't been prepared to take the lead – it had just happened, and in the heat of battle the men had listened and followed. But now would come the real test. If they followed Jules, he felt certain they had a good chance of walking straight into an ambush.

'We should go north,' Terry said as calmly as he could. Jules was incredulous.

'North? Deeper into Korea? You're fucking barking, man.'

Danny chipped in on Terry's side. 'I reckon Terry's right. It's exactly what they'd least expect. We could hook south later.' He looked around at the others. 'I'm with Terry.'

Ken stepped forward. 'I'm sorry, Terry. Jules gets my vote. I think it's worth trying for the dinghies. Even if that fishing boat doesn't turn up, they'll get us further down the coast and closer to home.'

One by one, the other mercenaries declared for Jules and the boats until Terry shook his head in desperation. 'You're mad, all of you. Raving fucking mad.'

But there was no more time. As Jules gathered the men together and prepared to set out for the boats, the sound of renewed firing came from the main gate where the surviving officers had finally regained control of their men and had restarted the assault. Finding the mercenaries gone, they were moving rapidly through the compound.

'Move out,' Jules ordered. Turning to Terry, he asked: 'Are you coming with us?'

Danny looked at Terry. 'I'd rather strike out on my own than go with this asshole. Will you come too?'

Jules's men were already snaking down into the forest away from the compound. Maybe Jules was right, Terry thought. Maybe they could give the paratroopers a wide berth and arrive at the beach to find the boats intact. Then, as Ken had said, they could be well down the coast by daybreak, even with those little motors.

'Well, are you coming?' Jules prompted.

'Come on, Dojo,' Ken called over, setting off down the hill. 'Leave Tonto to dance with his shagging wolves on his own.'

Terry looked at Danny. 'Maybe they're right,' he said, glancing away to avoid the look in Danny's eyes, which was too painful to take. It was a mixture of contempt for a professional who has taken a wrong decision, but tempered with pity for a middle-aged man trapped in a younger man's profession.

'OK, Terry. Good luck. I'll see you in Seoul, Danny said, and without a backwards glance he cradled his M16 in the crook of his arm and set off for the north, his long, steady stride taking him away from the boats and into the teeth of the enemy.

Throughout the journey to the beach, Terry was tormented by doubts. What the hell was he doing tagging meekly along at the back of the column like some Tail-end Charlie raw recruit, mind in neutral, a lamb to the slaughter? His every instinct told him that he had made the wrong choice, but now it was too late. Perhaps it was time to admit that he was simply too old for this game. When the crunch had come, the lure of a nice easy boat trip down the coast had been too great a temptation to resist. He had weighed it in the balance of his judgement against the prospect of a hard slog through mountains and forests with Danny and the soft option had won. What was the old saying about the road to hell being the easy downhill one?

However, about half an hour out from the compound, they heard the sound of an almighty fire-fight in the north, a deafening and continuous roar from a hundred Kalashnikovs and the thin, pathetic reply of a single M16. There were a couple of muffled thuds from detonating grenades and then silence. So that was the end of Danny Grey Wolf. Terry didn't doubt he had gone down fighting.

Jules fell back alongside him. 'No hard feelings, Dojo. We all make mistakes.'

'Fuck off and leave me alone.'

'Have it your way, man,' he said with a shrug, returning to the head of the column.

The wide hook added at least two hours to their journey but shortly before first light they came over the crest of a hill and saw the shimmer of the Sea of Japan below them.

'We've done it.'

Terry turned to see Andy beside him. His face was the usual impenetrable mask, but in his own feelings of isolation Terry sensed a new kinship with the tough little Scot.

'You're thinking about Danny, aren't you?' Andy asked.

'I'm wondering why I didn't go with him,' Terry replied. 'It was my idea.'

Andy chortled. 'Fucking stupid one too. No offence, mate.'

'Well,' Terry said thoughtfully, his eyes scanning the peaceful beach laid out below them. 'We'll see, won't we.'

Winding down the steep hillside, the exhausted mercenaries made quickly for the beach. There was no sign of the fishing boat which should have been there to pick them up, but that came as no surprise. But even without it they estimated that the outboard motors of the dinghies would be sufficient to get them out of the immediate danger area before running out of fuel. If their luck was in they might even make it past the 38th Parallel and then they could land safely on South Korean territory. If not, they would have to attempt a crossing of the land border. Either way they would be beyond the reach of the Communist paratroopers.

Terry didn't like it one bit. They were moving much too fast, lowering their guard, convincing themselves that the dinghies were clear and the enemy far behind. He dropped back from the main body, Andy staying with him, and carefully surveyed the beach as the lead man stepped out of the cover of the trees and on to the bare sand.

'Come on, lads,' the man called back, 'it's as clean as a whistle.'

He broke into a jog with the others following him, heading for the hiding-place where the dinghies had been concealed in the mangrove. Reaching it, he tore at the branches.

'They're fine!'

A couple of the men cheered.

'Let's get cracking.'

'Seoul here we come!'

Andy moved out on to the beach. 'Come on, Dojo. Better get a shift on.'

Terry was still uneasy, but why should he be? The Koreans had fully expected to catch them in the compound. The wide hook of their escape march had probably worked, taking them round the edge of the paratroopers' ambush. For all Terry knew the Koreans were still sitting back there waiting for them and in a few minutes they would be out on the water and hurtling down the coast towards home. Sure, it was wise to take precautions but it wasn't always necessary. Not every enemy soldier was as cunning as that.

With a sickening roar, the detonating booby-trap sent the mercenary's body cartwheeling into the air with the force of the explosion, ripping him apart and shredding the inflatable rubber dinghies. The fuel tanks ignited and burst in a series of lesser explosions, but by the time the lifeless body slumped back on to the sand everyone's attention was on the line of scrub-covered sand dunes from where a fusillade of gunfire was pouring.

The sand at Jules's feet danced with impacting bullets and as the mercenaries returned fire, they were forced back towards the waterline, bunching together involuntarily, defenceless in the open and at the mercy of the ambushers.

Concealed at the edge of the trees, Terry looked on in horror. But as he watched he noticed that apart from the single man killed by the booby-trap, none of the others was hit. The hail of bullets had driven them into a tight bunch like sheep herded by a dog, until they stood helpless in the water, the sea foaming with bullets around them.

As suddenly as it had started, the firing stopped, and a loud-hailer barked at them from the cover of the mangrove.

'Lay down your weapons.'

No one moved. Terry shrank back out of sight. The voice was not Yi Soong's. Presumably he was still back at the compound and the paratrooper commander was in charge of the ambush.

A second hail of bullets struck the ground at the mercenaries' feet and Andy doubled over, hit in the leg.

Again the firing ceased and again the loud-hailer blared out.

'Lay down your arms. This is your last chance.'

One by one the mercenaries dropped their weapons and raised their hands in surrender. From the cover of the dunes a line of North Korean paratroopers emerged, their Kalashnikovs at the ready, levelled at the mercenaries in case of any tricks.

Cursing himself, Terry ducked back deeper into the trees. He would now have to make it on his own, without even the help of Danny Grey Wolf, whom he had deserted and left to die on the hills behind the compound.

'And where do you think you're going?'

Terry spun at the sound of the familiar voice. With his full attention concentrated on the plight of his comrades on the beach, he had missed the approach of someone behind him. As he spun he tried to execute a precautionary block as he had done in the park in Seoul, but the strap of his Colt Commando was looped on his wrist for a safer grip, and his feet were shifting on the loose sand. The vicious roundhouse kick caught him full on the jaw and he went down, his last sight being the focused concentration on the face of Yi Soong.

The first thing Terry saw when he regained consciousness was the naked light-bulb in the middle of a bare ceiling. His head was pounding and his eyes felt as if someone was inside his skull trying to push them clean out of his head.

'Ah, Sleeping Beauty awakes.'

Recognizing the voice of Yi Soong, Terry tried to get to his feet but discovered that he had been securely tied to a wooden chair, his arms straight down by his sides, wrists and ankles tightly bound with cord.

Lifting his head, the first person he saw was Jules, similarly tied, his face swollen and bleeding, his head hanging limply down. On either side of him, two other prisoners stared back at Terry: Andy and Ken. Terry noticed that no attempt had been made to dress Andy's wound and although the blood had crusted and dried, fresh blood seeped from the gash, running down his ankle and on to the floor, where it was forming a dark pool.

From somewhere else in the building a piercing scream was cut suddenly short, followed by raised voices shouting some unintelligible command.

'What the hell's going on?' Terry asked.

From behind him, Yi's voice answered calmly. 'You're being tortured, what do you think? You're safely back at the resort.'

Ken raised his head. 'They want us to admit we're an American special forces unit on an authorized mission. They're trying to pin the murder of all those people in the resort on us.'

Terry tried to turn his head to look at Yi, but the Korean remained out of sight.

'But you know that's not true. You were in on the recruiting as well as Babs Butler.'

'Why, so I was. Perhaps it's all been a mistake and you can go home. Do forgive me.'

A fist slammed Terry's head forward, then grabbed him by the hair and yanked him back. Yi stared contemptuously down at him.

'What do you take me for? I don't give a damn who you really are, or what particular kind of scum. You'll say what I tell you to say.'

Terry sucked his lip and tasted blood. 'OK. What's so difficult about that?'

Yi chuckled. 'Let me clarify that. Your confession will be televised and broadcast to the world.'

'I see.'

'I doubt it, Mr Williams. Or can I call you Dojo?'

Again Yi's fist crashed into Terry's head.

'I've been looking forward to this little chat.'

'I bet you have,' Terry said, spitting blood on the floor. 'This is the only way you'd dare hit me.'

'You're not trying to goad me into untying you, are you? I can beat you any time I choose. I don't give a damn for your insults.'

'Good, 'cos that's all you're going to get out of me.'

'Wonderful! I was afraid you were going to do what we wanted and that would have spoiled my fun.'

Yi shouted for the guards and two men burst through the door and moved to the side of Terry's chair, tipping it back until he was lying on the floor staring up at the ceiling.

'You'd better agree to say what they want, Terry,'

Ken shouted. 'We all have. They've killed Dave Bedford.'

Terry felt himself go hot with anger. He struggled against the ropes, but the guard stepped on the chair back, fixing him in place.

'You bastards!'

'Really, Dojo. I didn't realize you were as stupid as David. I finished with him just before you came round. Let's see if you're prepared to go the distance.'

As Terry struggled on the floor, Yi took a sodden towel from a bucket of water and wrung it out. After shaking it loose, he draped it over Terry's face, straightening the ends so that his eyes, nose and mouth were all covered.

'You've heard of the Chinese water torture, I suppose? Well, we like to flatter ourselves that they got it from us.'

As Terry tried to inhale, the damp towel tightened on his face, suffocating him. The only way he could loosen it was by blowing out, but as he did so he emptied his lungs, which were already gasping for air. As he gulped in again, the towel once more tightened, choking him slowly.

'Fun, isn't it?' said Yi as he took a metal cup from the bucket and poured a trickle of water on to the towel. Soaking through the saturated material, droplets of water ran into Terry's nose and throat. He coughed and choked as it penetrated his windpipe, but whenever his aching lungs contracted, struggling for air, the towel was sucked closer to his face in a merciless grip.

When Terry's body started to convulse, Yi plucked the towel away and Terry gasped and choked. But before he had properly regained his breath, Yi flopped the towel back again, having poured a fresh cup of water over it.

'You see, we can go on like this all day if you wish. As they say in the old movies, we have ways of making you talk.' He laughed, enjoying the sport immensely.

Steady, Terry thought, fighting to control his mounting panic. He had steeled himself to face the physical pain of a beating, but this was beyond his wildest nightmares. While his lungs screamed for air his mind battled for control. Drawing on his inner reserves of will-power, he forced his muscles to relax, countering every desperate survival instinct and reflex. Focus on the mind, he thought. The mind is apart, separate. It doesn't need to breathe. He had almost managed it and felt himself slipping into the blissful release of unconsciousness when the towel was removed and, against his will, his body gulped in the air, undoing all the efforts of his concentration.

Eventually he lost track of how many times the towel had been placed over him until, finally, his body showed him the mercy that his captors would not and he passed out.

He was woken by Ken, who was kneeling beside him and holding a cup to his lips.

'Here you are, mate. Have a drink of this.'

Terry choked as the water slipped down his throat. 'A drink's the last bloody thing I need, you daft Aussie bugger.'

'Well, it didn't take you long to get back to your old self, did it?'

Leaning against the far wall of the cell, Andy

chuckled. Slumped against him, Jules was in a bad way.

'What did they do to him?' Terry asked as he crawled across the floor.

'Old Julesey wouldn't say what they wanted him to,' replied the Scot. 'I guess he felt responsible for going against you and leading us into this shit.'

Terry examined the South African. 'There don't seem to be any bones broken.'

'No, but he's been unconscious for too long. He should have come round by now. I reckon his brain's fucked.'

Andy gently turned Jules's head and showed Terry the bruising on the back and side of the scalp.

'That bastard'll pay for this. Somehow,' Terry said.

Ken laughed. 'We've got to get out of here first.'

His mind racing, Terry just nodded.

Right now, Yi Soong and his goons held all the cards, he reasoned. They had said what they wanted: a confession. So what if it was all a load of crap? Unless the mercenaries did what they were told they were going to die. Dave had already been killed, Jules was badly hurt, and Terry himself wasn't sure how much longer he could hold out. Just before he had passed out he had felt himself cracking. Next time perhaps he would break and then where would all his stubborn resistance be?

OK, give them what they want. But then what's to stop them simply killing the prisoners when they have made their confession? Perhaps they couldn't just finish them off that easily, though. Yi had said that the confession would be televised to the world. If the mercenaries were then murdered, the North Koreans would lose their propaganda victory. They wouldn't be able to set them free because they would tell the truth as soon as they reached the South, so the mercenaries would probably be imprisoned in a labour camp in the hope that the outside world would eventually forget about them. But at least if they were prisoners they would be alive. And if they were alive, they could find a way to escape.

'Right,' he said. 'Let's give them their confession.'

When Yi next visited the cell he found Terry in a more co-operative frame of mind.

'OK, you win. Just keep that towel away from me, that's all,' Terry said as he huddled in the corner, staring at the floor.

'Well, this is a surprise,' Yi replied. 'You disappoint me. I'd thought you were tougher than this. I was looking forward to our next session. In fact I'm almost tempted to continue with it regardless.'

Terry looked up, tears welling in his eyes. 'Please, no! I'll say whatever you want, just leave me alone.'

Yi stared at him with contempt. 'And you were so full of bullshit. The big *karateka*, grovelling in the corner like a whipped dog.'

He lashed out at Terry with his foot, hitting him in the ribs. Terry cried out with the pain and rolled away from the towering Korean.

'Be ready in an hour. Here's what you've got to say.' Yi threw a sheet of paper into the middle of the room. 'Learn it by heart or you'll be having another little drink with me.'

'Tell me one thing,' Terry asked. 'Why did you go to all this trouble?'

Yi stopped in the doorway. 'Why? I would have thought even you could work that out. When the world witnesses the blatant aggression of the United States on a tiny Asian country, the UN will forget its demands to inspect our nuclear facilities.'

'Only for a while, surely?'

Yi grinned. 'That's as long as we'll need.'

'And us. What'll happen to us?'

'You'll be released, of course. After a brief time as our guests.'

Terry thought for a moment. 'Who were the people outside in the compound? The bodies?'

'Trash, like you. Political prisoners. You might even find yourselves occupying the labour camp they've vacated.'

Laughing, Yi left the room, then shouted an order to the guards to take the prisoners for a shower and to bring fresh clothes for them to change into.

Thirty minutes later the mercenaries were hand-cuffed and lined up in a corridor. Chains bound their ankles, linking them together like convicts, but they had all had a hot shower and been dressed in brand-new prison clothes. When all was ready Yi and a paratroop officer marched slowly along the line to inspect their charges, stopping here and there to comb someone's hair or straighten a shirt collar.

'We want you looking smart for the world's press.'

Jules, still unconscious, was propped between Andy and Ken. When Yi came to the South African he rounded on the paratroop officer.

'What do you mean treating a prisoner of war in this way?'

The officer blinked in confusion as Yi's hand lashed across his face.

'Take him to the medical centre immediately.'

As two of the guards dragged Jules away, Yi smiled

sweetly and said: 'You see, we are men of principle too.'

He strode to the end of the corridor and with a final glance at the line of mercenaries, opened the door and led the way into the glare of lights. Emerging into the room, Terry was dazzled by the storm of flash bulbs and spotlights. The prisoners were led on to a stage and ushered into seats at a long table covered with a white cloth on which stood jugs of water and glasses.

A North Korean officer stepped up to a microphone and began his address, detailing with the aid of maps, diagrams and slides the American plan to assassinate the country's élite nuclear scientists. Projected on the screen, Terry saw the bodies, photographed where he had seen them in the bedrooms and on the lawn outside, but photographed at an earlier time when freshly killed, before they had become swollen and discoloured.

Minute by minute the evidence of the massacre was spelt out to the assembled press, all of whom had been carefully selected from countries or organizations sympathetic to the North Korean regime, or at least antagonistic to the United States.

Finally, a microphone was passed along the row of mercenaries, who one by one admitted that they were members of an American special forces unit, infiltrated in from the South with the full connivance of the South Korean puppet regime.

When it was over they were hustled away before the journalists were able to ask further questions. But instead of returning to the cells, they were led out into the compound, where a large crowd of civilians had been assembled. Still in the glare of the television cameras, they were made to walk through the crowd as women and children jeered and spat at them. An American flag was ceremoniously burned, but as an old woman leapt forward to attack Terry with feeble kicks and punches, a Korean guard restrained her, assisting for all the world to see, the inhuman butcher who had slaughtered the innocents in the resort.

When Andy stumbled, another guard leapt to his aid, supporting him under one arm and evoking a storm of protest from the civilians, who were now hysterical and screaming for vengeance. But the paratroopers moved in to bar the way, shepherding the criminals of the US special forces team to the safety of a waiting bus. There, as they were ushered to comfortable seats, the briefing officer explained that the criminals would now be taken for a fair trial by a panel of independent judges, after which they would be sent back to South Korea or sentenced to a term in prison to atone for their murderous crimes.

The United Nations should desist from its absurd claims that the peace-loving people of North Korea were constructing a weapon of mass destruction. It was absolute nonsense. Instead it should focus its attention on the clandestine activities of the so-called free world and on the United States of America in particular. They were the real enemies of world peace. He made a special appeal to the non-aligned nations of the Third World, urging them to free themselves from the capitalist yoke that had kept them economically enslaved since the end of the colonial era. They were being dominated even more than before, he proclaimed, his voice rising to fever pitch and breaking with emotion.

Under careful supervision the cameras were allowed forward to film the captured special forces unit through the bus windows. Ken shoved two fingers up at them and a guard went to restrain him, but Yi Soong, mingling inconspicuously with the crowd, gestured to him to leave the prisoner alone. Having butchered innocent children in the resort, it was fitting that the unrepentant American soldier should demonstrate his contempt for world opinion so graphically. It had all turned out better than Yi could have wished, and as the bus drove off he allowed himself a moment of self-congratulation.

The only thing that puzzled Yi Soong was the sudden breakdown of Terry Williams. The Korean was seldom wrong in his judgement of character and it had truly surprised him when the Welshman had caved in. Still, Terry Williams wasn't motivated by political conviction like Yi himself. In fact, Yi couldn't imagine what did motivate him. But then, Dojo was only a mercenary after all. Worthless trash.

8

In his Washington office, Alex Leitner had never known it so busy. Since the news had broken of the armed incursion into North Korea by an alleged American special forces team, the phones had never stopped ringing. He had heard it rumoured that the President himself had been grilling the high-ups. Probably even missed his lunchtime jog, Alex chortled.

One thing was for sure, Eliot Masterson was looking a worried man. Alex didn't have a clue what the son of a bitch had been up to but because he had been dismissed from the great Masterson's office the other day, he didn't give a damn about his fate.

Leaning back in his chair, feet on the desk, he tried to pitch another ball of screwed-up paper into the waste-bin, missed and idly rolled up another. Yes, nothing would please him more than to see Eliot in the shit, the deeper the better.

He knew that the idea of the CIA being behind the whole caper was absurd. Why the hell would they want to insert a band of cutthroats to massacre nuclear scientists and their families while they were skinny-dipping in the Sea of Japan. Hell, the UN had almost gained admittance to the goddam country by the front door. The whole thing just didn't make any sense.

He looked at his watch and tossed another ball of paper at the bin.

'Ah, Alex, I'm glad you're here.'

Alex leaned round to see who it was and sprang to his feet as Masterson walked into his office and shut the door behind him.

'I've got some bad news and I see it as my duty to give it to you personally.'

Looking into his boss's cool blue eyes, Alex felt as if a hand had reached inside his chest and grabbed hold of his heart. The concerned expression that had masked Masterson's face since the news first broke had vanished and in its place had returned his customary icy arrogance.

'I'll come straight to the point. When I was appointed to this job I was given a free hand to improve efficiency and get results. I know you've been with the organization for most of your career, but I've come to the conclusion that you're in need of a rest.'

Alex stared at him dumbfounded, the hand tightening its grip on his heart.

'This is as hard for me as it is for you, believe me, but I'm sure it's for the best. This is a job for younger men and I'm sure you'll agree it's time you moved over and gave someone else a chance.'

Masterson paused a moment, somewhat perturbed by the sudden paleness of Alex's complexion.

'It's got nothing to do with this Korean business. In fact I'm leaving for Seoul in a couple of hours' time to find out what the devil's going on. I expect they've got a mole in their organization. You know what the gooks are like. Anyway, I'd like you to clear your desk and be out of the office by . . .' – he looked at his watch – 'let's say three o'clock. I hate doing things in such a rush but it's standard procedure, as you know. Security. We can't afford a leak like the Koreans. There's a guard outside who'll help you tidy up. Alex?'

But Alex could no longer hear what he said. He was fishing in Chesapeake Bay with his son, joking about the time when Stephen would be an officer cadet at Annapolis. Nor did he hear the hurried steps of the security guard as Masterson flung open the door and screamed down the corridor that Leitner was having a heart attack.

After leaving the compound, the bus carrying the mercenaries wound its way painfully out of the valley, escorted by two truckloads of paratroopers. But when it came to a fork in the road just out of sight of the resort, instead of taking the main highway north to the city, it turned down a narrow lane that led through ever-thickening forest.

Staring blankly out of the windows, the prisoners were still in a daze, bewildered by the events of the last hours, most of them in deep shock. Only Andy and Terry took careful note of the route, wondering why the column was heading into the heart of a forest on a track that both of them knew from their map briefings led down to a steep-sided river and a dead end.

Without alerting the guards Terry glanced across the aisle and caught Andy's eye. The Scot frowned and raising his chained hands, drew a finger across his throat. Terry nodded solemnly. So this was how it was to end. He had miscalculated again. Yi Soong had got his confessions and no longer gave a damn what happened to the mercenaries. By the time the world woke up to the fact that they had been massacred, if

142

it even cared, the North Korean nuclear-weapons programme would be complete and, thanks to them, the
UN would have been outmanoeuvred and the South
would be wide open for ransom. Accept Communist
rule or face destruction.

Terry desperately tried to think of a way out but it
seemed hopeless. Each truck would be holding about
fifteen paratroopers, each armed with a Kalashnikov
and a plentiful supply of ammunition and grenades.
One truck was leading the way, the other following the
bus, escorting it to a new and terrible killing ground.
Perhaps there would even be others already waiting to
receive them on the river bank.

Although in the bus itself there were only the
driver and four guards, they were fully alert, their
weapons levelled at their prisoners, safety-catches off
and fingers on the trigger. The slightest pressure would
let loose a torrent of fire. Furthermore, the mercenaries
were chained together and without so much as a
toothpick between them. They were exhausted and
Terry wondered if any of them had any fight left. He
would have to find out.

On the seat in front, Ken was starting to doze.
Slowly Terry edged forward.

'Here, Ken. Wake up, you dozy bugger.'

'Fuck off.'

'Listen, mate, if we don't do something we'll soon
be having the big sleep.'

Ken shifted and without turning round, leaned
closer.

'What do you mean?'

Terry explained about the track and the dead end.

'Pass it on.'

Ken yawned loudly and leaned forward as if going

back to sleep, muttering instead under his breath to the man in front. God, don't go on the stage, Terry smiled to himself. You'd never win an Oscar like that.

While the message was being passed round the bus, Terry tried to figure out a way to distract the guards. The sun was pouring in through the windows and inside it was warm and comfortable. Although the mercenaries had been chained together, the chains were long enough to allow each of them to sit in a row on his own, the loose chains trailing down the central aisle. There were two guards at the front of the bus beside the driver, and two at the back. OK, Terry thought, here goes.

'Come on, lads, what about a little sing-song,' he said heartily, and before the guards could react, he began.

Row, row, row your boat, gently down the
    stream,
Merrily, merrily, merrily, merrily, life is but a
    dream . . .

Ken turned round and winced with horror. 'Is that the best you can do?'

'Sing, you bugger!' Terry hissed at him, and burst into the next repetition.

Row, row, row your boat, gently down the
    stream,
Merrily, merrily, merrily, merrily, life is but a
    dream . . .

One by one the others joined in. The guards were on

their feet immediately, shouting at them to stop and lashing out with their feet and rifle butts.

The bus had reached the steepest part of the descent and was winding laboriously down the hairpin bends through the forest. The turns were now coming every sixty or seventy yards and were so sharp that the bus was almost doubling back on itself. But more importantly, Terry had noticed that for long stretches at a time they were out of sight of the escorting trucks.

By now every prisoner was singing and, despite the beatings of the guards, they persevered, endlessly repeating the simple tune. Then, as the bus rounded another bend and lurched forward down the next stretch of track, Terry realized that both escorting trucks were out of view, the one in front having rounded the next bend and the one in the rear not yet having appeared from behind. He estimated that he had only a few seconds in which to act.

'Sing up, lads,' he shouted and shrugged at the guard who rushed to silence him. Terry smiled sweetly up at him as he raised the butt of his Kalashnikov.

'Now or never,' he said. The guard paused, a puzzled frown creasing his brow, and Terry's foot shot up between his legs, driving the guard's testicles deep into his body. His eyes bulged and he doubled forward, collapsing across Terry, who looped his handcuffed wrists over the man's neck, gripped his temple with one hand and his shoulder with the other and twisted viciously, breaking the neck with a loud crack.

'Rumble!' Ken shouted. 'Now that's what I call a sing-song.'

Before the other guards could react, the mercenaries struck. In their attempts to silence the prisoners the guards had carelessly spaced themselves along the bus, leaving their positions of relative safety at the front and back. Swamped by the mercenaries, they were dragged to the floor and killed before they had a chance to fire a single shot.

At the front of the bus the driver tried to bring the bus to a halt, but Andy's fist swung out of nowhere and spread him across the steering wheel.

'No you don't, mate. This isn't my stop.'

Lifting the stunned driver out of the seat, Andy flung him aside for another mercenary to finish off. But, as he clambered into the driving seat himself, he found that with the chains on his ankles he was unable to reach the brake and stop the bus from careering out of control down the hill.

'Dojo, get these fucking chains off!'

Ken rummaged desperately through the guards' pockets.

'Forget it,' Terry shouted. 'They won't have a key. Where we were going they wouldn't have needed to take them off – just dump us in the river.'

'Then shoot the bastards off!'

Ken grabbed at the dead guard's Kalashnikov but Terry snatched it from him.

'No. The escorts'll hear the shot.'

'Do something!' Andy screamed. The bus was now hurtling towards the next hairpin bend and at its present speed would go straight over the edge and down the precipice into the trees below.

Tugging against his own chains, Terry shuffled forward to Andy and raising the butt of the Kalashnikov over his head, brought it down with all his might on a single link of the chain an inch short of Andy's ankle. The chain sprung apart and Andy jerked his foot free and hit the brake, spinning the wheel to regain control of the bus and bring it into the turn. A cheer went up from the rest of the mercenaries as it lumbered round the corner and entered on the next stretch of road.

'Here, put this on and keep your face down,' Terry said, stuffing the driver's cap on Andy's head. 'Don't get too close to the truck in front. If they see your ugly mug behind the wheel it'll all be over.'

Back in their seats the mercenaries were smashing their chains. One of them had found a way of using the bayonet clasp to break open the handcuffs and went from man to man springing them free.

'Right, back in your seats everyone, quick. Everything's nice and normal,' said Terry.

Donning one of the guards' hats, he sat at the front of the bus beside Andy, cradling a Kalashnikov. Ken went to the back with another and sat in the guard's seat, checking that no one in the rear truck had noticed anything. When it rounded the bend a moment later sixty yards behind, it was motoring easily as if nothing had happened. The driver in the cab gave Ken a cheery wave.

'Up yours too, mate,' Ken murmured as he waved back.

Two of the other mercenaries also now had weapons but with half their number still unarmed, Terry didn't like the idea of getting embroiled in a fire-fight. The bus guards had only been carrying four spare magazines apiece and two grenades, and the driver had been unarmed, so it was hardly an arsenal with which to take on the escorting platoon of paratroopers.

'Think, man, think,' Terry murmured to himself. You've taken over the bus but it won't be long before you reach the clearing at the bottom of the hill and then it'll be too late. Sure, you would have the element of surprise and in the first few seconds you might be able to account for half a dozen of the paratroopers, but even with surprise your fire-power's no match for their greater numbers. The odds are they would eventually win.

OK then, what if we stop the bus? If we time it right the truck in front won't notice and will carry on and the four of us with weapons can ambush the one behind. With only fifteen of the buggers to deal with the odds are better. But the front truck would hear the firing and be on us before we could get away into the forest. It would only take a couple of survivors from the rear truck to keep us pinned down until their mates arrived.

He was just wrestling with a third option when Andy shouted down the bus.

'Hang on!'

A second later they were shooting down a footpath, Andy's foot hard on the accelerator, branches whipping and cracking against the windscreen.

'What the fuck are you up to?' Ken screamed from the back.

Andy stamped on the brake and the bus skidded and slewed to a juddering halt, flinging everyone to the floor. He sprang to the door and flung it open, shouting: 'Shut up! Listen.'

As the dust settled and the peace of the surrounding forest reimposed itself, they could all plainly hear the sound of the truck engines receding, the front one continuing steadily down the zigzag road, the other bringing up the rear. Suddenly Ken burst out laughing.

'You canny Scottish git.'

Andy shrugged modestly. Noticing a path leading

off the main track, he had reacted on impulse. Seeing that the lead truck had already rounded the next bend and glancing in the mirror to check that the other one hadn't yet appeared, he had swung the bus on to the footpath and ploughed deep into the thick forest.

Picking himself off the floor, Terry grinned and clapped Andy on the shoulder. 'Nice work. Of course I was just about to suggest something like that myself.'

Ken's hat spun the length of the bus, hitting Terry on the back of the head, and everyone cheered. But Terry realized there wasn't a moment to lose. As they negotiated the bends, the truck drivers would only have to miss a few more glimpses of the bus to become suspicious, and when the rear truck caught up with its partner at the bottom of the hill the game would be up. Shouting for everyone to debus, he and the other seven mercenaries tumbled out into the heart of the forest, and as the sound of the trucks grew fainter the river's distant roar rose up from far below.

'What's the betting we'd have ended up floating in it?' Ken said as Andy limped up beside him, the wound in his leg smarting from the sudden exertion.

'Aye, pumped full of holes and strung together like a fucking daisy-chain.'

Back at the resort, the press had been taken to see the unconscious Jules in the medical centre before being given coffee and driven back to Pyongyang. Standing by the bed, the briefing officer looked at the wounded man with tenderness.

'We don't blame the men themselves,' he said. 'They have been brainwashed by their corrupt political system. It is their government that must answer for their crimes. This poor individual was wounded in the battle with our victorious forces, but he will have the best medical care that North Korea can provide.'

A correspondent from an African state asked what would become of him when he regained consciousness.

'He will receive a fair trial, like his comrades, but in the meantime our prime concern is to ensure his full and speedy recovery.'

The journalist nodded approvingly and one or two members of the gathering applauded.

'Now come this way, please. I'm afraid that I must now show you the bodies of the innocents they murdered, helpless men, women and children enjoying a holiday here at the resort.'

Leading the crowd of reporters and cameramen out of the ward, the officer took them to see the bodies of the dead, unrecognizable in their garish holiday clothes as the inmates of labour camps from which they had been plucked several days ago and taken to their deaths.

When the ward was quiet again a door at the far end opened and Yi Soong came in. Dismissing the nurse, he went to Jules's bed and sat down on the edge.

'Can you hear me, Mr Merkoen?' he said.

Then, with his thumb, he pulled open one eyelid, looked into the unfocused pupil and let it drop shut.

'Pity. I was hoping this would be more fun,' he said aloud.

With his fingers under Jules's chin, Yi gently tipped his head back until the windpipe stood out bare and exposed.

Now, Yi pondered, how best to do this?

He searched around the bedside table as if looking for some implement to help him.

'Oh, never mind,' he said, finding nothing suitable.

Turning to face the unconscious body, Yi braced his knee on the mattress and drew back his clenched fist, couching it level with his breast. With the speed and force of a whiplash, he snapped the fist down, pulverizing the cartilage of the windpipe, and as Jules Merkoen choked to death in his sleep, his murderer stepped back like an artist surveying his latest creation.

As he walked out into the bright sunlight, Yi looked around at the compound and cursed the wretched mercenaries who had made such a mess of the place. It would be some time before it was fit once again for the use of the President and members of the ruling élite. The walls were pock-marked with bullet holes and grenade splinters, there were phosphorus scorch marks on the flagstones, and the main gate had been completely destroyed by the Fireflash.

Nevertheless, the operation had been a brilliant success. The press were eating out of his hand and would soon be filing their reports to every corner of the globe. The nuclear-weapons programme would be completed in a matter of weeks and to add to it all, he had advanced his own career in the North Korean intelligence service immeasurably. He smiled. What would Kwang and his whore have to say about that?

He gazed at the surrounding hills. The forest and mountains were certainly beautiful at this time of year. By now the remainder of the mercenaries would also be dead, their blood-soaked bodies tumbled into the river to feed the fish. What a pathetic bunch they were. But something still niggled at the back of his mind and he couldn't pin it down, something about Dojo Williams.

'Comrade Yi, Comrade Yi!'

He turned to see an officer, red in the face, hurrying towards him across the compound, nervously waving a scrap of paper in his hand. The spectacle struck Yi as extremely vulgar and as he accepted the message he wondered why the officer was standing as far away as he decently could.

Terry first realized that the North Korean paratroopers were on to them when he heard the distant crack of two pistol shots down in the valley, where the trucks would by now have stopped.

'Some poor bastard getting the blame,' he said to Ken, panting as they pushed up the hillside.

'My heart bleeds for him.'

He could imagine the shock and panic when the rear truck finally closed up with the leader and they looked stupidly at each other, gaping at the empty space in between, terrified to admit the worst. Couldn't happen to a nicer bunch of blokes, he smirked.

After leaving the bus, he had sent two of the lads back to the end of the footpath where it left the track, to camouflage the tyre marks as best they could. It might just buy them an extra half hour if they could force the paratroopers to search the whole length of the winding road for the bus's exit point. They would find it eventually, but all the while they were searching they would be unable to start tracking the escaped prisoners themselves.

Andy was having a hard time of it, the gunshot wound from the beach ambush was bleeding again and although he had bandaged it as best he could with a strip of shirt from the dead driver, he was limping badly and had fallen back from his usual place at the front of any difficult tab.

Terry had taken the lead, with Ken close behind him; both were armed with Kalashnikovs. He had given the remaining Kalashnikovs to the two men at the rear, the three unarmed mercenaries and Andy walking in the middle in single file, feeling naked without so much as a knife. Whoever was at the front of the column had the unenviable role of pathfinder, forcing a way through the thick undergrowth and overhanging branches, and when they reached a part of the forest that was particularly dense and tangled, Terry decided to swap over the lead scouts every few hundred yards.

They had decided to march due west, heading deeper into Korea in accordance with Terry's earlier plan before the disaster at the beach. Eventually they would swing south and attempt a crossing of the land border, but to do so now would be to walk right into the blocking position that the paratroopers would be bound to place in their way as soon as a reaction force could be gathered together.

With neither compass nor watch, it had only been possible to estimate the direction roughly, but it would have to do for now. Terry regretted not having the time to get a more accurate fix by setting up a shadow stick. He could even have improvised a compass with a piece of wire and something magnetic from the bus, but the paramount need had been to get moving and put as much distance as possible between themselves and the hunter force. For now, a quick glance at the sun would have to do. When darkness came he would find a clearing and check the stars. Then, locating his direction of travel, he would seek out a prominent feature or landmark on the skyline and use it as a reference point by which to navigate.

'This is almost as bad as secondary jungle,' Ken

said, tripping over a hidden root and going down on his knees.

'Were you ever in 'Nam?' the man behind him asked.

Ken winked at Terry.

'Sure, mate. Birming'nam.' He spat in the dirt. 'Stupid pom. How old do you think I am?'

Terry chuckled. 'When were you really last in the jungle?'

'Philippines. Helping the government winkle the Commies out of the bush. You?'

'West Africa. Some stinking bloody bush that was, I tell you.'

Terry looked at the pines and silver birches, smelt the fresh air. 'This is luxury compared to that. We lost most of the team from malaria and some eventually went down with Aids after some R & R on the coast. Jesus, what a God-forsaken hole.'

'Lucky you kept your flies done up. Kept that Welsh willie of yours nice and clean. What do you feed it on?'

'Laver bread, what do you think?'

'Might have guessed. The original Welsh rarebit.'

'Don't you ever shut up?' Andy snapped, panting heavily.

'Not so long as there's someone I can piss off by talking,' Ken said, grinning at him broadly.

At the crest of the hill they stopped for a break, the four without weapons sitting miserably in a huddle while the others with Kalashnikovs kept their backs to the group, facing outwards and each covering a quarter of the arc.

'Don't just sit around, lads,' Terry said when they had rested. 'We can get some cam on at least.'

The clothes they had been given were brown prison fatigues, loose and shapeless but the right colour for a walk in the forest. Normally prisoners would have been issued with light canvas shoes, rope-soled and quick to wear out, but unable to find sizes big enough for the Westerners and wanting to create a good impression for the press, the Koreans had allowed them to keep their boots.

By smearing their fatigues with mud and streaking the material with crushed leaves and grass stains, they gradually converted their prison outfits into a passable set of combats. This done, Terry crawled forward and checked the terrain they were about to enter.

'Looks like the same mix of pine and birch. There's a fair bit of bracken too. Much like the stuff we've come through.'

Cutting branches and uprooting clumps of bracken, they worked in pairs to cam themselves up further, breaking the sharp outlines that could easily be identified at a distance, until at last they resembled a gang of runaway pantomime trees.

Finally Terry redistributed their small stock of weapons so that those without Kalashnikovs at least carried a bayonet and a grenade each.

'And if it comes to a fight make every one count,' he told them.

With this done, rested and feeling more like soldiers, they set off in a well-spaced single file, two Kalashnikovs front and rear as before.

As they marched, Terry put his mind to the question of food. Water was no problem: they had already forded several streams and it tasted beautifully fresh and cold. Looking around at the woodland, he reckoned that a man with the right training could live on the run for weeks or even months. They wouldn't be able to risk the noise of shooting game, at least not until they were deeper in the *ulu*, but they may be able to get some fish and there was an abundance of plants. They had found mess tins in the webbing they had taken from the guards, and if they could build a fire and boil the young bracken shoots and nettles, they could make an edible stew. Add in some berries and fungi and they could march all day. It might not give them enough protein to go the distance with Frank Bruno, but it would keep them alive.

It was towards evening that Terry began to feel uneasy. It started as a slight wariness. First he slowed the pace and increased the spacing between the men. Next he pushed two lead scouts fifty yards ahead. Then, as the sun got lower in the sky, he executed a standard ambush procedure, breaking track and doubling back to ambush their own trail; if they were being followed, the pursuer would walk right along the muzzles of their waiting guns. Nothing.

Andy edged closer. There weren't many men in the world he respected, but Dojo was one of them.

'What's up?'

Terry shook his head, puzzled. 'I'm not sure. Something.'

Ken shifted on the bed of brown leaves. 'Got the spooks, have you?'

Andy shut him up with a glare.

'OK, from now on we move for ten minutes, listen for five. I'll increase it if I have to.'

By now Terry was accepted by everyone as the natural leader. They had learnt the hard way that the shortest route is rarely the safest, and from now on, if Dojo said wait, they would wait. Half their number had already perished since landing in North Korea, and they knew that if Yi Soong had his way, the rest would soon follow.

'Get these miserable shits out of my sight.'

Yi Soong stood at the roadside in full combat gear, a new AK74 slung across his chest. The latest Russian 5.45mm assault rifle, it was the weapon borne by every man of the North Korean special forces company that had just deplaned from the Hip helicopters in the field behind him.

At Yi's feet, the two paratroop officers from the prisoners' escort lay in the dust, their faces bleeding from his interrogation.

'What do you want done with them?' the special forces officer asked with contempt.

Yi didn't even bother to answer, but shook his head in disgust as he walked away. Drawing his pistol, the officer stepped up to each man in turn and fired one round into the base of his skull.

Calling the platoon commanders together, Yi briefed them on the pursuit operation that was now in full swing.

'The paratroopers who allowed the mercenaries to escape have been sent on their trail. Having managed to lose the bus, they have now found it and are following up. If they fail to recapture the enemy, they have been told that they will be shot – a good enough incentive, I think.'

He spread his map on the ground. 'We are now here, some kilometres to the west of the escape point, and before any idiot asks me why we are not cutting off the direct route due south, let me say that I know now who's leading the mercenaries. I underestimated him once before and I don't intend to do it again. He'll be heading into the heart of Korea, probably intending to cross the rail line at Singosan and then cut towards the border opposite Kumhwa.'

Yi stared at the faces around him. 'Believe me, I know this man. Our border forces have all been alerted but apart from the miserable paratroopers, I have ordered everyone out of the area. I don't want us tripping over our useless infantry. They made a big enough mess of the attack in the first place. No. We, gentlemen, will track these fuckers ourselves.'

When he had dismissed the commanders and they had dispersed to brief their platoons, Yi folded his map and slid it into the pocket of his combat jacket. Checking his watch, he estimated that there was an hour at the most to darkness. Good. A hard night march into the hills would be an excellent warm-up for the company. Not that they needed one. These were the best troops in the country, better even than their opposite numbers in the American puppet state of South Korea. He should know. He had served in both, rising to the rank of officer in the ROK special forces, laughing secretly at their lax training under American instructors.

Their Achilles heel was their reliance on a sophisticated back-up. Without massive air support, packs full of the latest high-energy rations, satellite communications, instant casevac – without the trappings of civilization – they were like lost sheep.

But Yi Soong had always been the wolf. He realized that civilization itself was the enemy of the man of war. It softened him and if he relied on it for support it would betray him. Let the Americans keep their helicopter gunships and rations and casevac, their waterproof clothing and rucksacks crammed with candy bars and clean underwear. He had always trained his men to live with nothing but their wits. They could kill with their hands and feet, live off the land, navigate by the stars, sun and moon, and disappear like the wind itself.

Most of all he had trained their will, and when the final war came between the North and the South, it would be strength of will that would decide the outcome. His government would call the bluff of the southern regime, which, with its allies, would collapse. In their souls, Yi Soong knew, they were weak.

'And what of you, Dojo?' he said aloud to himself as he studied the moon rising in a dark, icy-blue sky. 'How strong are you in your soul?'

9

Half an hour before dawn Terry woke the others. They had stopped for the night on the side of a heavily wooded, steep-sided hill. Thrashing through the bushes, with branches whipping in their faces, some of the men had complained that they should find somewhere on flatter ground with easier access. But Terry was not to be moved; this was exactly the sort of place he had been looking for to harbour for the night. It was the type of country that no one would attempt to move through in darkness, and if they did the mercenaries would hear them coming from a mile away. Furthermore, it would be necessary for only one man to remain awake on stag. With eight in the party, the sentry would have to do no more than an hour on watch and everyone could therefore expect to get plenty of rest.

Terry had always loved the hour before dawn, a time of complete peace and stillness, so, reserving the last stag for himself, he enjoyed a good night's sleep before he was shaken awake at the start of his duty. Having risen and moved silently to one side of the others, he went through a simple warm-up routine to loosen his muscles, aching and stiff from the day before. He slipped into the *sanchin* hourglass stance, his arms coming up in the position of a double block, his breathing deep and powerful. Normally he would have used the thunderous *ibuki* breathing technique, but in the circumstances he executed each move in total silence.

Step by step he worked through the whole *sanchin kata*, feeling his mind come fully awake and the power flood back into his limbs. Each punch was executed in slow motion in perfect synchronization with the movement of the legs, hips and the breathing, Terry's concentration being on the complete focus of energy into the striking point of the two knuckles. At full speed it would smash bricks or shatter wood, but in the dark silence of the forest, Terry's fist moved with the controlled strength and precision of a stalking tiger, the energy locked deep within ready to be unleashed in a split second.

When he had finished *sanchin*, he worked through the fluid movements of the *tensho kata*. Here, instead of confrontation of power against power, the aim was avoidance, the deflection of the opponent's own strength and aggression back against himself. In place of the solid arm blocks, the defences were executed with rolling wrist movements, and gentle hooks that would gather in the enemy like corn to be cut down with open hand blows, each one capable of scything through bone.

Completing the routine, Terry shook himself loose and sat cross-legged to focus his mind, now fully awake. This day would be crucial. He hoped that a good march would take them out of the immediate danger area, but they could not afford to relax their guard for a moment. It was probable that Yi Soong himself would take charge of the hunt, for that was what it was. This was no exercise on the Brecon

Beacons or Dartmoor. This would be a savage, ruthless pursuit, with death the price of failure.

Terry knew that Yi would have limitless resources at his disposal, but would he use them? He thought not. Yi had tried that at the resort and the soldiers had made a complete mess of it. This time, Terry guessed, he would use the stealth of specialists. He might well use the army and border guards to throw some kind of cordon around his quarry, but cordons were easy to slip through if you knew how. The border would be another matter; Terry had heard that it was one of the most heavily guarded in the world, but that would be the problem for another day. For the moment they would have to concentrate on avoiding Yi's specialists.

When everyone was ready to move, they filed out of the harbour position and contoured round the hill. Then, breaking track, they climbed fifty yards and silently doubled back until they were above and parallel to their exit route. When they reached a position that offered good visibility down the hillside, they crept into cover to lie motionless and alert for fifteen minutes, observing their own tracks from this new ambush position in case they had picked up a tail.

Terry still didn't know why he was uneasy. Being on the run behind enemy lines was enough to unsettle anyone, but he had never been the jumpy type. Whenever he had felt like this in the past it had always been for a reason. This time as well, he was sure that his sixth sense was firing on all cylinders; he just hoped that he would discover the cause before it discovered him.

The fifteen minutes were almost up and the men were starting to shuffle restlessly, anxious to be on the move, when something caught Terry's eye, springing his senses to full alert. His hand signal for enemy contact instantly brought everyone back to the present and eight pairs of eyes strained through the undergrowth, seeking out the hostile tracker. The safety-catches of the four Kalashnikovs were silently eased down into the automatic firing position, and the remainder of the party clutched their grenades in preparation for the coming fire-fight.

On the track that they had created when leaving their night harbour, a single bush moved. Terry was right: there had been someone tracking them. But whoever he was, he had just made his last mistake. There was another rustle, and the sound of muffled voices, but just as Terry squinted through the aperture of his weapon sight, closing his left eye and tightening his trigger to second pressure, two thin boys stepped into the open.

Barefoot and filthy, they were dressed in rags and moving with the stealth and terror of cornered animals. The smaller of the two was stuffing into his mouth something that the elder boy had just handed to him. It was hard to be sure from fifty yards away but Terry thought it was a shoot of bracken that Andy had spat out as inedible the previous night.

Ken reached across and tapped Terry on the shoulder.

'What the fuck do we do?'

Terry looked back at the boys, but catching the movement of Ken aiming his Kalashnikov, quickly pushed the barrel aside. There had been enough killing of children at the resort. He was damned if he was going to kill any himself; leave that to Yi and his cronies.

Thinking through his options, Terry reckoned that

they could simply lie still and let the boys move on, but he was sure that they had been tracking him for at least a day now, and if they felt the mercenaries were going to leave them a trail of food, they would continue to follow them. Then, if they ran into Korean troops, the boys might give them away.

But the matter was decided for him by Ken, who angrily flicked his selector switch back to safe, disgusted that Terry had weakened and stopped him from firing. In the silence of the forest the metallic click resounded as a clear warning of another human presence, and before the mercenaries could react, the boys had whipped around and shot away into the trees.

'Get them!'

Bounding out of cover, Terry shouted and threw himself down the hill. Although the boys had had a fifty-yard start, the smaller of the two had caught his jacket sleeve on a thorn bush. Wriggling free, he darted underneath a bush but not before Terry was able to grab one of his ankles and drag him out kicking and screaming. Getting to his feet, Terry lifted the boy upside down by the ankles and held him at arm's length, as he struggled like a demon. But a second later something slammed him in the back and he staggered forward as the older of the boys leapt at him, flailing with his puny fists and bare feet.

'Help me, someone. Get these little buggers off me!'

The rest of the men gathered in an amused circle to enjoy the spectacle of Dojo Williams being beaten up by a couple of ragged kids.

'Now there's a sight,' Ken mused happily. 'Dojo and the Karate Kid.'

One of the men stepped forward and with a swipe of the hand sent the older boy sprawling.

'He's got some guts, that one. Coming back to save his little brother.'

The others nodded approvingly and as Terry dropped the smaller boy to the ground, the men crowded round to inspect their captives, who clung together with eyes as big as saucers, the older one gabbling something in Korean.

'What's he saying?' asked Ken.

'How the hell should I know?' replied Terry.

'Maybe it's Korean for "Take me to your leader."'

'Or "Who's that fat, ugly bastard with the big mouth?"'

Terry crouched in front of the boys and looked closely at their clothes, trying to examine the material underneath the layers of dirt.

'Prisoners? Are you prisoners too?' He fingered the hem of his own fatigue jacket and held it beside their own. The boys looked at Terry's clothes, then at the others standing around them and nodded suspiciously.

'Well what the hell do we do with them now, Dr bloody Barnardo?'

'I say finish them. The first sign of the gooks and they'll give us away.'

Terry looked round at the speaker, a big Geordie. 'Don't act as dumb as you look. They wouldn't be wandering around in the bush if they weren't on the run as well. I bet they're more scared of the paratroopers than you are.'

'And that's saying something,' Andy piped up.

'We'll have to take them with us,' Terry said after a moment's thought, raising his hand to cut the storm of protest.

'Listen, if we leave them behind they'll simply trail after us and then they're far more likely to give us away. At least this way we'll know where they are.'

Ignoring the grumbles from the men, Terry placed the two boys in the middle of the little column, allocating one mercenary to keep an eye on each of them. When they were ready to set off, he checked everyone's camouflage, detailed the order of march, nominated two lead scouts, and passed the word to move. For the next few hours he couldn't help turning round every hundred yards to check that the boys were still there and that the men hadn't quietly disposed of them along the way, but whenever he looked the boys appeared to be quite content. They moved completely without sound, in sharp contrast to the tall Westerners flanking them. Previously Terry had thought that his men's fieldcraft was second to none, but in comparison with the two Korean boys they sounded like a herd of elephants. Even the men themselves noticed it and began to view their captives with a new and grudging respect.

It was also the boys who, towards the middle of the afternoon, gave the first warning of the paratroopers. Handing over their positions as lead scouts, Terry and Ken were taking their turn at the rear of the column, enjoying a break from the constant tension of pathfinding, where every sense was on full alert for the slightest hint of ambush or contact. But they had barely settled into the new movement procedure, each one turning alternately to check their tracks for an enemy follow-up, when there was a scuffling further up the column and the mercenary guarding the elder of the two Korean boys let out a curse as he wrestled with the boy, who was kicking him vigourously in the shins and chattering away unintelligibly.

Leaving Ken to watch the rear, Terry hurried forward to put a stop to the row. In the silent forest the smallest noise was amplified out of all proportion and travelled far. Furthermore, the column had just left the thicker cover of the trees and emerged into a clearing of stumps where the felled timber lay stacked in neat piles. The mercenaries could ill afford to be heard or spotted by woodsmen who could then alert the local police as to the whereabouts of the escaped prisoners.

'What the hell's going on?' Terry asked.

'God knows. The little bugger went all quiet and then ran amok. Needs a good hiding,' the man said.

But Terry could tell fear when he saw it and the boy had clearly been terrified by something. Passing the word quickly up the line, he ordered the column to stop, but being intent on their own task, the lead scouts had missed the commotion behind them and were already well across the clearing, becoming ever more isolated from the others. Suddenly there was a shout, followed a second later by a burst of Kalashnikov fire.

'Contact!'

Terry cursed his luck as the cry echoed back from the lead scout. He had thought that they were travelling too fast for their own good but had let it go, happy with the good progress they had all made since the escape. He had even allowed himself to dream of reaching and crossing the border unhindered. Some hope.

What was more, he now had his fire-power split in two at the exact moment when he could least afford it: a frontal contact with an enemy force of unknown size. In the normal contact drill, he and Ken would have moved forward through the relative security of the bush to add the weight of their own fire to the two Kalashnikovs of the lead scouts. Lobbing a grenade, they would have been able to break contact and bug out; they weren't in any position to get embroiled in a fire-fight. But now it would be suicide to cross the clearing, leaving behind the rest of the party with only bayonets and a couple of hand-grenades to defend themselves. The thick tree stumps made it impossible for Terry or Ken to even see the lead scouts, let alone expend their valuable ammunition in a useless blanket of covering fire. The only way would be by standing up and firing short, accurate bursts over the stumps, but already the air around them was crackling with the enemy's return fire, indicating a force of at least section strength. Whichever way he looked at it, Terry kept returning to the same terrible conclusion: his scouts were on their own.

'Pull back.'

'What do you mean?' Andy shouted above the noise.

'Do as I say!' Terry barked. 'Back to the cover of the trees. Move!'

At the first sound of shots the two Korean boys had hit the ground and huddled together behind a thick silver-birch stump. Grabbing them both by the collar, Andy shoved them along the ground in front of him towards the edge of the trees. With his Kalashnikov slung across his shoulders, Ken crawled forward on hands and knees, dropping into position beside Terry.

'Bit of a bummer, eh?'

'You're not kidding. Those two have had it.'

'I was thinking more about their guns and ammo. The other lads could have used them.'

'Has anyone ever told you you're all heart?'

'Never.'

There was a scream from the far side of the clearing, where the two lead scouts had gone to ground, and a moment later the dull thuds of exploding HE sent showers of wood fragments into the sky as grenades bracketed the remaining scout.

'Get the lads back to the last rally point,' Terry snapped. 'I'll hold them up for as long as I can.'

For once in his life Ken didn't argue. Every few hundred yards Terry had nominated a prominent feature, rocky outcrop or distinctive tree as a rally point for use in just such an emergency as this. In the event of ambush and the party getting split up, everyone was to return to the last rally point and wait for the others. After ten minutes they were to assume that no one else had made it and they were to proceed on their own. Ken knew that without the delay that Terry would impose on the pursuing paratroopers, the fleeing mercenaries would be lucky to get more than a hundred yards before the enemy rushed forward and got in among them. They would be cut to pieces.

'Right, mate. Don't keep us waiting,' Ken said, then turned and was gone.

Searching anxiously around, Terry located a good firing position about thirty yards to his left. At present he was dangerously close to the place where the two lead scouts had been killed. It would only take the paratroopers a couple of minutes to regroup and continue the pursuit and unless he moved, he would find himself directly in their path. Somehow he had to slow them down and he reckoned that he could best achieve this and conserve his precious supply of ammunition by sniping at them from a flank.

'What I'd give to be another six hundred yards away with an L96 rifle and a gillie's suit,' he muttered under his breath as he leopard-crawled through the wood chippings that littered the soft earth. But there would be no time for that, and besides, the ground didn't allow for it. If he was any further than fifty yards the trees would prevent him from identifying his targets. Instead of the sniper's stealth and unwavering patience, he would have to rely on speedy footwork and snap shooting.

Having reached his selected firing position, he had barely checked his magazine when the first paratrooper stepped into the clearing and moved clumsily into Terry's new line of fire.

'Dumb bastard.'

Terry tightened the butt into his shoulder and aligned his Kalashnikov sights on the unwary soldier. Flicking his selector switch to single shot, he waited until the figure had paused as if wondering which way to go, and squeezed the trigger. The round caught the paratrooper squarely in the chest knocking him backwards.

'Wales, one: North Korea, nil.'

Rolling to his right, Terry changed his position, the clusters of tree stumps obscuring him from the enemy's view. There was a shout from the far side of the clearing, where he estimated the rest of the paratroopers were gathering, and a fusillade of random shots ripped through the overhead branches.

You'll have to do better than that, Terry said to himself as he prepared to take on the next Korean.

But with Yi Soong's threats fresh in their minds,

the paratroopers were desperate to prove themselves to their absent commander. In a wild rush they burst from cover and surged forward, firing from the waist as they ran. One of them stumbled over a root and went down, accidentally firing his Kalashnikov as he did so. Thinking they were being engaged from a new angle, the paratroopers froze and bunched, blazing wildly around them. Steadying his aim, Terry levelled his sights at the only figure wearing the rank insignia of an NCO and fired. The sound of his single shot was lost in the torrent of noise from the paratroopers' weapons and the NCO crumpled and dropped to the floor.

'Just a couple more ought to do it.'

Estimating that there were at most half a dozen men left from the paratrooper section, Terry flicked his selector switch to automatic. In their panic and without the guidance of an NCO, they had allowed themselves to become bunched in the open, presenting a tempting target for the opportunist. An accurate burst would have a good chance of taking out several of them. Drawing up his right knee, Terry shifted on to his side and primed himself for action.

Using the pistol grip of the Kalashnikov to screw the weapon securely back into his shoulder for a rock-solid aim, he jack-knifed into a kneeling position and squirted two five-round bursts into the packed soldiers. Three of them went down, at least two of them dead, but the remainder, in the flood of relief at seeing their assailant for the first time, screamed with a mixture of hatred and fear, and charged at the kneeling mercenary behind the tree stump.

Bounding over the roots and fallen trunks, they rapidly closed the gap, but keeping his breath measured and even, Terry aimed at the nearest man and fired again. Both shots of the two-round burst caught him in the chest, although his momentum carried him forward until he hit a stump and collapsed dead on the ground.

Switching his aim calmly to the next soldier in line, Terry again squeezed the trigger. Nothing happened. Flicking the weapon on to its side, he stared in horror at the empty brass cartridge case jamming the mechanism. The front end projected out of the ejector slot, but the base was held fast by the breech-block. Snatching at the cocking handle, Terry tipped the weapon over and shook it violently to dislodge the empty case, but even as he let the spring slam shut, carrying the next round into the breech for firing, he knew that it was too late. The paratroopers were upon him.

Ducking under the slashing bayonet of the leading man, Terry cursed himself for having given his own bayonet to one of the lads who had been unarmed. Swinging his Kalashnikov, he caught the paratrooper behind the knees and brought him down, then, reversing his grip on the wooden stock, he crashed the metal butt plate into the bridge of the man's nose. Glimpsing a blur of steel to his left, he flung himself aside just in time to avoid a vicious lunge from the second paratrooper. In a fit of rage, the Korean raised his rifle above his head and hacked at Terry, who edged away on his back, wriggling to right and left to dodge the rain of blows. Then, allowing the man to close within range of a hand grip, Terry brought his foot up into the man's stomach, gripped the lapels of his combat jacket, and using his foot as a lever, hoisted the surprised paratrooper over his head in a perfect *tomoenage* somersault throw.

Even as the man was landing with a grunt in the dirt behind him, Terry was on his feet, darting to the side of his fallen opponent. As the man tried to get up, Terry slashed downwards with a *shuto* open-hand blow to the jugular, instantly following it with three devastating drop-punches, one to the bridge of the nose, the next to the upper lip, and the last to the point of the chin.

The immediate threats neutralized, Terry dropped to his knees, gasping for breath.

'Jesus, man, you're getting too old for this lark,' he muttered as he mopped the sweat from his forehead and slung the extra two Kalashnikovs over his shoulder. He then rummaged through the webbing of the two paratroopers for the spare magazines and grenades, which he stuffed into his own pouches.

'These'll do nicely, thank you.'

He was just standing up to go forward and check that the lead scouts were dead and to retrieve more equipment, when a bullet snapped past his ear. Dropping into cover, he looked across the clearing to see an extended line of paratroopers advancing steadily towards him.

'Bloody hell, where did you lot come from?' he said as he snapped a fresh magazine on to his Kalashnikov. 'I reckon this could be it, Terry my lad. One fire-fight too far.'

By now he estimated he had bought enough time for the other mercenaries to make good their escape to the rally point. They would only wait a few more minutes before setting off without him, presuming him dead. But glancing round, he saw that he was a good fifty yards from the relative safety of the trees and his position had been clearly identified by this new force of paratroopers. He gritted his teeth, promising himself that the Koreans would pay dearly for his death.

Suddenly, there was a burst of fire to his right and he ducked by reflex.

This is it, mate, he thought. They've got you cut off now as well.

But as he searched for this new enemy, Terry noticed that far from pressing home their attack, the paratroopers had gone to ground and were returning fire, not at him but at the new fire position. Adding his own fire to the bursts from his unknown helper, he created an overlapping arc with the Korean paratroopers caught in the middle. But something else was bothering him: the sound of the rifle fire was different; it was not a Kalashnikov but an M16.

With the paratroopers hugging the ground and unable to hit him because of the stumps, Terry made his way slowly back to the edge of the trees. As soon as he reached the welcome shade of the towering pines and birches, he fired a last burst at the paratroopers and then turned to sprint away into the depths of the forest. But what was more, as if at a signal the M16 of the other firer fell silent, and Terry knew that he too, whoever he was, would similarly be running for his life. Since he had been in Korea it was a drill that Terry had only practised with one man: Danny Grey Wolf.

Even from a distance of several miles the sound of the battle was music to the ears of Yi Soong. In the forest shadows around him every member of the special forces team instantly froze, melting into the shapes and colours of the woodland, tensed and ready for anything.

Yi listened carefully, counting the guns, accurately

picturing the engagement in every grenade burst and return of fire as if reading a sheet of music, building his mental image into a precise symphony of battle. With closed eyes he saw the initial contact, the panic of the answering fusillade and the pinning down of the lead scouts with a series of short, sharp bursts. In the silence that followed he imagined the confusion among the escaped mercenaries as they matched their inadequate weapons to the task, and then, yes, just as Yi had known he would, Dojo Williams offered himself up as a sacrifice and Yi could imagine the deliberate sniper fire from the Welshman's rifle taking a terrible toll of the miserable paratroopers.

Nor could he help smiling when he heard the Kalashnikov fire from the second section of para-troopers, imagining Dojo's surprise in the face of this new and unexpected threat. But the smile froze on his lips when he heard the unmistakable crack of an M16, knowing that it could stem from only one man. When the paratroopers had contacted Danny Grey Wolf north of the resort, they had assured Yi that he had been killed; he had fallen into the river and been carried away. No, they hadn't found his body, but there had been bloodstains on the rocks at the top of the cliff on to which they had driven him, and in the water below they had seen his body, turning face down in the swell, pulled under by the current and swept out of sight. With a painful effort, Yi forced the episode from his mind. He would deal later with the officer responsible.

Jogging across to a bare knoll, Yi walked out on to the rock, unzipped a small pouch on his web belt, and pulled out a compass. Taking a fix on the direction of the firing, he noted the bearing, plotting it on the transparent cover of his mapcase, and matching it to the ground below him. Across the valley the roof of the forest was a brilliant sea of greens and golds, but today there was no pleasure in it for Yi. Today it was an obstacle to be crossed and the site of a possible future cut-off position to ambush the mercenaries when they neared the border.

He outlined his plan to the special forces officer.

'We won't catch them today. Maybe not even tomorrow. But we will catch them. Right here.'

His finger stabbed at the map on his knee, and the officer looked with some surprise at the point indicated, in the desolate wilderness of minefields and razor wire of the border DMZ.

After Terry and Danny met up, they made their way back to the rally point to find that the rest of the party had already given Terry up for dead and left. But with Danny's tracking skills they soon located the trail and by nightfall everyone was celebrating the return of not one, but two spirits from the dead.

'What about the blood on the rock?' Andy asked as Danny recounted his escape to the crowd of eager listeners.

'I killed a rabbit, slit its throat and daubed the blood on the ground beside my empty cartridge cases. Once I was in the water I reckoned if I could convince them I was dead they wouldn't bother coming all the way down to check me out. The current was pretty fast and by the time I had to stick my face up for air, I was in the clear.'

Ken whistled in admiration. 'I take back everything I said about you, mate.'

Danny smiled and reached into his bergen.

'You guys look like a bunch of skeletons. Don't they teach you anything in the army these days?' He pulled out a bundle and unwrapped the grubby cloth. 'I don't have any wampum, but how about some nice rabbit jerky?'

As he handed round the strips of dried meat, he grinned, for one by one the faces all about him glowed with the pleasure of the taste of meat. He waited until they had finished and then pulled out another bundle, this time of dried fish.

'I'm afraid I don't have any ketchup.'

There was a cough from the back of the group and Danny saw two huge pairs of eyes boring into the bundle of fish. He selected two of the largest strips and passed them to the boys, who stuffed them in their mouths and chewed ravenously. When they had finished, Danny fired a couple of questions at them in Korean.

After questioning the boys further, interspersing their answers with further bribes of dried fish, Danny repeated their story to the others, telling them of their time in the labour camp and escape from the trucks, their flight to a forest hide-out and eventual contact with the mercenaries.

'They thought you were ghost spirits,' Danny said, laughing. 'They had never seen Westerners before, and when you came clumping through the forest covered in twigs and camouflage, they reckoned their time had come and they were supposed to follow you into the next world.'

'It might still come to that,' Terry added morosely. 'Have you any ideas about how to cross the border?'

Danny thought for a while. 'Some. I did a number of tours of duty in different sectors, and the Rangers ran an escape and evasion exercise that might come in handy. We all learnt quite a few lessons.'

There was a buzz of excitement around the encampment.

'Thank fuck someone knows what to do,' Ken said, sighing with relief.

'What's that supposed to mean?' Terry asked.

'No, I didn't mean it to sound like that, mate. We wouldn't have made it this far without you,' Ken replied hastily to background murmurs of assent from the others.

'What about the boys?' someone asked. 'It'll be difficult enough for us to make it by ourselves, let alone bogged down with a couple of brats.'

'We can't just leave them here. The poor little buggers'll starve to death, or get shot by those Korean bastards.'

'Yeah, you heard what they told Danny about having the dogs set on them.'

Terry looked across at Danny. 'You know the border. What do you think?'

Oblivious to the turn of the conversation, the two boys were picking the last shreds of dried fish from their teeth, happy for the first time since being picked up by the mercenaries. Danny called across to the eldest of the two and asked him some questions.

'What did he say?' Terry asked when they had finished.

'Well, he doesn't seem to know the immediate border area, but they sure as hell want to come with us. They might even be useful. It's fine up here in the forest, but once we're out in the open we'll stick out like sore thumbs. If we have to go near any villages we could use them to scout out the land for us.'

'Can they be trusted?'

Danny shrugged. 'Why not? We were dumb enough to trust that asshole Yi and look where it got us. These kids have got a vested interest in escaping to the South, just like us.'

Terry looked around the gathering: everyone was nodding in agreement.

'OK, then. The boys come too.'

Danny called to the boys, translating the news. Liang sat up, wiping his mouth and beaming, and whispered hurriedly to Little Chiao.

'What's he saying?' asked Terry.

Danny smiled. 'He says they were right about you being ghost spirits. He says you are going to lead them into another world.'

10

When they came to the edge of the forest Terry ordered a change of cam. They had been marching due south for some time and when the trees at last began to thin out they knew that they would soon be forced to leave the relative security of the wooded hills. Putting the men in a temporary defensive harbour, Terry and Danny stalked forward to the brilliant sunlight that dazzled their eyes after days in the shadows and gloom. Danny had taken Liang and as they dropped into the grass to crawl the final yards, the boy surged eagerly ahead as if expecting to see the free world laid out before him.

Instead, he only just managed to duck back into cover as a truck thundered past, spraying clouds of dust into the air from the surface of the unmade road that skirted the forest. Grabbing him by the ankle, Danny yanked him back into the shadows.

'Someone's coming,' Terry whispered, and crouched as low as he could, hugging the ground. But a moment later, an old man sauntered past, leaning heavily on a walking stick, oblivious to the three people watching him intently.

'There must be a village near by,' Danny said. 'Let's see if we can get a better look.'

Using their sniper training, he and Terry leopard-crawled out of the trees, the boy following, imitating their movements. Peering across the dusty track, they saw a cluster of houses some two hundred yards away. Beyond them, the ground stretched into the distance, where a low line of hills rippled the horizon.

'According to my estimates, the border's just the other side of those hills,' Terry said, thinking back to the maps that he had studied and memorized back in the training camp. 'If we're going to cross tonight, we'll have to get over this farmland this afternoon.'

'In broad daylight?'

Terry shrugged. He didn't like it any more than Danny did, but he knew that Yi was likely to have located their approximate position from the noise of the contact battle with the paratroopers. Ideally he would have liked to lie up for a few days, march by night and attempt a border crossing in a totally different sector, but without proper food the men were getting weaker by the hour and their ability to cover long distances was now seriously curtailed.

'I think it's time for a little deception plan.'

Back at the harbour, the men were restless, anxious to get moving with the border and the freedom of the South so close. When Terry, Danny and the boy entered the clearing, they were met with a barrage of questions. How far was it? Would they get over tonight? Had Dojo spotted any more paratroopers?

'Hang on a minute, lads,' Terry said, waving for silence. 'First things first. Strip off your cam and wipe off as much of the shit as you can. We've got a couple of miles of fairly open farmland to cross and folks'll get suspicious if they see a shagging forest strolling along. When you've done that, use the bayonets to cut two or three stacks of saplings, the longer the better. Nice leafy ones.'

'I knew it,' Ken smirked, 'we're going to pole-vault over the fucking border. The Welshman's finally flipped his lid. Couldn't hack the pressures of command.'

'Shut it. There're some farm buildings and a small village off to the left and anyone in it will have a clear view out across the fields. We'll keep as far away as we can but there's no way we can stalk it. The only way is to brazen it out.'

Having gathered the men around him, Terry explained his plan, and half an hour later a tired but successful group of woodcutters emerged from the forest and walked happily back to their homes on the other side of the valley. Each pair of men carried a stack of saplings between them, balanced on their shoulders, their heads and faces hidden behind the bright-green leaves.

One farmer, pausing by his herd of cows on the outskirts of the village, thought it was strange how the shadows at this time of day made a person seem taller than he actually was, but then it was hard to tell when, like the group of peasants, they were bowed under the weight of such loads. Two of them had brought their sons, who played and sang in front of the work party. The farmer smiled to himself. It was always the same with the young these days. They had no sense of responsibility; not like in his day.

'I blame the parents,' he said to his friend, who had come out of his cottage to watch. 'If I was their father I'd whip them if they didn't help.'

His friend nodded. 'A spell in the army would sort them out.' And the two of them shook their heads in disgust and went inside to moan to their wives about the lax villagers of Hamdok on the opposite side of the valley, who had been cutting fence posts and beanpoles.

Sweating under his burden of saplings, Terry shifted the weight, careful not to dislodge the Kalashnikov, which he had secured by the shoulder strap in the middle of the bundle. He had thrown away his webbing, keeping only the belt, slinging the pouch with his spare magazines over his shoulder like a satchel. Reluctantly, Danny had also thrown away his bergen, and stuffed his pockets with the most essential items of survival kit.

'Just keep that haircut out of sight,' Ken called over. 'One look at you and they'll think it's the brush salesman.'

They were almost across the belt of open farmland when directly in front of them an old farmer appeared out of nowhere, ambling towards them along the same narrow footpath. At the front of the column Terry swore under his breath, turning round to see Danny slip his tomahawk from his belt. Why did the old fool have to appear just now? The last thing Terry wanted was to take an innocent life. Also, if there was a scuffle it might be seen from the village. And how long would it be before the old fellow was missed? In addition to Yi Soong and his men, they would have the whole district out hunting for them.

The old man had been dozing behind a low earth bund and had been invisible until getting to his feet. He looked up and squinted at the approaching woodcutters, narrowing his eyes to focus on their bowed heads, hidden beneath their loads. He wondered why they were hesitating. Still, maybe they could let him have some water, for he was thirsty after being out in the fields all day. He was just about to start towards them, when a small boy ran past and snatched his hat.

'Here, grandfather. See what I've got,' Little Chiao called out as he tossed the black stovepipe hat to his elder brother. The old man was apoplectic with rage. Raising his stick, he ran after the two boys, who remained just beyond his reach.

'Are you an old shaman?' the taller of the boys shouted to him. 'Well, we're not afraid of your spells!'

Halfway across the field, the old man stopped and leaned on his stick, panting heavily. Far from calling their sons to heel, the woodcutters had gone on ahead. He could hardly believe his eyes. With parents as uncaring as that, how could these two youths grow into anything but hoodlums and vagabonds? But when he turned back the boys had gone, leaving the old man's hat at his feet. Racing across the field, they chased after their fathers.

The old man shook his stick at them, shouting: 'Show more respect for your elders! Your fathers should be ashamed of themselves.' But it was no use. The woodcutters were out of earshot, approaching the low ridge of wooded hills that sheltered Hamdok, the last village on their side of the border.

In the command bunker at Point 763, Yi Soong was putting the final touches to his plan for the destruction of the mercenaries.

'On the contrary, Colonel, I don't want your border guards near them. These are not your ordinary renegades, and besides, it has become a matter of personal pride to me and my men.'

The colonel nodded thoughtfully. He could imagine the sort of fuck-up that was being avenged. It was always the way: something would go wrong up-country – a coup attempt, a mutiny or a local rebellion; the survivors would try to flee to the South and those most responsible for causing the unrest in the first place would be the ones screaming loudest for revenge. But of course revenge would always be cloaked up in talk of national security; the colonel had heard the same claptrap a hundred times before. But whoever these runaways were, it was no longer any concern of his. Comrade Yi had taken personal control of the interception operation planned for that night and it was to be repeated every night until the enemy had been terminated.

When the colonel had gone and Yi was satisfied that only his own special forces officers and NCOs were present in the briefing room, he checked that everyone knew his part in the plan.

'We don't know where they will cross, but I believe it will be in this sector. Our intruder alarms and ground sensors should give us ample warning of their approach but in the last resort we can only rely on our own skills. I've had a network of sensors laid to cover the entire front. The border fence system, with its razor wire, dog runs, mines and machine-guns, will be the anvil and we, gentlemen, will be the hammer. At the first sign we will move in with the Quick Reaction Forces and crush them.'

Once they were back in the cover of some trees, Terry moved the party into a lying-up position and made the maximum use of the remaining daylight. The boys had crept into the outskirts of Hamdok and returned with an armful of corn-cobs and some apples, but not being prepared to risk the smoke of a fire this close to the border, Terry ordered the men to crush the corn, soak it in water and chew it raw. Since proving themselves over the incident of the old man, the boys had become trusted members of the team and delighted in sharing out their stolen rations.

When everyone had eaten, they stripped their kit to the bare minimum, burying the mess tins and the few other items that had helped them to survive until now. In the night crossing of the border, stealth would be essential and Terry wasn't prepared to risk being given away by a clanking tin or shining spoon.

Next the weapons were checked and the ammunition evenly distributed. Planning for the worst case, Terry decided to split the party into two roughly equal groups in case they had to withdraw using fire and manoeuvre, but when Danny tried to explain to the boys that one of them would have to go with each group, they refused to be parted, Little Chiao sobbing as he clung to Liang.

'OK, OK,' said Terry, relenting. 'Put them both in my team, but shut them up before they give the whole game away.'

Along with the two boys, Terry detailed Danny and Andy to join his group. Both he and Andy would carry Kalashnikovs and Danny his M16. Ken would take the other three men, with the two Kalashnikovs captured from the paratroopers in the earlier forest battle. The grenades were split fifty-fifty.

Lastly everyone cammed up, checking each other to make sure that their faces were well blacked and that nothing would rattle in the silence of the night.

This done, they lay down and waited, each man

locked in the privacy of his own thoughts and fears until, when it was completely dark, Terry stood up and hand-signalled everyone to their feet.

'As Danny's the only one who's seen the border before, my group will take the lead. Also, if we're challenged, the kids can reply that they're lost or something. Ken, you keep an eye on the rear. Once we close up to the actual fences, we'll leapfrog you through, OK?'

Terry looked around at the anxious faces staring back at him in the dark.

'Good luck, lads. All being well, we'll be in South Korea this time tomorrow.'

A couple of the men laughed nervously and with a final check of his safety-catch, Terry led the way out of the lying-up position, contouring slowly round the hillside before crossing a narrow track and starting the climb towards the ridge and the first of the border fences.

Before the small green light had flashed a second time, the soldier had tugged on the communication cord linking his wrist to his section commander. Without a word the NCO woke instantly, checked the reference number beside the tiny bulb, pressed the switch on his pocket radio and spoke into the throat mike in a barely audible growl.

In the command bunker, Yi strode to the map.

'Say again reference.'

'Contact point three-two-zero, over.'

Yi plotted it on the map. 'Roger, out.'

His luck was in. Tonight he could feel it as sure as ever. He had known that Dojo was far too professional to follow an existing track, but there were so many in the area that at some stage in his approach to the border he would be forced at least to cross one. Yi had allowed for this in his plan by covering all the tracks in the sector with a thin spread of ground sensors. Lightly buried in the earth, they could pick up the slightest tremor and measure the strengths to distinguish between an animal and a man. But the NCO who had just reported in had picked up not one man, but two groups, each of at least four.

Speaking into another handset, Yi had to suppress the excitement in his voice.

'Move to Kilo Golf four, out.'

He wanted these bastards who had thwarted him. He wanted them dead and in a short while they would be, their blood seeping into the earth of the fourth of the twelve separate killing grounds that Yi had prepared with painstaking effort.

At the top of the hill the ground levelled out into a broad plateau, sloping gently down towards a distant row of lights.

'The border,' Danny said flatly. 'Some areas are covered by bright spotlights, but others are blacked out. They vary it every night to avoid creating a standard pattern.'

'And the dark areas?'

'Covered by night-vision devices, image intensifiers, thermal imagers, infrared – you name it. Just because you can't see them, don't assume they can't see you.'

Terry scanned the ground ahead, mostly undulating folds of scrub and gorse. The bulk of the taller trees had been cleared to give open fields of vision, but there were a few patches here and there.

Following Terry's line of thought, Danny pointed to a shallow drainage ditch.

'That will probably run all the way up to the border fence but you can bet it'll be covered by ground sensors and filled with razor wire and anti-personnel mines.'

'Any more good news?'

'It's probably our best bet. In the open, however well we stalk, we'll be sitting ducks. At least if we're in dead ground we're invisible to all the other devices except the ground sensors. There's no answer to them. Let's just hope they haven't deployed any and have relied on booby-traps instead.'

Terry agreed. From his training with surveillance devices he knew that darkness no longer provided cover from view. Image intensifiers drew on the ambient light from stars and expanded it into a glowing green picture of the landscape; thermal imagers gave an accurate heat picture, showing men, animals, engines and any other heat source as easily identifiable white shapes against a dark background; and infrared torches could bathe an area in light invisible to the human eye, but not to the ambusher lying in wait with special goggles and a machine-gun.

The only way to counter this array of highly sensitive devices was to treat night as day and move across ground accordingly, using every fold, depression and piece of cover, trusting that the hidden observer was tired or careless, prone to the same human weaknesses as his prey. It was the latest twist in never-ending game of cat and mouse.

Crawling back to the others, Terry briefed them on his plan to use the drainage ditch. The going would be painfully slow and they would be lucky to make it completely across by first light, but it was their only hope. Andy pushed to the front of the group.

'Let me go first, Dojo. I'm a qualified assault pioneer. I did the combat engineer course at Chatham. I know all about booby-traps and mines. If anyone can clear a way through, I can.'

Terry checked with Danny.

'OK by me,' Danny said. 'I'll give him back-up.'

'That's settled then. My team will lead. Ken, you be prepared to pass your team through when we breach the first fence. I reckon we'll be knackered by then.'

'Or blown to fucking kingdom come.'

Leaving Ken to deploy his team into fire positions ready to give covering fire in case Andy and Danny had to pull back in a hurry, Terry waited until the little Scot and the big Indian had wriggled across the scrub and slipped down into the drainage ditch, before moving out of cover himself. Behind him, the two boys slithered as silently as snakes, so that Terry had to keep glancing round to check they were still there. But whenever he looked, he saw their two blacked-up faces close behind, stuck to him like shadows, their fear and excitement visible through the dirt.

Reaching the lip of the ditch, he dropped into it and slowly crawled forward. Ten yards ahead of him, Andy was probing the ground with the tip of a bayonet, his fingers feeling gently for trip-wires or pressure pads – anything that might indicate the trigger of a mine or booby-trap. Clearing a yard at a time, he worked his way along the ditch at an agonizingly slow speed. Terry couldn't help admiring his courage. He might be a vicious bastard in war, merciless with his enemy and almost as ruthless with his own side, but it took the coolest of nerves to deal with a hidden mine that could explode and blow your hands off at any moment. It was a different kind of courage from the red-hot ferocity of an attack, and as he watched the painstaking operation in front of him, Terry felt a new respect for the man.

Crawling level with Andy's feet, Danny was flat on his stomach, pulling aside stray branches and smoothing the path for those coming up behind him. So long as they kept their heads and backsides below ground level, he knew that they would be masked from every surveillance device except a ground sensor, and he hoped that because this was a drainage ditch, subject to flooding, it would either have been overlooked or any sensors would have been washed away or rendered inoperable by the water. It was a hell of a gamble, but it was the best they could hope for.

After two hours Andy reached the first fence. Although the drainage ditch continued underneath it, the gap had been closed with a coil of razor wire. Deciding not to risk cutting the fence in case it was alarmed, he took each lethal strand of the coil as delicately as he could, wrapped a cloth around it, and piece by piece, clipped a way through. Sliding up alongside him, Danny used the crook of his tomahawk blade to pull the loose ends apart, forcing a gap wide enough for the largest in the group to crawl through. If anyone got snared on the savage barbs it would take valuable minutes to free them, time they could ill afford. This was only the first of several fences and when daylight came clearance patrols would be sent out to check every scrap of dead ground such as the ditch.

Coming up beside Danny, Terry signalled them to stop.

'Well done, lads. We'll let Ken pass through now. I think he's got the hang of it.'

Ken and his team had closed up behind, ready to leapfrog into the lead. As Terry hugged the side of the ditch, Ken slithered past, winking as he drew level.

'Had enough, have you? We'll show you how it's done, mate. Last one to Seoul's a poofter.'

'Just take it easy.'

When the last of Ken's team had cleared the gap in the razor wire, Terry set the boys to keep watch and crawled alongside Danny. It was a good fifty yards to the next fence, beyond which they could see the dog runs that they would have to tackle before reaching the third and last fence and the minefields on the other side. After that they would have to cross a stretch of no man's land before climbing towards the first of the South Korean defences and home. Danny intended to use his tomahawk to silence the dogs. With luck they would only have to deal with one of them. Each dog had its own run of several hundred yards, separated from the next one by a fence. A thin wire was suspended the full length of the run, with a leash attached to the dog's collar long enough for him to cover the entire enclosure. Inadequately fed, they were the dogs who had proved untrainable, too savage even as compound dogs, and anything that ventured into their territory would be instantly attacked and killed.

Terry knew that the drainage ditch was unlikely to run through all three of the fences; they were lucky to have had use of its cover this far. But soon they would be forced out into the open. Luckily they were midway between two watch-towers and Terry hoped that the guards would be concentrating on the ground directly in front of them, not suspecting that anyone could have penetrated into the fence zone itself. Leave the fence zone to the dogs, Terry thought, as if, by willing it with all his might, he could make it happen.

When Jimmy Haynes missed the hidden trip-wire, snagging it with his elbow, the small charge of the booby-trap exploded upwards, taking his left arm with it. In an instant the whole area was flooded with light, and to the background baying of the dogs, straining at their leashes, mad with rage and hunger, bipod-mounted RPK machine-guns opened up from both watch-towers, hosing the area of the detonation with fire.

Screaming with the pain, Jimmy stood up and staggered into the open before Ken could stop him. But he hadn't gone more than six stumbling paces before the Korean gunners found his range and put a swift end to his agony. Firing as they went, Ken and the other two survivors wriggled backwards as fast as they could, not stopping to aim but spraying the bursts randomly over the lip of the ditch in the rough direction of the guard towers. From the base of the towers came the sound of shouting and running feet as soldiers poured out of the underground accommodation bunkers and closed in on the trapped mercenaries.

Springing to his knees, Terry rested his elbow on the side of the ditch and brought his Kalashnikov into the aim.

'OK, guys, let's give them some covering fire. Danny, snipe at the lights. Me and Andy'll take on the guards.'

But as he caught first sight of the approaching Korean soldiers, Terry's blood went cold. For by their black combat suits and the controlled precision of their fire and movement, he recognized them as special forces, and he knew that Ken would be lucky to escape from the killing ground alive.

Yi was furious, screaming into the handset.

'Why the hell did you open fire? I wanted to get them all in the killing ground first.'

On the other end of the line the special forces officer stammered in reply: 'We didn't, Comrade. They set off a booby-trap.'

'I ordered the colonel and his border guards to remove them before handing over the sector to us.'

'He must have overlooked one.'

Yi cursed. Why did he have to do everything himself? Nevertheless, at least half the mercenaries seemed to be trapped and from the reports it appeared that the others were pinned down beside the outer fence. If he moved quickly he could still trap them. Calming himself, he paused before speaking again to the company commander.

'OK. It's not your fault. Get your cut-offs into position immediately. If Dojo is the man I think he is, he'll stick around to help his friends rather than run away and save himself. I'm on my way and together we can have him yet.'

But at the border fence the decision was not being left to Terry. A second member of Ken's team had been killed and a moment later the third mercenary was hit in the chest. Checking the exit wound, Ken saw that the man had only minutes to live. The ground between him and the fence was alive with impacting bullets; from their vantage point high on the watch-towers, the guards were able to angle their fire downwards, directly into the ditch. It was only a matter of time before Ken himself was hit. Meanwhile, Terry and the others were making themselves into sitting ducks, doing their best to cover him, but Ken knew what he was up against and that if the Korean special forces were as good as they were supposed to be, they would be putting in a long-stop to block Terry's escape route even now.

He shouted at Terry and waved him away frantically, but although Terry could hear him he ignored the message. Realizing there was only one thing for it, Ken gritted his teeth and stood up, tossing aside his Kalashnikov and holding his hands high above his head.

'No!'

He turned at Terry's scream, stared across the open killing ground at him and grinned.

'Guess I'm the fucking poofter, mate,' he shouted. 'Clear off, there's a good fella.'

As Terry looked on in horror, the fire continued unabated, dancing in the raging earth at Ken's feet until it found the lone Australian and cut him down. Terry felt Danny's hand on his arm.

'Come on, Terry. Let's get out of here. Ken's given us a break. Let's make the most of it.'

Andy shot to his feet, blazing from the hip.

'The bastards! The fucking bastards!'

After pulling him back into cover, Terry and Danny dragged him back along the ditch.

With the last of Ken's team dead, the tower gunners redirected their fire at the furthest party of mercenaries while the special forces pursuers unlocked the gates and hurried through the safe lanes in the minefield towards the other side. When they entered the dog run, the raging beast leapt at them but was shot down with a burst from an AKM. Speaking into his throat mike, the commander checked on the progress of the cut-off teams.

'In position, over.'

'Roger, out.'

The commander sighed with relief; no one survived in Comrade Yi's bad books for long. Deciding to risk the casualties that his men would take if they ran into their own cut-off groups, he urged them on. Better that than lose the mercenaries again.

Terry reached the end of the ditch, burst into the open and led the way across the scrub towards the ridge line. Sprinting over the top, he careered down the hillside until he came to the first of the trees near the lying-up position that they had left only hours before. He crouched down and waited for the others to close up, frantically organizing his thoughts.

Steady, man, he thought, fighting to calm his breathing and clear his mind of the life-threatening panic that clawed for supremacy. He had seen that these were special forces troops, so Yi Soong was probably somewhere around. What would he be doing at this moment? Think, man, think. Of course! Nothing. If he had prepared one killing ground for the mercenaries to enter, there would be a network of others. He would already have back-stops out, using his forward troops to drive Terry back into the cut-offs. But the Welshman wasn't some pea-brained pheasant to be easily frightened straight into the muzzles of the waiting guns.

'Which was the way to Hamdok?' he asked as Danny skidded to a halt beside him, followed a moment later by Andy and the two boys. Trusting

Terry's judgement and knowing better than to question a commander in the white heat of battle, Danny pointed across the hillside.

'Two hundred yards. Path. Go left. Three hundred yards. Hamdok.'

'Roger. Move!'

Without giving anyone time to catch their breath or wonder where he was taking them, Terry led the way diagonally across the hillside, moving through cover whenever possible, hoping that the pursuing troops would carry on straight down the hill to the open fields. If he was Yi Soong, that's where he would have sited his cut-offs, writing off the village or at most covering it with a thin manpower screen.

When they were within fifty yards of the path, the bare earth glowed like a silver ribbon in the moonlight. Veering sharp left, they moved parallel to it, following it like a road sign down towards the village.

Hurrying through the night with his heavily armed escort, Yi paused to take the message from his radio operator.

'Ground sensor contact, Comrade. Kilo Golf eight.'

Yi smiled. So far so good. If Dojo was hoping to find something in Hamdok, be it a hiding-place, a hostage, transport or whatever, he would be sorely disappointed. Every villager had been evacuated and the streets converted into a viper's nest of interlocking machine-gun arcs, Claymore directional anti-personnel mines, booby-traps and razor wire, making Killing Ground Eight the one that Yi was most proud of.

A hundred yards out from the village outskirts, with

the first of the houses silhouetted against a peaceful backdrop of paddy-fields, Liang pointed excitedly at a thick grove of bamboo on the other side of a wide, fast-flowing stream. When Andy grabbed him by the scruff of the neck and tried to drag him away, he jerked loose and rushed over to Danny, whispering urgently.

'What's the hold-up?' Terry hissed, anxious to be getting on.

'I don't know,' Danny replied, frowning as he tried to calm the boy and translate using his sketchy Korean.

'We haven't got time. Thump him and let's get on.'

'No, hang on. This might be worth having a look at if it's what I think it is.'

Before Terry could stop him, Danny and the two boys had darted off towards the bamboo and plunged into the stream.

'Jesus Christ, this had better be good,' Terry groaned. Slipping into the stream, he and Andy gasped as the icy water soaked them to the skin. Their Kalashnikovs above their heads, they waded across, leaning into the current to avoid being swept off their feet. Danny and the boys were already across and heading into the shadows, from where a tall brick structure loomed out at them.

'What the fuck's that? It looks like some kind of shrine or something,' Andy asked when he and Terry caught up. But Danny had found a small alcove where a statue of a Buddha was poised on a stone plinth.

'If I'd known this was a shagging sightseeing tour I'd have brought my sodding camera,' said Andy.

Danny cursed the weight of the statue as he set his shoulder to it and shoved.

'Shut up and lend a hand.'

'What is it, Danny?' asked the Scot.

But before he could answer, the statue slid aside and Danny almost toppled headlong into the gaping darkness below.

11

Falling back on to the grass, Danny grinned up at Terry while Liang and Little Chiao danced with excitement.

'What's that? The door to the bloody underworld?'

'That, my fine Welsh friend, is our passage to freedom.'

'What do you mean?'

As Terry peered into the dark abyss, Danny explained how for years the North Koreans had been tunnelling under the border to allow infiltration teams to carry out sabotage and suicide missions.

'We've known for years that the border's honeycombed with these, but the problem's been finding them. When I was in the Rangers we had to track down a sabotage team that had taken out a whole desalination plant on the coast. We drove them back into their tunnel but before we could get at them they had blown it up and buried themselves alive. The Communists use labour gangs to dig them. Liang here recognized the village and remembered the shrine.'

'I thought you said he didn't know the area.'

'He doesn't. They were trucked in in covered vehicles and he didn't have a clue where he was. He only recognized it just now when he was virtually on top of it.'

Andy shoved them aside. 'Fuck me. Are you two going to stand there gabbing all night?'

'Hang on a minute, couldn't it be booby-trapped? Panji stakes or something?'

But before Terry could stop him, Liang had ducked between the three Westerners and dropped down into the hole. His voice came back to them out of the darkness.

'He says it's all clear.'

'Well, that's one way of finding out.'

One by one they lowered themselves gingerly into the hole. There was an eight-foot drop to the floor of beaten earth and when the last of them was in, Danny balanced on Terry's shoulders to ease the Buddha back into place as best he could. In the pitch-blackness he fumbled for his cigarette lighter, flicked it open and struck the flint. The small, yellow flame that sparked into life threw a thin glow on the five tired and dirty faces, the outer reaches of its weak light playing on the damp, earthen walls of the chamber. Liang pointed out the entrance to the tunnel itself, the roof of which was little more than four feet high. Out in the night, muffled and sounding far away, they heard the unmistakable sound of gunfire.

'Those assholes have run into their own cut-offs,' said Danny.

'Yeah, but it won't be long before they sort themselves out and pick up our tracks. We'd better get on,' Terry replied.

Liang tugged at his sleeve.

'He says he wants to show us the way,' said the Indian.

'Fine by me. Give him the light.'

With Liang and Little Chiao in the lead, the party

ducked into the tunnel and set off, the impenetrable blackness retreating grudgingly in front of the lighter, but swiftly closing in behind them so that the last two men had to feel their way forward along the slimy walls. Whereas the two boys hurried along with ease, Little Chiao barely having to bow his head, the three men had to double over, hobbling and cursing, going down on one knee every few yards to stretch aching limbs that rebelled with the effort.

After what seemed like an age, Liang suddenly stopped and called back to Danny.

'Go easy, gents,' Danny said, 'the buggers have rigged up a panji pit.'

Peering between the two boys in the flickering light of the flame, Terry saw that the floor of the tunnel dropped abruptly into a two-foot-deep pit. Sharpened bamboo stakes had been driven into the bottom, their fire-hardened tips black and deadly, waiting in the dark to spear the unwary.

'Nice work, Liang,' Terry said, patting the boy on the shoulder.

Danny laughed. 'He said it was him who had to fix them in the first place.'

With the butt of his Kalashnikov, Terry smashed a path through the forest of bamboo, moving stealthily across the six-foot gap until Liang was able to take the lead again at the far side. But after that progress became slower. As the tunnel went further under the border the booby-traps became more frequent. Liang found a trip-wire attached to the pin of a grenade that had been fixed into the tunnel wall at waist height. Then they came upon another panji pit, longer than the first, and this time the ground in between the stakes was sown with a scattering of anti-personnel mines. It took a full half hour to clear a way through and no sooner had they set off again than they almost blundered into another trip-wire, set to activate a necklace of four grenades embedded in the tunnel roof. The panji pit and the grenade necklace worked as a pair, each complementing the other, so that anyone clearing either obstacle could be expected to have their guard momentarily relaxed just in time to hit its waiting partner.

'Proper little theme park, isn't it?' Terry said as he stepped over the hair-thin wire.

By now they were all suffering badly from the strain, a combination of delayed battle shock, physical exhaustion and the agonizing tension of the dark, cramped tunnel packed with its lethal secrets. As he pulled himself painfully forward, Terry couldn't help admiring the stamina of the two boys, probing up ahead in the flickering light, chattering to each other, seemingly oblivious to the fact that they could all be blown to kingdom come at any moment. He found himself waiting for the sickening twang of a trip-wire or the metallic spring of a grenade pin and the five seconds of mad panic and confusion that would follow as the detonator fuse burned its way into the heart of the shrapnel-encased explosive.

Miraculously it never came. Further minutes went by and more ground was painstakingly covered. Terry had no idea where the boys had come from or how long they had been starving in the hills before the mercenaries had found them, but he was almost certain of one thing: they had saved his life. Even if he had been able to lead the party away from the immediate danger of the pursuit, they would have been forced to attempt another crossing of the border at some stage, and with the North Koreans alerted to their presence, their chances of success would have been minimal. The tunnel had come as a miracle – the one saving grace in a disastrous operation. Somehow he would have to find a way of repaying them.

Suddenly, a few yards in front of him, the boys stopped and Liang called back excitedly. They had reached the end of the tunnel.

On the outskirts of Hamdok, Yi Soong was consulting with his commanders. On the open farmland to the east of the village, one of the special forces platoons had taken four casualties when they had blundered into their own ambush party. In the darkness the fleeting figures had been mistaken for the runaway mercenaries and the machine-gunners had opened fire without a preliminary challenge. To add to the confusion, the platoon that was caught in the killing area assumed that they were being ambushed by the mercenaries and had immediately gone to ground and returned fire, while their depth sections executed a wide hook that caught the ambush in the flank and attempted to roll it up from the side. It had been precious minutes before the chaos had been unravelled, the parties disengaged and the bodies counted.

But what bothered Yi more was the apparent disappearance of Dojo and his team from the face of the planet. The losses suffered by his own men were due to their own incompetence, but if the surviving mercenaries managed to slip through his fingers again, he would not only lose face but his superiors would start asking some awkward questions that he would be sorely pushed to answer.

He had gambled that Dojo would go for Hamdok and had prepared a reception accordingly. The ground sensors had indicated that the mercenaries had indeed been going in that direction, but somewhere along the way they had apparently stopped and nothing more had been seen or heard of them since. Several hours had passed and at first Yi had assumed that they had gone to ground. But why? The eastern sky was already brightening and in full daylight it would be an easy task to comb the area. Cover was sparse and if the mercenaries were lying up in a patch of scrub or bamboo it would be no great problem to locate, isolate and destroy them. The logical thing to have done would have been to seek the deep cover of the forest again, regroup, move to another sector of border and try again. Failing that, Dojo might well try his luck along the seashore; find a fishing village, steal a boat and slip down the coast and into South Korean waters by night.

But the network of ground sensors had indicated nothing. Yi himself had checked on their deployment, ensuring that the entire area was adequately covered. In addition, he had placed covert teams of surveillance specialists with image intensifiers, night-vision goggles, thermal imagers and ground-surveillance radars in a broad arc covering every possible exfiltration route out of the killing grounds. Ever desperate to appease their commander, one of the surveillance teams had even reported the ambling passage of a fox. Lastly, a thin spread of snipers had been superimposed over the whole interlocking network, each man being allowed to select his own position. If anyone could catch a man with sniper training it was another sniper. Set a poacher to catch a poacher.

Nothing. If Dojo and the others had tried to leave the area Yi would have received word by now. Instead, they had simply disappeared.

It was only as the light strengthened and the tracker dogs were deployed that the scent was picked up and the mercenaries' trail was found. Starting from the last-known point of contact at the drainage ditch, the dogs easily followed the scent to the lying-up position and then down the track towards Hamdok. Losing the trail when confronted with the stream, they were urged across by their experienced handlers and after scanning up and down the far bank, quickly recovered the scent and followed it up to the shrine. Excited and confused, the dogs yelped and bayed at the mute stone which their puzzled handlers surrounded, waiting for Comrade Yi Soong to arrive.

Striding through the water, Yi shouted up at them.

'Tear it down, you morons. Do I have to do everything myself?'

'But, Comrade, the shrine belongs to the local village.'

Unfastening the flap of his holster and drawing his pistol, Yi was wild with rage, and in seconds the dog teams and their escorts were ripping at the stones with their bare hands while urgent messages were sent to bring picks and shovels.

Fighting to control his temper, Yi sat on the grass and threw stones into the water. Why hadn't he guessed? A tunnel. He had used them himself often enough in the past. But how the devil had the wretched mercenaries discovered it? It couldn't simply have been luck; it was too well concealed. They must have had intelligence that even he wasn't privy to. The details of the North Korean tunnel system were accessible

206

to only a handful of the most senior intelligence officers, and the labourers who dug them were usually eradicated once the work was complete.

Be that as it may, the fact was that in all probability his quarry was now safely home and dry in South Korea. Of course they might well have fallen foul of one of the booby-traps with which the tunnels were always laced, but Yi discounted the possibility the very moment he thought of it: Dojo was far too clever for that.

One of the dog handlers approached him warily.

'We've found it, Comrade. It's a tunnel.'

Yi sighed heavily and smiled up at him. 'Well I never!' Getting wearily to his feet, he called across to the men working feverishly to dismantle the shrine.

'Forget it.'

'But Comrade, we can follow them.'

'I said forget it. Get your stupid dogs back to their kennels. They're pissing on the Buddha.' He turned to his radio operator. 'Call in the surveillance teams and the ambushes.'

The man blinked up at him uncertainly. 'Is it over?'

'For now.'

Brushing the grass from his combat trousers, Yi slung his assault rifle over his shoulder. There would be no more shooting today. The bodies of the dead mercenaries in the border fence zone had been identified and their details passed to Yi. As he walked back towards the Hamdok track, three names and three faces hung almost tangibly in the air before him. Andy Buchan. Danny Grey Wolf. Dojo Williams. Yi Soong knew that he himself would now be going undercover again.

*   *   *

Emerging into a chamber similar in size and proportion to the entrance under the Buddhist shrine, Terry breathed a sigh of relief as he stretched to his full height and felt his knees and joints crack into place. Seconds later, Danny popped out of the tunnel beside him, helping Andy, whose old leg wound was throbbing painfully from the exertion of the long, damp scramble underground. Little Chiao was already balancing on Liang's shoulders, scrabbling at the earth overhead with his small hands.

Danny took the lighter and held it up. Long tendrils of tree root dangled from the ceiling and as Little Chiao's efforts brought a shower of loose earth down on their heads, Danny and Terry reached up and joined in the excavation.

'It'll probably come up in a wood or somewhere,' Danny said. 'The one I saw before with the Rangers seemed pretty much like this. They put all this effort into digging them but only ever use them once. The surface shouldn't be more than about four feet up, and it'll be reinforced so that anyone walking over the spot by accident won't cave it in.'

Sure enough, after some more digging they came upon two sturdy wooden beams, which they man-handled to one side. They had only been digging for a few more minutes when there was a groan, a cascade of loose earth, and they were squinting up into the harsh daylight.

Little Chiao fell back into the hole and Liang picked him up, dancing and clapping with delight.

'OK, lads. Keep the noise down,' Terry cautioned them, unable to suppress a huge smile. Even Andy chuckled at the smell of the fresh, cool air that flooded into the chamber.

With a leg-up from Terry, Danny eased into the breach and cautiously poked his head through the opening.

'Yep. Middle of a wood,' he called down, and after pulling himself out of the hole, he reached down to help the others. Once the two boys had climbed out, Terry cupped his hands under Andy's boot and hoisted him up. Then, when Danny and Andy were both lying flat on the overhead grass, reaching down into the hole, Terry pulled the pins from two hand-grenades, rolled them as far as he could back down the tunnel, and grabbing the outstretched hands, was lifted bodily out of the hole just as the grenades detonated, collapsing the tunnel behind him. As the shock waves expanded, magnified in the confined space, they triggered the nearest of the booby-traps and anti-personnel mines, until a full hundred yards of roof had come crashing down, sealing the tunnel to all but a well-equipped party of engineers.

Rolling away from the opening as a cloud of dust and earth sprayed into the air and settled on the surrounding undergrowth, Terry felt the clean smells of the forest flood his nostrils and the dazzling light prick at his clenched eyelids. Looking at the broad smiles all around him, he sat up on the lush grass and spat the dirt from his mouth.

'I don't like to put a dampener on things, but how do we know we're in South Korea and not still on the wrong side of the border?'

'This,' Danny said simply, handing him a small piece of dark-brown plastic. 'US Army ration pack.' He brushed the inside with the tip of his finger and tasted it. 'Mm. Peanut butter.'

Terry laughed. 'I suppose you'll give me an eight-figure grid reference of our position next?'

'Well, let's see. We're probably well into the South Korean side of the DMZ. The gooks would have wanted their tunnel to penetrate far enough to avoid a messy clash with our own border troops. As the tunnel ends here you can bet there'll be an easy covered exit to a highway or something where they could have met up with their own agents or gone straight on to their target. It's a game they've been playing for years.'

Andy massaged his stiff leg. 'So what's the problem? We just walk to the nearest guard post and tell them who we are, right?'

Danny saw that Terry was deep in thought.

'I think Dojo's got other plans.'

'Oh shit,' said Andy.

'Well, what do you make of it?' Terry asked. 'We don't really know who set us up.'

'What do you mean? Yi did. He was some kind of double agent.'

'Yes, but who was controlling him?'

'Who the hell cares?' Andy growled. 'They can do what they damn well like. I'm going home.'

'I wouldn't bet on it. We don't know what story they've been putting around. For all we know the South Korean government might be after us too. We've caused them a fair bit of bother, after all.'

Danny kicked at a loose stone. 'Shit. He's right, man. We've been out of circulation for too long. It'd do no harm to check out the lie of the land before we go surrendering to anyone.'

'And what about Babs?' Terry added. 'How much did he know? I can't speak for you guys but I want some answers. We owe it to Ken and all the others who haven't made it back.'

'Fuck the answers. I want my money,' Andy said bitterly.

'Right. And there's only one bloke who can give it to you.'

Danny looked across at the two boys, who were listening intently to the conversation without understanding a word.

'What about them? Do we take them with us?' he said.

'You bet we do. If it wasn't for them we'd still be in North Korea, or worse. They stick with us until we've sorted this out and then we'll see if we can help them dig up some relatives in the South.' Terry smiled grimly. 'And you might find that Babsy wants to make a sizeable donation to their future welfare; a sort of orphan's fund.'

Making their way out of the clearing, they moved through a forest that was tamer than the sprawling wilderness they had become used to over the last days. Being close to the border it had been used for military exercises and the evidence was visible wherever they looked: bits of ration pack, blank cartridge cases, discarded scraps of military clothing, pieces of link from machine-gun ammunition belts.

'Don't think much of their field discipline,' Andy observed scornfully. 'These your boys?' he added with a wry grin at Danny.

'No way. You don't see the Rangers until they've got a knife to your throat, and the ROKs would be crucified if they left a heap of shit like this. These'll be the GIs – bums and college kids.' He spat in disgust. For years he had trained his men to move inconspicuously, taking out their rubbish or burying it too deep for wild pigs to dig it up again.

On reaching the edge of the forest, they located a farmstead and lay down to observe it until they were reasonably confident that they could account for all the occupants. The whole family was busy in the fields on the far side of the farm buildings. So, while the three men remained out of sight on the edge of the trees, Liang and Little Chiao crept forward and disappeared through a window into the farmhouse, returning ten minutes later with armfuls of clothing and food.

While everyone stripped off their prison fatigues, now caked with dirt and stinking, Terry made a note of everything taken from the house.

'Babs might also want to send the farmer an anonymous cheque repaying him for his kindness.'

In their new outfits they felt even more conspicuous than in their fatigues. It had been impossible to find anything big enough to fit Danny; in his borrowed jeans and sweatshirt he looked like the Incredible Hulk, his chest bulging through the Pepsi slogan and the trouser legs halfway up his shins. Andy, Terry and the boys had been easier to kit out and once they were happy that they looked as normal as they ever would, they put their weapons in a holdall that Liang had stolen and stepped out on to the metalled road.

'Right,' Terry said, trying hard not to laugh at Danny's ridiculous appearance. 'Erm . . . bus or taxi?'

'What about surfboard?' Andy said innocently, pointing at Danny's newly cut-off jeans, huge boots and skin-tight sweatshirt, and starting to whistle a Beach Boys number.

Later that same morning the cheque from Francis

Kwang was cleared and Babs discovered that he was richer than he had ever been in his life. He nipped out to the local supermarket and bought some Asti Spumante, the closest thing to champagne he could find, then rang Michelle and told her to come round immediately. She pressed him for the reason but Babs delighted in making her wait; he wanted to see the expression on her face when he told her of his plans for their future.

The sparkling wine was still warm when Michelle arrived, but unable to contain himself any longer, Babs popped the cork, filled two whisky tumblers to the brim, offered her one and then proposed a toast.

'To us.'

'What is it, Babsy? Tell me, tell me,' said Michelle, pulling at his jacket sleeve like a child wanting attention.

Babs pulled a slip of paper from his pocket and handed it to her. It was a printout of his bank balance.

Michelle went pale. 'This all yours?' she said with staring eyes.

'No, it's ours,' Babs said warmly. 'I've done it, my love. I've finally done it. You and me are going to take a little trip and we're not coming back. Bin that revolting job in It'aewan, bring your stuff round here and we'll fly out next week.'

Michelle stared blankly at him. 'Where we go?'

'Hell, I don't know. Anywhere away from here. We'll go to Tokyo first.'

'Oh, Babsy, I always want go Tokyo!'

He put his glass down and pulled her to him, her waist trim and slight in his plump hands. She had come straight from the club and was wearing a bright-red dress split up both sides to the thigh. He slid his hands underneath, drawing her closer, feeling her hips press against him.

'Then maybe we'll fly on to Hawaii. Cathay Pacific. First class, of course.'

The wine spilled from Michelle's tumbler as she kissed Babs full on the lips, feeling his mouth open and his tongue penetrate her. Arching her back, she ground into him until she felt him respond, then slipped a hand between them, fumbling with his trousers. When she had him in her hand, she slid to her knees, caressing him with her tongue until she heard him moan. Easing him down on to the carpet, Michelle pulled aside the flaps of her dress and manoeuvred herself delicately on top.

'You been good to me, Babsy. I repay you rest your life. You see.'

But Babs was beyond hearing. As he ran his fingers through Michelle's ebony hair, his body pulsated with every move she made, each motion slow and teasing, seeking out his weakness and pleasure with hips and hands until he longed for release. For the first time in her life, Michelle too found herself being carried away beyond her own control, lost in an unknown world where the pleasures of the body met the fondness of the heart, the two continuing together to explore the strange new region where neither she nor Babs had ever ventured before.

When the mid-afternoon sun pushed its lowering beams through the window blinds, slashing the room into thick strips of shadow and golden light, it found them in bed, Michelle's head resting on Babs's bare chest, her eyes open and wondering. Listening intently to his gentle snoring, she marvelled at all that had happened. He had been telling her the truth after all. Like many of her clients, Babs had always been full of stories. Some men needed to impress her, as if by filling her ears with their importance and exploits they could explain away their presence in a whore's room, assuaging some hidden guilt. As if she cared. Others compensated with a hostile silence, treating her as a sly enemy who had somehow lured them in and entrapped them; their lovemaking was savage and brief, and they seldom allowed their eyes to meet hers lest they be forced to confront the fellow-human beneath their brutal thrusts.

Babs had always been different. Sure, he had been full of stories, but somehow he had let Michelle know that he didn't really believe them himself either. It had been a game and she had grown to love it. But what surprised her now was the discovery that, in the process, she had grown to love him.

Slipping out of his arms, she dressed hurriedly, resolving to start their new life together as she meant it to go on. When Babs awoke he would find a cooked meal waiting for him. The apartment would be alive with the smells of the food and the noise of their laughter. She tiptoed into the kitchen, opened the fridge and surveyed the empty shelves. Finding the cupboards likewise bare, save for a packet of biscuits and two empty whisky bottles, she slipped on her shoes and took some money from Babs's wallet. The store on the corner would have everything she needed for now. In future she would dress like a proper housewife and shop at the market, haggling with the fishmonger and the vegetable man until they gave her their best produce at a reasonable price. Of course, she wouldn't haggle too much; that would be vulgar. No, she would do exactly what was expected of the wife of an ex-army officer and man of honour.

With a final check on her sleeping lover, Michelle eased out of the door, closing it behind her soundlessly. Once out in the corridor, she bounced down the flights of stairs, humming to herself with unbounded joy, stepping to one side when she reached the second floor to let a group of Westerners pass. A number of them lived in this block, though most of the inhabitants were middle-class Koreans, bank clerks and junior managers. She smiled generously at a strangely dressed giant, and winked at a couple of mischievous boys. Perhaps she would have sons of her own one day.

Last in line, an athletic man of medium build greeted her pleasantly. 'Morning, miss.'

'Morning.'

Babs had told her to drop the 'Good', making it sound more natural. As she looked after the strangers, Michelle wondered whether they would soon be neighbours. Perhaps she would pick up her things from the club that evening. Continuing on down the stairs, she resumed her humming, daydreaming of Tokyo, Mount Fuji and Honolulu.

12

'Darling!'

The bowl of ice-cold water struck Babs's face, waking him instantly.

'How simply wonderful to see you. You fucking bastard.'

Andy dragged the terrified man from the bed and threw him to the floor.

'Jesus, what a sight for sore eyes. There's more flab on that bum than on the dance floor of a gunner officers' mess.'

Terry pulled Andy away and hoisted Babs to his feet. 'Get a chair, Andy. We've got some questions to ask our friend here before we decide what to do with him.'

Behind Babs, Danny tested the blade of his tomahawk.

'Can I have first shot?' he asked.

'Sure. Why not. Add his foreskin to your scalp collection.'

When Babs had been tied to a chair, he stared forlornly at the three men looming over him.

'Listen, boys, I didn't know anything about the operation. Kwang simply hired me to recruit the best mercenaries money could buy.'

'Who's Kwang?'

'He's the bloke who put up the money. Yi was only his sidekick.'

'Keep talking.'

'He's something big in South Korean intelligence.'

'Then why would he cause his own government all this bother?'

'I don't know. You've got to believe me. He was probably fooled by Yi Soong, like the rest of us.'

Andy sprang forward. 'Us? Don't you dare count yourself as one of the team. You seem to have come out of it all right, don't you? And where's our money, and the money for all the boys who didn't make it back?'

'I haven't got it.'

Andy's fist slammed into Babs's mouth, splitting his bottom lip.

'Honest I haven't. Kwang's only paid me my share. The arrangement was that you would all be paid direct by him. I gave him your details and that was that.'

'And you can bet he hasn't parted with a fucking dollar since,' Danny added.

Terry walked over to the window and drew the blinds shut.

'Where's this Kwang guy now?'

'I'm not allowed to tell anyone.'

In an instant, Danny was beside the chair, his tomahawk resting lightly between Babs's legs.

'How do you want it, Babsy? Diced or sliced?'

Babs stared in horror at the big Indian and swallowed hard.

'Dojo, explain to him. You know how it is . . . if I break a confidence I'm finished.'

Terry shrugged helplessly. 'Danny-boy's got a mind of his own, I'm afraid. When he's set on something, there's no stopping him.'

Babs gritted his teeth as Danny moved the savage blade closer to his penis.

'All right, all right. He's got a country villa at Sorak-san, but there's no point contacting him – he's untouchable. When the news broke about the raid there was an investigation and Yi Soong took the wrap. If Kwang is a double agent – and I'm not saying he is, mind – but if he is, he's already covered his back. If you try to get to him he'll have the entire South Korean defence establishment down on you before you know what's happening. Believe me, Dojo. Don't mess with him.'

'What's his address?'

Babs sighed. 'You can't take no for an answer, can you?'

Terry put his face close to Babs's. 'Not when there's thirteen other blokes out there pushing up daisies. If Yi was a double, then Kwang fucked up with his screening procedure and I'll see that the widows and families get every penny that's owed to them. And if Kwang was in on it himself, then I'll find a way of getting even with the bastard.'

Babs nodded to a dressing-table. 'In there.'

Rummaging through the drawers, Terry came across an address book.

'This it?'

Babs nodded.

Sinking into the armchair, Terry began to leaf through the pages.

'Danny, why don't you see if you can find something that fits you in Major Butler's wardrobe. I'm sure he wouldn't mind. Andy, take the boys into the kitchen and get a brew on.'

'Right, boss.'

Stopping at one of the pages, Terry raised his eyebrows in surprise. 'Is Mike in town?'

'Mike Adams? Yes. He's with CNN now. Seoul desk.'

Terry whistled. 'He's come a long way since Angola.'

'Haven't we all?'

'No. Look, do you want some clothes? I don't like the way your prick's staring at me.'

'You don't like it? What about me?'

Cutting Babs loose, Terry kept an eye on him as he dressed, ordering him to sit again when he had finished.

'Ah, here we are. Kwang, Francis. Sorak-san. That's the National Park, isn't it?'

'Yes, but you're wasting your time.' Babs thought for a moment. 'What do you intend to do about yourselves? I mean, how are you going to get out of the country?'

'British Embassy. We discussed it on the bus on the way here. We reckon we'll give the Korean authorities a wide berth.'

Babs coughed lightly. 'And what about me? I really didn't know about any of this. Look at it from my side: why would I have set you up? First, I know that no bugger on earth could ever hold you for long, and second, the word would be out that Babs Butler was a turncoat. If I wasn't fixed in the night by some old chum of yours, I'd never be able to recruit anyone ever again. I'd be ruined. We were both stitched up, Dojo. You, me, the others, all of us.'

'Except you got paid.'

'I suppose Kwang reckoned it would throw me off his trail. Make it all seem legit.'

'Seems to have worked.'

Terry leaned back in the chair and looked at Babs calmly. He had worked with him before and in his heart he knew that it didn't add up. Babs could be selfish, stupid, idle and greedy, but he wasn't a double-crosser. And he wasn't imaginative enough to fall in with a devious plan like this. The odds were that he had been used as well. But perhaps that wasn't good enough. After all, Terry's life was still on the line.

When Andy and the boys had come back with mugs of sweet tea and Danny had found some clothes that looked almost normal on him, Terry had just tied Babs to his chair again to stop him escaping or raising the alarm, when the door opened and Michelle came in, screamed and dropped her shopping. Lunging past Andy, who tried to catch her, she flung herself protectively across Babs's lap, shouting insults at the three men and the two staring boys.

'Who the fuck's the tart?' Andy said, rubbing his cheek, which Michelle had clawed on her way past.

'Well, well, well,' Danny grinned, 'Babsy's got himself a squaw.'

'Leave her alone, lads,' Babs pleaded. 'Michelle knows nothing about all this.'

'You needn't worry about us,' Terry said. 'Our business is with Kwang.'

When they had calmed Michelle, Terry left her kneeling beside Babs's chair and went to call the British Embassy from the phone extension in the bedroom. After some minutes, the languid, disinterested voice that had first answered was replaced by the clipped, precise tones of another person who refused to give either his name or position.

'I think we can help you, Mr Williams, but you

221

mustn't come to the Embassy building. Nor can I say any more on this line. Do you know the Central Post Office?'

'No, but I can find it.'

'Good. Be outside it at nine-thirty tomorrow morning. We'll take it from there.'

'Want us to come too?' Danny asked afterwards as Terry pored over a street map of Seoul.

'Yes. But not with me. Babs, have you got a car?'

'No.'

Terry turned on him and glared. Babs sighed.

'A Blue Honda Civic, down in the basement. The keys are in my coat pocket. Dojo, please be careful. I only got it a few days ago.'

'Babsy, I used to drive armoured personnel carriers.'

'That's what I'm afraid of.'

'Danny, I want you and Andy to shadow me. Bring the hardware, just in case.'

'What about the boys?'

'They can stay here and keep watch. We'll make Babsy and Michelle nice and comfortable before we go and the kids can watch them for us. See they come to no harm.'

Andy was doubtful but Terry reassured him.

'Don't worry. The way I'll tie them up I doubt we'll even be able to undo the knots when we get back.' He turned to Babs. 'And when we do, I'll have to relieve you of your cheque card and account number. Simply as a precaution until things are cleared up and Mr Kwang's seen the error of his ways and paid all his bills.'

'Please, Dojo,' Babs pleaded, 'Don't take my money. It's all I've got. Me and Michelle were going away.'

Terry smiled, patting him on the back. 'Don't worry, mate. If you're clean and you've told us the truth, I'll buy you a wedding present and drive you both to the airport myself.'

'And if you've been lying to us,' Andy said severely, 'I'll put a match to the place with both of you in it.'

The next morning they were up at first light. As it was the first night they had spent under cover for some time, it had taken a while to get used to the soft mattresses spread on the floor. Michelle had been given the bed with Liang on one side of her and Little Chiao on the other; whereas Terry could trust the boys to keep an eye on her and no more, he wasn't so sure about the other two men. Babs was secured in his armchair and Terry, Andy and Danny slept on the floor, taking it in turns to keep watch in the event of any unwelcome visitors.

After an early breakfast that finished the last of Michelle's shopping, the three men prepared to leave, tying Michelle and Babs securely back to back using a combination of knots that even Houdini would have been unable to wriggle out of.

'Be good, now. As soon as we're back, we'll fix lunch.'

Turning to the boys he added: 'And you've done all right. We'll sort something out for you too, don't you worry. Tell them what I said, Danny.'

The Indian smiled. 'I think they got the drift.'

Once out in the street, Terry set off at a brisk pace for the centre of town. Feeling lost in one of Babs's jackets, he felt in the pocket for the 9mm Browning that he had taken from the major's desk, along with two spare clips of ammunition. As he touched the black plastic grip of the butt like a lucky charm, he was glad to have it in easy reach should things go wrong. He was too experienced to trust anyone at this stage in the game, and certainly not some posh-sounding diplomat or whoever he was, British or not.

As he sauntered along Chungmu-ro Street, he stopped to look at a display of Gucci shoes, checking in the shop window's reflection for the reassuring shape of the Honda Civic idling a block away. Moving on, he crossed over another street and found the Central Post Office opening for the day's business.

Stamping up and down in the fresh morning air, Terry scanned the crowds of shoppers and tourists. It didn't seem a day since he and the others had first arrived in Seoul at the start of the mission. Remembering the crowd of faces at Babs's reception party in the private dining-room of the restaurant, he felt anger mounting inside him. None of them had been saints, but they hadn't deserved to be butchered like that. No one did. He vowed to himself that he would get to the bottom of the whole affair if it was the last thing he did. If Kwang had merely been incompetent and Yi Soong had slipped through the South Korean screening process, then Terry would ensure that every last dollar reached the dependants of the dead mercenaries. If, on the other hand, Kwang himself was a double agent, Terry would sort him out personally. Francis Kwang might be able to pull the wool over the eyes of the South Korean intelligence community, but he would find Terry Williams and his mates a different kettle of fish.

Out of the heavy traffic, a sleek white Mazda pulled up alongside the kerb and the man in the passenger seat wound down the window and called across to Terry.

'Mr Williams?'

Terry nodded and made towards the car as the driver reached over and opened the back door. A second man was in the front passenger seat.

'Good morning.'

Terry recognized the passenger's voice as the cool one from his telephone call. The car pulled out into the traffic and turned north up Sogong-no Street.

'Presumably now that you've caused a major political embarrassment to our South Korean allies, you want us to clear up the mess and get you out of the country incognito?'

'I couldn't have put it better myself,' Terry replied, angered by the man's arrogant tone.

'Who are you, anyway? British intelligence, I suppose.'

The man smiled.

'As regards getting you out of the country, I'm afraid it won't be quite that simple.'

'I didn't think it would.'

'We'd like to know everything you can tell us about the whole operation. Who hired you, how you came into the country, who met you, your method of entry to the North and so on.'

Terry looked around at the bustling city streets. 'Here?'

'Here. We don't want you to be seen at the Embassy, I'm afraid, so this will have to act as the debrief.'

'And if I don't want to tell you.'

The man swivelled round.

'I hardly think you're in any position to refuse. You're going to need travel documents and identification papers. Were you the only one to escape?'

Terry was about to give him the names of the

other two but on the spur of the moment changed his mind.

'Yes. The rest were all killed.' It would be no big problem for the Embassy to arrange further papers for Andy and Danny later. For now, Terry wanted to see the lie of the land, as Danny had said.

The interrogator relaxed. 'I see. Congratulations,' he said grudgingly. It's no mean feat to get in and out of North Korea at the best of times, let alone with their security forces after you.'

Terry let the compliment pass and as the unmarked embassy Mazda toured slowly through the streets of the capital, he recounted the story of the Korean contract. The intelligence officer stopped him a couple of times, to slip a new cassette into his recorder or ask a question on a point of detail.

'So perhaps you should tell your friends in Korean intelligence to have a closer look at Francis Kwang,' Terry concluded.

'They already have and as far as they're concerned his name's been cleared.'

'And in your books?'

Without answering Terry's question, the man continued. 'Your operation was compromised by his assistant, Mr Yi Soong.'

Terry snorted. 'Tell me about it!'

'There was an investigation and Kwang was cleared of all blame. Once Yi had warned the North Korean government of the attempt to kidnap Professor Lim Choy, they decided to capitalize on the operation and turn it into a propaganda coup for themselves. It worked very nicely. Of course none of us seriously believed that American special forces would be involved in any massacre, but there were enough states in the UN that did believe it to cause severe embarrassment.'

'And the UN inspection of North Korean nuclear facilities?'

'Put on hold, I'm afraid. It seems that for the time being the Communists have won.'

Red-hot anger surged through Terry as he thought of the dead civilians at the resort, massacred by Yi and his men; of the dead mercenaries; of Dave, Ken, and in all likelihood Jules. Perhaps this man was right and Kwang was innocent, simply an incompetent who had allowed his organization to be penetrated by a double agent.

After driving in silence for a while, Terry remembered the money owed to him and the others, and broached the subject.

'Not my problem, old chap,' the intelligence officer replied. 'And if you know what's good for you you won't go near Kwang. Think yourself lucky to be alive, and get out of the country. We can have identification papers and travel documents ready in a couple of days.'

Terry's mind raced. He would be able to get money from Babs but it would never be enough for the dependants of the dead mercenaries. But was there any point in approaching Kwang? Perhaps he should take the man's advice and cut and run.

He was about to come clean and tell the officer about the existence of Danny and Andy, when he noticed the driver glancing in the rear-view mirror. They had come to a halt in a solid queue of traffic at a major intersection. The man in the passenger seat looked across irritably.

'What is it, Simon?'

The driver chuckled. 'The way these Orientals drive! Some impatient arsehole back there flashing his lights. Can't he see the red lights?'

Terry twisted round and saw the blue Honda Civic some way back in the queue. The headlights were flashing and the horn blaring. The doors were open and Danny and Andy were diving out of the car.

'Get out!' Terry screamed.

'What the . . .?'

The intelligence officer never finished his sentence. A burst of machine-gun fire raked the car, catching both front-seat occupants in the chest and face. Even as he screamed, Terry was flinging himself to the floor, fumbling for the handle and kicking open the door.

Slithering out on to the road, he pulled the Browning from his pocket and curled into a ball with his back to the car, clenching the pistol in a firm, two-handed combat grip. He glanced down the row of cars, but there was no sign of either Danny or Andy, though he could hear the sound of the Kalashnikov and M16 answering the much heavier bursts of fire coming at them from several directions.

Flat on his stomach, Terry scanned the ground underneath the cars, still jammed nose to tail in parallel queues. Most of the drivers and passengers had stayed in their vehicles, huddling for shelter and screaming with terror, but some were attempting to bolt for cover. To Terry's trained eye, it was obvious which of the people whose feet were visible under the packed cars were running in fear of their lives, and which of them were moving methodically towards him, pausing to fire, then moving still closer at a crouch.

Realizing that the attacking gunmen probably considered him dead or at least badly wounded, Terry watched silently as the nearest pair of feet approached round the side of the neighbouring car. Easing himself up into a kneeling position, he aimed the Browning, sighting with both eyes open ready for a close-quarters engagement. When the man appeared, his attention was on the occupants of the Mazda; he was doing a quick body count. Both rounds of Terry's double tap hit him in the middle of the chest, knocking him backwards too fast for alarm to register on his face.

Pivoting on his heel, Terry whipped his pistol round just in time to fire a second double tap at another Korean as he aimed his AKM. Again the man toppled backwards, but not before Terry had recognized him as one of the snipers from Yi Soong's team that had accompanied the mercenaries to the resort and that had later ambushed them.

'That one's for Ken,' Terry said bitterly.

Tumbling into a forward roll, Terry came up level with the Mazda's rear bumper and aimed round the corner seeking his next target.

'Dojo, catch!'

Looking up at the cry, Terry saw a grenade arcing towards him through the air, the pin pulled and the lever spinning free as if in slow motion.

'Shit!'

Keeping a hold on the Browning, he caught the grenade in his hands, hearing the fizz of the detonator in its lethal core.

'Behind you!'

Without looking, Terry flung the grenade over his head like a hot potato, hitting the tarmac as it exploded in an airburst of deadly splinters, showering down on the two gunmen who had been about to take him out.

He looked round at Danny's anxious face several cars away.

'Sorry, buddy. I couldn't be sure of reaching them from here.'

From a couple of blocks away the sound of sirens filtered through the noise of the machine-gun fire. The attacking AKMs faltered and fell silent as the ambushers pulled out, with shouted orders and the squealing of tyres on the cartridge-strewn tarmac.

'Better make ourselves scarce,' Terry shouted.

'Fine by me.'

Finding Andy blazing off a last volley after the retreating cars, Terry and Danny bundled him into Babs's car and Terry shunted back and forth until they had cleared a space big enough to slip through.

'Hope Babs is insured more than third party.'

Once they were out of the traffic jam, Terry gunned the engine and raced away with the tyres smoking. Swinging the car round a corner, he shot up a side-street, raced straight across two intersections, then slowed at the end of another side-street before turning lazily into a busy main road and losing himself as just one more frustrated motorist amid the Seoul traffic.

Several blocks away the sirens wailed as heavily armed police tumbled out into the killing ground to puzzle over the carnage and the slaughter of two British Embassy officials and several unidentified gun-men.

'Well, we can't go back to the flat,' Andy said, clipping a fresh magazine on to his Kalashnikov.

'Keep that fucking thing out of sight, will you? We don't have a choice. Babs, the kids and the bird are there. And another thing, I recognized one of those fuckers back there as a goon from Yi's sniper team.'

Danny stared grimly out of the window. 'So he's back in town. It didn't take him long, did it? You don't think he's taking it personally, do you?'

Terry turned into the road outside Babs's apartment. 'I hope to God he is. That way we can expect him to make a mistake.'

Instead of stopping at the main entrance, Terry drove straight past and went round to the back, pulling up by the fire escape that snaked up the side of the building. Getting out of the car, the three men moved away quickly, splitting in three different directions, checking every angle to ensure that their approach had been unobserved. Only when Terry was content that the coast was clear, did he hand-signal the others to cover him towards the fire escape.

Bounding up to the first level, he crouched by the rusty metal steps until Danny and Andy had joined him. Then, as they watched, Terry moved again, and so on, leapfrogging through the levels until they came to Babs's floor. He forced the lock on the window, eased it open and slipped into the corridor. As soon as Danny and Andy were crouching beside him, he moved stealthily past the other apartments and peered round the corner. At the end of the corridor Babs's door was ajar. Terry felt the hair on his neck bristle and without taking his eyes off the entrance, he gave the thumbs-down signal for enemy contact.

Leaving Andy to cover the rear, Terry and Danny sidled along the corridor, hugging the walls on opposite sides. Danny had flicked his M16 to automatic and Terry held the Browning in a combat grip, eyes wide open and every sense alert to the slightest hint of trouble.

Reaching the door, Terry signalled Danny into a

position a few yards back, where he knelt down and aimed his M16 at the centre of the doorway. Then, taking a deep breath, exhaling, and breathing again, Terry tensed like a spring and burst through the door into the middle of the sitting-room, coming up from his forward roll at the foot of Babs's chair.

'Who do you think you are? The man with the Milk Tray?'

Babs's fat white cheeks shuddered with laughter as Terry flopped back on to the carpet with relief.

'You stupid fat bastard,' Terry exploded. 'Why was the bloody door open?'

'Ask those two little devils you set to watch us. Michelle's been pleading with them to cut us loose but the swines told her to shut up. The eldest one even put his bloody hand up her skirt. Where did you find them? Biting the heads off kittens?'

Calling Danny and Andy into the apartment, Terry went through into the kitchen and found the boys stirring a huge pan of rice and meat.

'They went through my wallet and sent out for a bloody take-away! How's that for covert? Leave the recruiting to me next time.'

Terry took a knife from the worktop, went back into the sitting-room and cut Babs and Michelle free. In a blur the woman was on her feet and dashed into the kitchen. A second later there were howls and screams and it took two of them to pull her off Liang, who collapsed on the floor nursing his head, which she had clubbed repeatedly with the heavy wooden spoon from the rice pan.

When a modicum of order had been restored and Little Chiao had served out the food, everyone sat on the floor to eat, Michelle glaring at Liang over the top of her bowl, muttering curses in between cramming her mouth with rice. Terry reached across and switched on the television for the midday news bulletin. The screen was instantly filled with footage of the battle site in town.

'My, my,' Babs drawled, 'you boys have been busy. It says that two British Embassy officials were attacked and assassinated by three escaped criminals. I wonder who they mean?'

Danny slammed his bowl on the floor. 'Have we got to take on the whole of goddam South Korea as well?'

Terry stared at the pictures of the blood-soaked bodies of the British intelligence officer and his driver, referred to by the media as 'registry clerks'.

'So what do we do now?' Andy asked morosely. 'I don't reckon the Embassy will want to hear from us again.'

Terry wrestled with the blur of facts. How on earth had everything gone so terribly wrong? Obviously the Embassy's phone had been tapped and once he had got word, Yi Soong had decided to eradicate Terry and the others as soon as they had been forced out into the open. They would have been safer walking straight into the Embassy and asking for shelter, but the intelligence officer had insisted on playing his pathetic secret-agent game of intrigue. The poor sod had paid for it with his life.

Now, even though his men had bogged up the ambush, Yi had capitalized on the situation. The word had been sent out and Terry and the gang were down to take the rap. In addition to Yi's own hit team, the South Korean police and intelligence services would be after them, anxious to catch the murderers of two foreign diplomats and to regain the face they had lost by hosting a full-scale fire-fight in the heart of their capital city.

But the more he thought about it, the more Terry found himself coming back to Francis Kwang. Who else would have had the contacts both in the security services and the media? Yi had been discredited, at least publicly. Unless the whole edifice of the South Korean government was rotten, riddled with Communist sleepers, Yi would have been unable to pass the word himself. It would have had to have come from someone who was trusted, whose name had been cleared of any complicity. It must have come from someone at the top.

'I think it's time we paid a visit to Mr Kwang,' Terry said.

Danny looked at him thoughtfully, following his reasoning. 'I'd say it was overdue.'

Andy stabbed his thumb at Babs. 'What about this useless fucker?'

'I say!' Babs protested.

'That's just it,' Terry answered. 'He *is* a useless fucker. But he's not the bastard who set us up. The North Koreans are the most paranoid, security-conscious arseholes in the world. The last person they'd let in on their little plot is a foreigner. No. This is purely home-grown. Babs was used, like the rest of us. Kwang paid him off to cover his own back with his intelligence bosses here in Seoul. Made it seem above board as though he had intended to get the scientist out just like we were briefed. God, what fools we were! To think we fell for it.'

'And to think Kwang's got away with it as well,' Danny added.

'Sure. Why not? It was the easiest thing in the world

for him to finger Yi. So what if there was an investigation? The old-boy network probably runs as smoothly here as it does anywhere else. Kwang could have used his connections to get himself off the hook and before you know it, he's back in business. Probably planning his next little gem – trucking a nuclear bomb into the heart of Seoul and holding the government to ransom, for all we know.'

Terry snapped off the television,which was showing mugshots of Andy, Danny and himself, along with their names and details, and stalked to the window.

'We'd better get out of here fast. Babs, you're coming too.'

'Dojo, I . . .'

'Shut it. This is going to take every one of us. We'll need explosives. Can you get them?'

Babs sighed. 'Yes.'

He had seen Terry in this mood before and he knew there would be no escape until things had run their course, even though it was unlikely that by then anyone caught in the way would be left alive.

'Demolition charges. TNT. OK?'

'Got it.'

'Tetrytol boosters, det cord, electric detonators, masking tape – all the trimmings. And mines. Claymores and grenades.'

As he scribbled down the shopping list, Babs mumbled: 'Are you planning to start a war?'

'I hope I'm going to prevent one.'

'I get it,' Babs answered. He looked up and smiled. 'And I suppose this "useless fucker's" going to help you?'

'You've got it.'

'Just like old times.'

13

For the journey to Sorak-san, Babs gave Michelle some money and sent her out to hire a Toyota minibus. By now the police would be looking for the Honda and if Kwang was able to pull strings, there would undoubtedly be roadblocks on every approach to his country villa. Apart from that, if, as Terry insisted, they were all going to make the trip, it would take a minibus to hold the seven of them and all the hardware.

From the bottom of his bedroom cupboard, Babs unfolded an ancient pair of combat trousers.

'Hello, boys,' he said quietly as he held them up against himself in front of the mirror. 'It's been a long time.'

After putting them on, he went back into the sitting-room to hoots of laughter from the others.

'Blimey, it's Danny La Rue. How'd you squeeze into that little number? Dacron, isn't it?'

'Looks more like chiffon.'

Babs smiled good-naturedly. 'Actually they're jungle OGs. These were used in combat when you, Mr Buchan, were in kindergarten. Or was it the Glasgow branch of the Hitler Youth?'

They had spent an afternoon of feverish activity; Babs had been out with Terry's shopping list, to which he had added a few items of his own, and when he had returned he had staggered up the stairs with an enormous holdall in each hand and a bergen over his shoulder stuffed with still more hardware. For the next hour Terry and Danny sat cross-legged in the middle of the floor, preparing a variety of explosive charges. As the minutes passed the pile grew, and with it, their range of options. There were steel-cutting charges for severing metal beams or fences, charges for cutting timber, road-cratering charges, and breaching charges for attacking reinforced concrete.

'There,' Terry said at last, sitting back and admiring their handiwork. 'That ought to do the trick.'

Meanwhile Andy and Babs had been preparing the weapons. In addition to the two Kalashnikovs, the M16 and 9mm Browning pistol, all of which they stripped, thoroughly cleaned and then reloaded, Babs had brought back an M60 machine-gun, an M203 rifle with attached 40mm grenade-launcher, three more Brownings, grenades and plenty of spare ammunition.

When everything was ready, Terry went over each item of kit, checking and double-checking, before supervising the repacking of the holdalls.

It was late afternoon by the time they loaded the van and set off, Michelle driving, the two boys in front with her, and the four men tucked out of sight in the back.

'Just look like any mother out driving with her sons,' Babs called to her. She glared with distaste at Liang and his grubby companion, who both smiled back innocently.

Reasoning that the main roads were likely to be under surveillance, they turned away from the east–west Yongdong Expressway and selected a route that took them across country on a network of back roads. Once out of the city, Babs clambered up into the front passenger seat between Michelle and the boys and navigated from a map that he spread on the dashboard. Heading north-east towards Uijongbu and then east to Chunchon, they planned to approach the Sorak-san National Park by the lesser-used northern route.

Nevertheless, as they finally neared the park's outer boundaries later that night, Michelle pulled the van over to the side of the road when she saw a queue of cars ahead and the flashing blue and red lights of a police roadblock. In accordance with a pre-arranged plan, the four men piled out of the back and, shouldering the bags of weapons and explosives, disappeared into the night. Swinging back into lane, Michelle eased the minibus forward until she had closed up behind the queue of cars, to sit waiting her turn. She lit a cigarette, stuck her elbow out of the window and blew smoke in the face of the policeman who came up to ask her where she was going.

'Naksan beach.'

'At this time of year?'

'I need to get away with the kids.'

The policeman shone his torch on the two boys, by now curled up asleep in the back.

'They don't look anything like you.'

'No. Everyone says that. They take after their father.'

The policeman looked her up and down, taking in the dress and the make-up. He grinned at her. 'Which one?'

Michelle winked at him. 'A girl's got to earn a living.'

Further up the line a police sergeant shouted for

the minibus to get moving. The policeman stood back reluctantly and waved her on. As Michelle selected first gear and moved forward, she blew him a kiss. Weaving through the armoured cars, she noted the heavily armed police and a chill ran through her when she saw a handler restraining a sniffer dog close to her rear bumper. Her only experience of them had been when the police had raided the brothel for drugs, but she was sure that they could sniff out the scent of explosives just as easily, even if the TNT was no longer actually in the minibus.

In her rear-view mirror she saw the dog tense, its nose spinning round to the back of the vehicle. Seeing that the handler was looking the other way, chatting to a friend, Michelle gunned the accelerator and simultaneously trod hard on the clutch a couple of times, bouncing the van forward in a series of kangaroo jumps like a first-time driver. Now firm on the scent, the dog barked and strained at the leash, but Michelle jerked the van into a couple more violent lurches.

'Goddam useless fucking piece of shit!'

The policemen burst out laughing. 'Nice language for a lady.'

The dog tugged and yapped. Michelle turned on the officers.

'What the fuck are you staring at, idle sons of bitches! Can't you shut that fucking dog up?'

The boys woke up and Little Chiao burst into tears, terrified by the barking and the noise. But the handler just grinned and waved after the retreating minibus, pulling his dog to heel.

'Even my dog thinks your driving sucks, lady!'

'Screw you!'

Stepping on the accelerator, Michelle shot away from the roadblock, gripping the steering wheel with all her might to calm her shaking hands. Liang came up beside her, picked her cigarette off the floor and put it between her lips.

'Here you are, Mum.'

Two hundred yards up the road, with the police out of sight, Michelle pulled over again, turned off the lights and waited. After a while four figures emerged out of the darkness and Terry and the others climbed into the back of the minibus, Babs breathing heavily from their fast cross-country march, which had bypassed the roadblock in a wide hook.

'OGs pinching a bit, Grandad?' Andy smirked as he clambered past.

Babs wiped away the sweat cascading down his cheeks. 'Let's just see who's still standing when this lot is over,' he said quietly.

Lying in the darkness, Kwang listened to the light fall of rain outside. It had only started in the last half hour and he loved the sound of it on the wooden roof and the skylights. Feeling Lulu's naked body the length of his, snuggling safe and warm in their sheets, away from the night's discomforts, he found it reassuring to know that the villa was fully manned, his own guards reinforced by a complete police SWAT team.

He felt like a spider at the centre of a sprawling web, towards which the unwary fly was being inexorably drawn. The moment he had heard of the escape of Terry Williams across the border he knew that they would eventually be meeting. Dojo sounded an extraordinary man and Kwang regretted being unable to make use of his obvious talents. Such professionals were rare and it would be a pity to waste his expertise. But that was how it had to be. His own security came before everything. Williams had chosen the wrong man to make an enemy of.

Shifting gently on to his side, he looked at Lulu's face, her hair spread across the pillow like a Chinese silk fan. It would be morning in a few hours. Lulu would make breakfast for them both and if the rain had stopped they would later go for a walk in the compound. It would be unwise to go farther until the remaining mercenaries had been apprehended or killed, but Kwang didn't expect to have long to wait for that. Roadblocks were covering every approach to the secluded villa and his men had had every opportunity to recce their positions in daylight, carefully selecting their arcs and checking that every angle was covered.

Dangling the tip of his finger on the hollow of Lulu's throat, he lightly traced a line down between her breasts. She moaned in her sleep, turning slightly, then slipping back into her dreams. Her mouth opened and she moistened her lips. Pausing to feel the beat of her heart, the finger continued over the taut, smooth skin of her stomach, down past the well of her navel to the eternal secrets of her thighs under the white sheet.

As Lulu blinked awake, yawning, she smiled at Kwang with half-closed eyes and guided his hand. He thrilled at the touch of her, watching all the while with a detachment that she always found tantalizing. Outside, he knew that the web lay taut and waiting, its deadly arcs fanning out from the hub where he and Lulu were making love. It would take an army to storm the defences.

Moving beneath the sheet, Lulu's body writhed, her

fists clenching above her head, tightening on the pillow as she bit her lip to keep from crying out. Unable any longer to deny himself the same pleasure, Kwang eased himself on top of her, fighting to hold back the waves that shuddered through his body, kissing her breasts until she parted beneath him.

When the minibus got to within a mile of Kwang's villa, Babs indicated a side road leading off into the trees. Winding steeply up a hill, it soon became little more than a forestry track. Cutting the lights, Michelle edged the vehicle slowly forward, leaning over the steering wheel with her nose on the windscreen to make out the ribbon of track, almost invisible in the darkness. Terry thanked his lucky stars. The night was overcast and the light rain would not only interfere with any night sights that Kwang's guards would be using, greatly reducing their effectiveness, but in the thick undergrowth it would also muffle the sound of their footsteps on the forest floor.

'Perfect. We couldn't have planned it better ourselves.'

Babs grinned. 'You'll probably find that Kwang's pulled his men in close to the compound, shoulder to shoulder in a daisy-chain. He doesn't trust the wilderness. Never been in it.'

'Well, the wilderness is about to come to him. You know your position?'

Babs hoisted the M60 out of the carrying case. 'Don't worry. I'll be there.'

'Take Michelle and the boys to carry the ammunition.'

After backing the minibus into a thicket, Andy cut several boughs and camouflaged it as best he could. When they were ready, he, Terry and Danny shouldered the holdalls and set off on foot, Babs and the others disappearing into the trees in the opposite direction.

It took Terry a good hour to get his charges in place. Moving in a wide circle, he gradually worked his way around the villa, stopping whenever he came to a track. At each location, while Danny kept watch, he planted cratering and tree-cutting charges, so that he would be able to isolate his target from the outside world. While reinforcements tried to penetrate the network of demolitions and booby-traps, Terry would be dealing with the man in the centre.

Beyond and around the demolitions, Andy set trip-wires attached to Claymore mines, and in the trees on either side of the roads, he scattered anti-personnel mines so that anyone trying to outflank the obstacles would be forced to think twice. It would not be impenetrable, but it would cause sufficient delay and give them the time they needed to get to their man.

Shortly before dawn the three mercenaries dropped silently into a ditch fifty yards from the wire fence. Checking the defences, Terry decided on an entry point and crawled forward through the tall grass until he was close enough to attach a steel-cutting charge to the main fence post. Withdrawing as carefully as he had approached, he slipped back over the rim of the ditch and checked the demolition firing circuits on the panel of his control box. He looked up at the sky. Despite the dark blanket of clouds, the sky was lightening, but the drizzle was getting heavier and looked like persisting throughout the morning.

'We'll wait until it's fully light and then hit them.'

Terry knew that the change from night routine to

day routine was always a time of maximum vigilance for any defensive force. Kwang's guards would probably be going through some sort of stand-to drill, but once the day had fully broken they would be preparing to change shifts and thinking of breakfast.

As if to confirm his reasoning, a lone figure came into view, walking calmly around the inside of the compound. When he came to a hut, he paused beside it and Terry saw his lips moving, although the man kept his face to the forest. Terry glanced at Andy.

'Got him,' Andy replied, noting the concealed sentry position and slipping a 40mm grenade into his M203.

When the guard commander had disappeared around the corner to visit his next sentry post, Danny leaned across.

'Did you see the outfit? He's police. Kwang's got a SWAT team in there.'

'What's the strength?'

Danny shrugged. 'Could be eight, maybe twelve guys. They could be pretty good too.'

'Body armour?'

'You can bet on it.'

'Go for head shots then.'

Dressed in a trim pair of slacks and T-shirt, Kwang smiled at Lulu across the breakfast bar. He sipped his decaffeinated coffee and then deftly sliced the ripe papaya that Lulu had prepared with segments of fresh lime. It was a shame about the rain. They would have to spend the morning indoors, but casting his eyes over Lulu's tight cotton blouse he was sure they would find some way of passing the time.

The police commander had just been in to report that everything was secure, but Kwang didn't like the man. He was far too cocky and overconfident. Kwang had also noted that his men's uniforms had been immaculately ironed; normally he would have been the first to admire neatness, but somehow it didn't sit well with a SWAT team who were supposed to be hardened professionals. He hoped it wasn't an indication of a narrow, parade-ground mentality.

Feeling uneasy, he got up and walked across the room.

Lulu looked up, catching some lime juice on her chin. 'What is it?'

'I'm just going to check something, kitten.'

There would be no harm in checking that his own man was equally happy with the situation, even if he had been put under the command of the police.

Kwang pressed the intercom. 'Hello? Chun Jo, isn't it?' He laughed. 'Listen, Chun, will you have a look around? I don't trust that idiot police captain. Report back when you're satisfied.'

Feeling better already, Kwang stretched lazily. Walking briskly up to Lulu, he put an arm round her and kissed her tenderly.

'What was that for?'

He was just about to reply that he loved her, when the large glass doors that covered most of the wall leading out on to the terrace shattered in a hail of lethal shards.

As soon as Terry pressed the button to fire the cutting charge attached to the fence post, Babs Butler opened up from his position on the hill above. He had done his job well, finding a commanding position that gave him a broad view right across the compound and buildings, enabling him to direct the fire of his M60 into any part of the villa, dominating the battle with accurate machine-gun fire in close support of Terry's assault group.

Working through the buttons, Terry pressed one after another and from all around the valley came the answering reports of the detonations, echoing through the mountain passes as if the villa was being engaged by a battery of medium artillery. On every track and approach, explosions sent chunks of dry earth into the sky, as huge craters appeared, rendering the tracks and roads useless. As the tree-cutting charges shattered the trunks, giant pines toppled across the roadways like latticework, adding to the craters and the waiting booby-traps, cutting Kwang off from the outside world.

Before the roar of the last explosion had died away, Terry was on his feet and doubling towards the breach in the fence. The severed post had taken a good thirty yards of wire down with it, and the three men cleared the tangled mess in a single bound. Firing from the hip, Andy pumped his 40mm grenade into the hut where the police commander had given away the position of his own sentry. Splintering in an orange ball of flame, the hut and the man inside disintegrated.

Two men in police uniforms appeared round the corner. Had they been Kwang's men, Terry would have finished them with head shots. Instead, he engaged them with bursts of fire from his Kalashnikov aimed at the chest. Although their body armour saved their lives, the force of the bullets smacking into them at close range flung them backwards and smashed their ribs, knocking them unconscious.

The next one wasn't so lucky. Diving out of cover in a forward roll, he was scythed down by a long burst of fire from Babs's M60. Up on the hilltop, Babs couldn't afford the luxury of distinguishing between the enemy targets. For him, every one of them deserved and got the same concentrated hail of 7.62mm bullets.

Terry waited until Danny and Andy had both closed up beside him before pressing on to the centre of the compound, where the main villa was situated. With Babs raking the ground ahead of them, they made rapid progress until coming up against the first of Kwang's own men. Secure behind a wall of sandbags, he sprayed them with a burst from his AKM. Andy cried out and dropped the M203, blood soaking his right arm. Unable to retrieve the grenade-launcher, Terry and Danny hugged the ground, desperately trying to place their rounds through the narrow firing slit in the sandbags.

From his firing position on the hill, Babs spotted the target and swivelled on his belly, bringing his M60 to bear as Liang clipped on a fresh belt of ammunition.

'That'a boy,' Babs mumbled, his cheek squashed on to the butt. 'We'll make a soldier of you yet.'

Firing a long, continuous burst, he noted the line of tracer, adjusting his aim as if hosing a garden plant, until he found the bunker and, with finger firmly on the trigger, let the endless stream of copper-plated bullets chew their way through it.

Lying a few yards back from the sandbag emplacement, Terry and Danny cursed and hugged the ground as the bullets cracked past their ears. But in front of them the sandbags were dismantled, torn and finally ripped apart. Realizing that his shelter was disintegrating, Kwang's guard suddenly sprinted away from it, but once in the open he was cut down by Danny's M16, two well-aimed shots smacking into his back.

Retrieving the M203, Terry clamped a tourniquet

on Andy's arm. Although the wound wasn't severe, Andy had lost a lot of blood and Terry noted the first tell-tale signs of shock.

'Better sit this one out.'

'Fuck that,' Andy replied, struggling to his feet. 'I can still use this.'

Drawing his Browning, he limped after Terry and Danny. He had made it this far. There was no way he was going to let his mates down now. That was one of the reasons he was here, after all. To fight alongside men like Dojo Williams and Danny Grey Wolf, and to call them mates. If he deserted them now to sit beside the wall, he'd be nothing, a nobody. It was what drove him up the hill every time. It was what pushed him on.

By now Terry and Danny were out of sight, inside the villa itself. Lurching forward, Andy tightened the tourniquet on his arm, but fumbling with the knot, he dropped his pistol. From the hilltop, Babs Butler saw the figure emerge from a doorway behind Andy, and struggled to free the stoppage that had just silenced his M60. Liang and Little Chiao screamed for all they were worth, but their voices were lost in the vast, empty valley.

'Mr Buchan, isn't it?'

Andy froze at the sound of Chun Jo's voice. His hand was only inches away from his pistol but as he felt his heart go cold he knew that it might as well be a mile. The first kick caught him full in the ribs but it was the second that made him scream, landing on the gunshot wound in his arm. Rolling on to his back, Andy lashed out with his feet, but Chun Jo stepped aside easily.

'You Westerners really have no idea how to fight, do you?'

A barrage of kicks disabled the Scot, leaving him at the mercy of his attacker. When the final kick landed, it cut into the back of his neck. Tumbling on to his face, Andy started at the dirt as Chun Jo pulled back his fist and released the death blow. Up on the hill, Babs had cleared the stoppage and squeezed off a burst. But it was too late. The bullets found only empty space and the loose earth around Andy's body.

Having recovered a little from the shock of the explosion, Kwang had armed himself with the semi-automatic pistol that he kept in the drawer of his desk, and pulled Lulu into the relative safety of the corner farthest from the terrace. Rain slanted in through the shattered sliding doors, and crouching behind the bar where the remains of his uneaten breakfast lay covered with bits of glass, he cursed the police commander and wondered why his own guards hadn't come in to give him the close protection he wanted.

Entering the ground floor of the villa, Terry and Danny found themselves in a large vestibule. Tropical fish stared stupidly from a long ornamental tank and potted palms fringed the reception area. With his finger on the rifle trigger of the M203 combination weapon system, Terry edged round the side of the wall, eyes wide and senses alert. Standing hard up against a tall rubber plant, he covered Danny as he crept stealthily towards the corridor entrance, which led into the heart of the luxury building.

In the heated tank, a brilliant-turquoise fish swerved suddenly, alerted by a movement that Terry had missed. Swinging his weapon on to the source, Terry squeezed off a burst, the 5.56mm bullets ripping through the furniture and finding behind it the guard, who was aiming his AKM at Danny's back.

As if at a signal, the vestibule was suddenly alive with men, springing from cover to tackle the two intruders. Three of the SWAT team policemen burst from a side room, Heckler and Koch MP5 sub-machine-guns blazing. Dropping on to one knee, Terry knew that he had barely half a second before the tightly packed group fragmented into separate fleeting targets. Aiming at the centre man, he fired the M203's grenade-launcher. The snub-nosed 40mm round hit the policeman in the centre of the chest and exploded, cutting him clean in two and dismembering both his neighbours.

Pumping the barrel open, Terry ejected the spent casing and slammed in a fresh round, as Danny blazed at another of Kwang's men, who had darted between two chairs. But the man came up uninjured and hit Danny's M16 with a round from his AKM, smashing the stock, before rolling forward again, unwittingly giving Danny time to recover. Rather than go for his Browning, Danny pulled his tomahawk from his belt, and launched himself over the top of a sofa and on to the stunned Korean.

Seeking a clear shot, Terry didn't dare fire in case he hit his friend, but after a savage struggle Danny pinned the guard to the floor by the throat with one hand, while the other raised the tomahawk over his head and brought it down mercilessly on the man's grimacing face.

He wiped the blade on the man's shirt. 'It might not be high-tech, but it doesn't suffer from stoppages.'

At the top of a flight of stairs they came to a single wooden door, and kicking it open, entered a large comfortably furnished sitting-room. One wall had been of glass but it had been shattered either by one of the explosions or by Babs's M60.

Scanning the room, Danny tensed at the sound of whimpering coming from behind a bar in the far corner.

'Stand up. Now. Slowly, with your hands above your head,' he said, then, repeating it in Korean, moved in the opposite direction to Terry, his Browning trained on the beautiful Korean girl who came into view. He looked across at Terry, both of them realizing that they were at the heart of Francis Kwang's empire.

'Come on out, Mr Kwang,' Terry called, kneeling behind a chair and levelling his M203 at the bar. 'If you try anything, both you and the bird get it. I don't know what kind of peashooter you've got, but there's a 40mm grenade over here just begging to be fired.'

Slowly Kwang stood up, the pistol sliding from his fingers as his hands rose above his head.

'Don't shoot. I'm sure we can come to some arrangement.'

'I doubt it.'

'How much do you want?'

'Just what's owing to us and to the guys you had murdered in North Korea.'

'I knew nothing about that,' Kwang replied in an even voice.

Danny looked across at Terry. 'Cool bastard, isn't he? Staring down both barrels of an M203 and still lying his shit-filled heart out.'

'I told you, I knew nothing about it. I was cleared by a full investigation. You were hired to do a job. I'm sorry if it went wrong, but that's war.'

'And Yi Soong? He was your man.'

'Yes. But he double-crossed us all.'

Terry and Danny closed in on Kwang. Tossing his M203 aside, Terry knocked him to the floor. Lulu screamed and ran forward, but Danny caught her, holding her by the arms in a vice-like grip. Terry pulled Kwang to his feet and punched him again, holding his sagging body upright like a rag doll.

'You hired him, you fucker. Even if you're not working for the Communists, you let that murderer lead us into a trap.'

With the renowned Mr Kwang in his hands at last, Terry felt the rage surging through him, blinding him as he remembered Ken, Dave Bedford, Jules and the others. He drew back his balled fist.

'That'll do, Dojo.'

Fast in Terry's grip, Kwang twisted round to see the speaker. 'Chun Jo! Where the fuck have you been? Where are the police and the other guards.'

'Dead, I'm afraid. These devils have turned out to be really rather good.'

Rooted to the spot, his back to the speaker, Terry looked across at Danny, his alarm mounting.

'If either you or the Indian moves a muscle, you're dead. Release Mr Kwang. Now!'

Letting Kwang go, Terry turned round slowly until he was standing face to face with Chun Jo.

'Chun Jo, is it now?'

Yi Soong shrugged. 'Call me what the fuck you like, but keep it polite, please. There's a lady present.'

Cradled in his large hands, Yi Soong held a semi-automatic shotgun, short-barrelled especially for close combat. Terry knew that, however fast he moved, he could never hope either to recover the M203 or to draw his Browning. Likewise he knew that Danny too had fallen into the trap. With Lulu still locked in his arms, he could never get his pistol into the aim. Yi would cut them both down at the first twitch, probably not even caring to avoid the girl. He cursed himself for being so stupid. Just when they had made it to the centre of the lair, they had allowed their emotions to get the better of them. His only hope now lay in playing for time. Somehow he had to find a way of parting Yi from the shotgun.

'So. You win,' Terry said amiably.

Yi laughed, his eyes never moving or even blinking as he kept the shotgun barrel trained midway between the Welshman and the Indian, ready to switch and take out either target.

'You don't expect me to fall for any more of your little ploys, do you?' he said. He was clearly thinking hard, tilting his head on one side as he did so. He beckoned Kwang to move towards him.

'Shoot them!' Kwang screamed. 'That's an order!'

Yi glared at him. 'In my own time. Communist equality, remember? I'll do this my way.'

Ordering Danny to sit cross-legged on the carpet with his hands on his head, Yi had Lulu and Kwang bind him securely, keeping his gun trained all the while on Terry. Then, when Danny was secure, Yi directed Kwang to disarm Terry, throwing the Browning aside and checking that he had no further weapons.

'There now, that's better, isn't it?' he said. He moved across to Danny and slipped the tomahawk from his belt, grinning at it and shaking his head. 'You really haven't progressed very far from the caveman, have you? How does it work?' Testing the weight of the blade in his fist, he suddenly lashed out at Danny, hitting him in the face with the flat metal. With blood pouring from his nose, Danny tipped over backwards, gasping.

Terry lunged forward, but found himself staring down the shotgun barrel.

'Easy, Dojo, easy.'

Tossing the tomahawk through the window, Yi ordered Kwang to pull back the loose rugs that covered the floor.

'What are you playing at?' Kwang said, irritated by his subordinate's growing lack of respect in front of the two Westerners, but more particularly in front of Lulu.

With his eyes still on Terry, Yi handed the shotgun to Kwang. 'Here. Take this.'

But before releasing his grip on it, he added very slowly, the menace barely concealed: 'You will not use it. I will want it back when I've finished with him.'

Like a scolded child, Kwang took the shotgun and moved to one side, the peeled carpets and rugs laying bare the polished wooden boards underneath.

Yi smiled at Terry. 'Well, Dojo. What are you waiting for? Here I am.'

Slipping off his shoes and socks, Yi padded to the far side of the cleared area. Danny propped himself upright, spitting the blood from his mouth. 'Don't do it, Terry.'

But Terry knew there was no other way. Perhaps he had known since his first meeting with Yi Soong that one day the two of them would have to fight. Not in the detached blur and confusion of a fire-fight, but like this, across a cleared space of open ground, with only their natural weapons of hands and feet.

Keeping his eyes on Yi, he bent down and unlaced

his boots, stuffing his socks inside them. Testing the wooden surface with the balls of his feet, he noted the grip; although the boards were highly polished, there was a good enough purchase. Almost as good as the gym, he thought. But then in the gym he had never fought *sutemi*: to the death.

14

Facing Yi Soong across the cleared sitting-room, Terry couldn't help admiring the man's coolness. He moved with the grace and agility of a cat, a faint, ironic smile on his lips. In his eyes, however, Terry saw only the chill glint of death. Steeling his nerves, he drew on all his experience and training, forcing every other thing from his mind, bringing himself wholly and completely into the present. All the events of the past days since his arrival in Seoul, and the fire and mayhem of the contact battle only minutes before in the vestibule – everything was purged from his mind as he slipped into the total concentration of unarmed combat.

Yi appeared to be in no hurry to start things. He circled almost lazily, but Terry refused to be taken in by it, knowing full well that behind the semblance of carelessness a ruthless killer lay in wait, ready to pounce if given the slightest opening.

Sinking into a *kamae* fighting stance, Terry placed his hands to guard against both lower and upper attacks. Alternating between open-hand blocks and closed fists, he glided to the right, changing his stance and blocks as he went, his eyes following Yi's own counter-clockwise steps. Terry had fought Taekwondo experts at all-styles tournaments before and had learned a healthy respect for their superb kicking techniques. As Yi had twice been the world champion, it was painfully clear to Terry that he couldn't afford a single mistake.

However, although the Taekwondo kicking techniques were the best of any combat style in the world, he had also noticed how their hand techniques were less impressive. Concentrating on stunning leaping and jumping kicks, they often neglected basic hand blows. The result was that, while they were most proficient at the longer ranges, in the closest contact when punches were being traded, they tended to lack the variety of most Japanese karate styles. But more particularly, being used to enjoying the tremendous momentum of vast sweeping kicks, they had also neglected the development of *kime*, the focus that gave even the shortest karate hand blow its devastating power.

Focusing on the middle of Yi's chest, Terry concentrated on observing his every move. With his eyes on the centre, everything was visible, a change of stance, the lifting of a heel or a shift in balance that might signal the start of an attack. But as hard as he tried, Terry saw nothing, Yi was far too proficient to telegraph his intentions.

When the attack came, Terry only just managed to react in time, darting aside as Yi's heel spun past his face, the rush of air stinging his cheek. Jesus, this bastard's fast, he thought. He had known Yi would be good, but not how good.

No sooner had his kick failed to contact, than Yi was the far side of the arena again, his breath as steady as if he hadn't even moved. By comparison, Terry felt like a ton weight, fatally slow.

Wake up, you idle bastard, he thought. Wake up

or die. He knew that he couldn't play Yi at his own game and win. His own style concentrated on strength and power, solid stances and lightning hand blows. When Terry moved it was like a glacier, calm and unstoppable. Sure, he could deliver stunning kicks and rush at an opponent as fast as a cobra, but not with an enemy like Yi. Yi was the master of speed. Somehow Terry had to capitalize on his own strengths, combining them with Yi's weaknesses, to bring the bastard crashing down.

Yi's next attack started as a roundhouse kick, but halfway through it he switched and spun the other way into a jumping back-kick, seeming to defy gravity and hang in mid-air as his foot shot out, catching Terry in the chest and knocking him backwards across the floor. Aware that Yi would be on him the moment he landed, Terry forced himself to ignore the searing pain that shot through his ribcage, rolling to one side and up again to his feet.

Halfway to him to deliver a drop-punch, Yi skidded to a halt and backed off as he saw the speed of Terry's recovery.

'Not bad for an old man,' he mocked. 'Still, we're only just beginning.'

The next moment Yi was hurtling through the air towards Terry, his legs bunching for a flying side kick without having betrayed any sign of preparation, a feat that was only made possible by superb fitness and muscle control. Sliding aside in a *tae sabaki* body shift, Terry used the heels of both palms to deflect the lethal knife edge of Yi's foot, seeing an opening for the first time. As Yi landed and recovered his balance, Terry shot forward with the *kiai* shout welling from the depths of his midriff, firing a punch straight at Yi's waist. Catching the left floating rib, Terry felt it crack and saw the pain register on Yi's face. But even so Yi slipped smoothly out of reach, turning on his heel.

Not this time, Terry thought. If you're expecting me to follow up my attack and walk straight into your counter, you've got another think coming.

'No more smart-arsed remarks?' Terry said.

The last hint of a smile had gone from Yi's face. Instead the skin was drawn tight across the cheekbones and his lips were set in a thin line.

Terry wished with all his might. That's it, lose your temper, Mr bloody Soong. Terry smiled sweetly, changing to *neko ashi*, the cat stance, the rear foot taking his body weight, his front leg poised on the ball of the foot. At the same time his hands came up into a high guard position. Judging the time to be right, he edged forward, shifting his weight to his right foot and raising the left into the cat stance, his hands maintaining the guard at all times.

He was halfway across the floor when Yi struck. Even with a broken rib, the kick came at lightning speed, wheeling round. Despite Terry's block, Yi's foot scythed through and slammed into his cheek. Staggering to keep his balance, Terry reeled backwards, catching the look of triumph in Yi's eyes. Instantly another kick followed, and again Terry's guard was too slow to stop it powering into his stomach. With the breath knocked out of him, Terry shot backwards across the floor, executing the *ibuki* breathing technique to regain his wind, parrying Yi's increasingly ferocious kicks and punches as he did so.

This is it, Terry realized. The horns have been locked and only one of us is going to be standing at the end. Yi's seen I'm hurt and he knows that if he lets me recover he might not get another chance this good. He knows he has to close and finish it now.

It was the chance Terry had been waiting for. Lured on to his prey by the success of his attack, Yi pounded forward with a lashing series of punches. Backing away all the time, Terry blocked some but allowed others through until he was reeling, blood pouring from his nose and mouth.

I can't take much more of this kind of punishment, he thought, willing Yi to give him the only opportunity that could save him. Come on, you bastard, come on.

And then it happened. Blind with rage, the pain from his broken rib jarring through his body, Yi smelt the blood of his opponent and knew that he had him where he wanted. Now was the time to close in with his fists, now that he had the Welshman at his mercy. At last, after so many failures, and after so much loss of face.

Driving forward, intent upon his own attack, Yi ran straight on to Terry's *mae geri* front kick. As the *josokutei* ball of Terry's foot shot forward with the massive power of his hips and leg muscles, it found its path clear and open, straight through Yi's attacking move and drove deep into his solar plexus, Yi's own forward momentum doubling the power of the crippling blow.

Crumpling to the floor, Yi tried to freeze the pain in a superhuman effort to drag himself out of range before it was too late. But it was already too late. Dojo Williams was on top of him. Raining out of the sky like bolts of lightning, Terry's carefully aimed punches dismantled the fallen Korean, one by one destroying his ability to resist, until at last he lay broken and bleeding at Terry's mercy.

Glaring down into Yi's eyes, Terry gripped him by

the blood-soaked collar of his shirt, drawing back his right hand for the *nukite* finger-thrust that would bring instant death.

'This is for all the lads you killed, you bastard,' he said through gritted teeth, spitting out the words with the venom that was consuming him. But as he looked at the ruined creature on the floor, despite the pain and suffering Yi had inflicted, Terry's hand remained quivering at his side, ready and vibrant with death.

As he exhaled slowly, Terry's hatred left him, dissipating with his breath in the stale air of the room, rank with blood, sweat and the smell of cordite. Releasing his grip, he let Yi's head fall back on to the floor, unconscious. Straightening up, he turned towards the doorway, but instead of Kwang and the shotgun, he found himself looking into the soaked, filthy but triumphant face of Major Babs Butler. At his feet, Kwang cowed, holding his head in his hands, blood seeping between the fingers where Babs had clubbed him with the butt of the M60.

'I didn't like to disturb you, old boy. Didn't seem the sensible thing to do.'

Terry fell to his knees, his knuckles cut and bruised, the nauseous taste of blood in his mouth. Michelle had Lulu against the wall, the barrel of a Browning pistol stuck in her back, and beside the shattered windows, the two boys were busy untying Danny. With the situation once more under control, Terry knew that there was only one more thing to do.

'The CIA?'

'Who else is big enough to handle this? The South Koreans think Kwang's clean as a whistle and even once we show them that Yi was here, there's no saying how they'll react.'

Babs came back from the drinks cabinet with a bottle of whisky and some glasses. 'I agree with Terry. Don't forget, we've just taken out a Korean SWAT team. There are bits of policemen all over the place out there. I don't know about you, but I'd rather hand Kwang over to the CIA than to his own erstwhile colleagues, even if we can convince them he's a Commie plant.'

Danny took a long drink of the whisky that Babs was passing around. 'OK. The CIA it is, then. How do we get hold of them? Directory enquiries?'

Terry looked at Babs. 'You must know someone, don't you?'

'Yes, I think I can help. One of my drinking chums is CIA. Of course, he's never been so crude as to say so, but like all these sneaky-beaky fellows he can't resist dropping the occasional hint, especially when he's pissed. I'll give him a call and set up a meeting.'

While Babs went off to search for a phone amid the wreckage of the sitting-room, Danny secured Yi's hands and feet with a length of flex ripped from the back of the television. With another length he then bound Kwang's wrists.

As Michelle similarly tied Lulu, she winked at her. 'I bet the old man does this to you as well, eh?'

Lulu spat at her. 'Slut! Take your hands off me.'

Wiping the saliva from her face, Michelle gripped Lulu by the chin and sneered at her. 'The only difference between you and me is a couple of years of screwing. Where do you think you'd have ended up?'

Lulu jerked her head away. 'Francis, order them to let me go.'

But Kwang was staring morosely out of the window, his eyes glazed and baffled by the turn of events.

'I don't think they'd listen to me. So why don't you just shut the fuck up? There's a good kitten.'

Lulu burst into tears.

Escaping into the fresher air of the courtyard, Terry went to retrieve Andy's body. Babs had told him how he had watched helpless as Yi had slain the young Scot. Terry was glad that he hadn't heard about it until after he had won his fight with Yi; the anger might have destabilized his concentration, giving the vital edge to his opponent and altering the whole balance of skill between the two men.

When he found Andy, he was lying where Yi had left him, face down in the dirt. Rolling him over, Terry closed the eyes and brushed the earth from the face and hair.

'Poor sod,' he said quietly. 'Not much of an innings, was it?' He wondered what combination of circumstances had made Andy Buchan into the fierce, angry man he had been. Tucking his arms under the body, Terry lifted it and carried it back towards the villa. He was surprised to find it strangely light, as if the vanished life-force had somehow contained a weight of its own instead of the insubstantial mix of qualities, traits and quirks that together had composed the dead mercenary.

Laying the body on a sofa in the vestibule, Terry placed the M203 across Andy's chest and folded his arms across it as if on the stone tomb of a knight. Searching around, he discovered in an outhouse some jerrycans of petrol. He dragged them back into the house, opened the caps and emptied the contents on the walls and furnishings.

Babs and the others came down the stairs, bringing Kwang and Lulu with them. At the back, Danny half carried and half dragged the semi-conscious Yi Soong.

'It's on,' Babs said proudly. 'My chum says they would be delighted to get their hands on the bastards. They'll square everything with the South Koreans.'

Danny hoisted Yi Soong over his shoulder like a sack of coal. 'Let's just get rid of this shit soon. I'm going to need a shower to get myself clean after handling him.'

Taking their prisoners across the compound and out through the fence, Danny and Babs set off for the hidden minibus on the far side of the ring of demolitions that had isolated the villa before the main attack. In the vestibule, Terry took two grenades from his pocket and was about to pull the pins when he paused a moment, laid them on a table and disappeared back up the stairs to Kwang's sitting-room. It was a full ten minutes before he returned and took up the grenades again. With a last look at Andy, he strode out into the open air, pulled the pins and lobbed the grenades back into the villa.

Following hard on the twin explosions, a raging fire swept through the building. Halfway up the hillside, Babs and Danny turned to watch the mounting blaze, and the distant figure of Terry jogging away from the compound towards them. In the bowels of the villa, the searing heat detonated the ammunition of Kwang's dead guards like the crackling of Chinese firecrackers. Catching at the wooden terrace, the flames leapt into the sky, firing a shower of sparks above the waving tops of the pines. And lapping at the sofa where Andy lay, they found at last the M203 locked in his stiffening arms, a solitary grenade silent and waiting in the black metal chamber, waiting for the touch of fire to detonate and consume its dead master.

When Joe Lacorde heard what Babs Butler had to say, he had to pinch himself to make sure he wasn't dreaming. Privately he had had his doubts about Francis Kwang from the very first, but the South Koreans had insisted he was one of theirs, so who was he, a relatively minor CIA desk officer, to contradict them? Now here, if he was to be believed, was that drunken old bastard Babs Butler, a washed-out mercenary and professional bar bum, saying that he could hand Kwang to him on a plate. What was more, to clinch it Babs said that he had captured the North Korean agent Yi Soong and could link him with Kwang. It was as good as in the bag. All Joe had to do was arrange the pick-up.

The moment he put the phone down he informed his boss and then got on to Operations. He would need to put a team together immediately if they were going to collect the two Communist double agents before Babs and his friends ran into the South Korean police. If a complete SWAT team had been eradicated Babs could expect little in the way of understanding from the gooks.

With the preliminaries taken care of, Joe sprinted down the corridor of the Seoul office and stuck his head round the door of the Ops room to check that the boys were getting ready to roll. A dozen square-jawed operatives were strapping on shoulder holsters and passing round the Ingrams, the snug close-quarters weapon with the highest rate of fire in the business.

Jeez, Joe thought to himself, they must stamp these guys out of a mould. No matter where they came from, they all ended up looking the same, mean sons of bitches without two scruples to rub together.

Carrying on down the corridor, he slowed to a walk outside his boss's door. He knocked on the frosted glass panel and when he heard the deep, growling voice of Felix Carlson he went in, to find another man already there.

'Oh, sorry, boss,' Joe stammered. 'I just wanted to say that we're almost ready to go.'

'That's fine, Joe. Get the guys into the briefing room. We'll be along in a minute. This is Mr Masterson. He's going to be in charge of the Op.'

Two hours out from the RV, Babs swung the minibus on to the Sokch'o road and reached across to pat Michelle's knee. The daylight was fading and by the time they met the CIA they would be conducting the hand-over in darkness. That suited Babs fine. He felt himself to be a creature of the night, not in any flattering combat sense like Dojo Williams or Danny Grey Wolf, but because that was usually the time that Babs would set off on one of his drinking binges in It'aewan.

Michelle put her hand on his and squeezed it. She was a good girl, Babs thought; they would be very happy together. He was also happy because in addition to the money that he had received from Kwang, he had arranged with Joe Lacorde for a handsome pay-off from the CIA. After all, why shouldn't they reward him and the others for exposing the North Korean plot that had so embarrassed America and delayed the access of the UN inspection teams to the Communist nuclear facilities? OK, so the idea of going direct to the CIA had been Dojo's, but Babs couldn't help feeling a certain pride for having capitalized on the opportunity as a means of making a few more bucks.

In the back of the minibus, Kwang had given up his attempts to bribe Dojo. Keeping his eyes on the road, Babs called over his shoulder.

'Aren't you going to make us any more offers we can't refuse, Francis? I can call you Francis, can't I?' He chuckled merrily.

Kwang sat on the floor with his eyes closed, trying to doze, Lulu curled at his side, her head in his lap.

'Shut up, Butler. You'll always be a loser, however much money you make. You're in this way over your head and you've no idea what you're getting into.'

Danny prodded Kwang with the toe of his boot. 'Is that so? Seems to me you're not doing so great yourself.'

Chuckling to himself, Babs glanced in the rear-view mirror and in the light of a passing car, saw Terry at the back of the minibus. At first he thought he was sleeping, but as the headlights swept across his face, Babs saw that he was gazing out into the dark. The old mind's working away, Babs thought. What a man; after all that's happened, he's still plotting, evaluating, asking himself the essential 'what ifs' that have kept him alive all these years and through all these battles. What if an enemy machine-gun opens up from those bushes on the right? What if I reach the open ground and encounter a minefield? What if a meteorite's on a collision course with planet Earth and I've only got five minutes to save civilization as we know it? Babs smiled. Dojo Williams: he was truly one of a kind. Thank God.

The rest of the journey was made in silence, each person locked into their own thoughts. Yi Soong regained consciousness to find Danny grinning down at him, a firm grip on the end of the flex that bound the Korean's wrists and ankles. Lulu woke and sat up beside Kwang, who was staring out of the windows wide-eyed. Liang and Little Chiao sat behind Michelle, to whom they had stuck throughout the day; leaning together, their heads lolled in sleep as the minibus rolled round the corners. Michelle held the map up whenever Babs needed to check a turning, glancing over, one hand on her knee, the other on the wheel. In the back seat, Terry sat alone. Looking at his watch, he took the Browning from his pocket and checked the mechanism, stuffing the pistol in his waistband when he was happy that there was a round in the barrel and a dozen more in the magazine.

'Looks like party time.'

Babs eased the minibus down a gear, slowing as the headlights cut through the pitch-black of the quiet side road, picking out the isolated lay-by and the four black limousines strung out in line.

'That'll do, Babsy,' Terry called. 'Stop short.'

Pulling to a halt fifty yards from the front limousine, Babs switched off the engine. Terry and Danny kicked open the back door and jumped to the ground, pulling Kwang, Yi, and Lulu after them.

'Give us some light, Babs,' said Terry.

Pulling their prisoners by the scruff of the neck into the corridor of light that appeared, illuminating the lay-by, Terry and Danny went towards the limousines, stopping halfway there. Babs, Michelle and the boys got out of the minibus and came forward to join them, the nine figures casting long shadows towards the opening doors of the limousines.

Babs peered at the faces of the suited men who

sprang out of the sleek black cars and jogged towards them. 'Joe, is that you?'

Joe Lacorde came up and shook Babs firmly by the hand. 'Nice work, Babs baby. You sure as hell know how to play an ace.'

Babs and Michelle laughed with relief and Danny relaxed his grip on Yi as two CIA operatives jerked him away roughly. Another two took hold of Kwang and Lulu.

'Thank you, sir. We'll handle things now.'

Terry let go.

'We'd better relieve you of these,' one of the men said, taking Terry's Browning and Danny's M16. 'Just routine.'

'Fine by me,' Danny said, yawning. It had been one hell of a long day and he felt reassured by the familiar sound of his fellow-Americans, even if they were overly precise and polite. It was the same in the military, he thought. All these guys had a pole up their arse.

When the three prisoners had been removed to one side, another two men got out of the front limousine, stepped into the light and came towards Terry.

'You'll be Mr Williams?'

'Yes.'

'And Danny . . . Grey Wolf?'

Danny's eyes narrowed, catching the tone in the man's voice. 'You got it.' Whoever this man was, he didn't like Indians. But so what? There was nothing new about that. The military was full of bigoted fuckers.

'My name's Eliot Masterson. This is Felix Carlson. You've done a really terrific job here.'

He looked at Yi Soong. 'Well, well. Nice to meet you at last.' Balling his fist, he punched Yi hard in the stomach, dropping him to the ground. ''Cuff the son of a bitch.'

As two of the operatives pinned Yi to the ground and another slapped a pair of handcuffs on him, Masterson went across to Kwang and looked him up and down, shaking his head.

'What a mess. What a sorry fucking mess.'

He took a knife from his pocket and cut the flex binding Kwang's wrists, then turned to Lulu and freed her.

'I'm really sorry about this, Francis.'

Handing Kwang his own Walther pistol, Masterson waved his hand and the remaining CIA operatives surrounded Babs and the others, now unarmed and dumbstruck in the beam from the headlights. Standing in a semicircle, each of the CIA men cradled an Ingram sub-machine-gun in his hands, nursing it close to the hip ready at the touch of a finger to spray their helpless victims with a hail of bullets.

Joe Lacorde shrugged in apology as Babs gaped at him questioningly. 'Orders, Babs baby. You know how it is.'

With the comforting weight and feel of the pistol in his hand, Kwang rubbed his wrists, bruised from the flex. Walking over to the kneeling figure of Yi Soong, he looked down at the large man, humbled and broken at his feet. As Yi's expression turned from puzzlement to understanding and rage, he tried to struggle to his feet, but the hands of his CIA captors held him firmly in place. Without a word, Kwang put the barrel of his Walther to Yi's temple and blew his brains on to the tarmac.

Michelle and Little Chiao started to cry; Liang put a protective arm around them and stared defiantly at the closest of the CIA men. Out of the corner of his eye, Terry signalled Danny to freeze. He had caught the first tell-tale movement that told him Danny Grey Wolf was preparing to go into action and he knew that, against the CIA Ingrams, it would be the last move he ever made.

While one of the CIA men escorted Lulu to the waiting limousines, Kwang and Masterson conferred over the dead body of Yi Soong. After a few moments, they walked across to Terry and the others, but being careful to keep behind the semicircle of Ingrams.

'You've caused us a great deal of inconvenience. You don't know it, but you've screwed up our plans and I'm afraid there's only one thing to be done.'

Stepping back, Kwang signalled to the CIA men, who cocked their weapons and braced themselves to fire.

'Surely you're not going to leave us in suspense,' Terry called out.

'Not at all. I'm going to have you shot.'

'Without an explanation? Don't you think we deserve at least that?'

Kwang turned to Masterson and exchanged a weary smile with the American.

'We really don't have time,' Masterson called across to Terry. 'But seeing as it's the last thing you'll ever hear we'll indulge you. Francis is exactly what he always said he was, a senior officer in the South Korean intelligence service. Some time ago, however, he was recruited by the Communists to work for them. Yi Soong was sent across to act as his number two and, secretly, to keep a check on him. Yi was already a double agent working for Pyongyang; he had been planted in the South Korean special forces some years earlier but he was always a dyed-in-the-wool Commie.'

He glanced at the crumpled body on the floor, a dark pool of viscous liquid spreading from the head.

'But things are never what they seem, are they? I'm sure you can appreciate that now, Mr Williams. Because over and above all of that, Francis was working for us. He was our man inside the South Korean intelligence network, reporting to us on everything the Seoul government intended to do, and then the bonus fell out of the blue when he was suddenly able to give us inside information on the Communists as well.'

Terry shook his head. 'Clever, really clever. A triple agent. So what was the mission to the resort all about and who was Professor Lim Choy?'

Masterson laughed. 'There never was any such person. The North Koreans decided to stage the massacre of their so-called top nuclear physicists and their families to throw the UN off their trail. They reckoned that if they could finger America they could delay UN inspections of their nuclear facilities long enough to complete a bomb.'

'But surely you've helped them achieve that? You've seriously embarrassed your own government, even if they weren't behind the raid.'

Masterson smiled. 'You really don't get it, do you? I don't give a fuck about my own government. Because Francis set up the Korean contract, hired you and executed the mission, he convinced the North Koreans that he was truly their man. He was proving himself. Sort of like a stamp of guarantee. The embarrassment will blow over and we don't reckon the gooks have got the know-how to produce a bomb yet, anyway. But with the Commies fully confident that Francis was loyal to them, we would have had our man at the centre of the intelligence networks of both North and South Korea. Smart, eh? The CIA could have looked forward to a stream of the most tightly guarded secrets from both governments: their nuclear programmes, military strengths and deployments, their sleepers in Seoul and Pyongyang.'

Terry stared at him steadily. 'And what do you get out of it?'

'What do you think?' Masterson answered. 'Promotion to the top of the most powerful organization in the world.'

'And the innocent political prisoners who were butchered at the resort? The men that Babs hired in good faith but who were double-crossed, tortured and killed?'

'Small fry. Dross. Disposable waste. Sad by-products of our modern society.'

'I think I get the message. But why can't you leave Kwang in place and let us go?'

Masterson and Kwang swapped smiles. 'You must think us very stupid. After your conversion of Mr Kwang's country home into a latter-day Valhalla, I think even the North Koreans would feel the need to ask awkward questions. Even they might suspect that Francis had been compromised.'

'You blew my cover, Dojo,' Kwang added.

'And as for letting you go on your way,' Masterson cut in, 'I don't think that even merits a reply. I'd love to go on talking to you all night, and in other circumstances you're a man who could have worked for me, but not now. I'm afraid the lot of you are going to have to join your comrades in your own little twilight of the gods right here and now. You see,

Mr Williams, you've fucked up a seriously brilliant master plan.'

Terry glanced around at the dark trees beyond the reach of the harsh white beams from the minibus and the figures silhouetted in their glare. When he spoke, it was not with the voice of a man who was about to die.

'You've no idea just quite how much.'

In the CNN newsroom in Seoul, Mike Adams could hardly believe his luck. After years as an investigative reporter he had acquired a nose for a story. It was like a sixth sense. But to sniff out a lead took contacts, and Mike had always been one to recognize a good contact. It seemed to him that conflicts attracted two kinds of men, reporters and mercenaries, and of all the mercenaries he had ever met, none was as worthwhile a contact as Terry Williams. In Africa Terry had given Mike the tip-off when a guerrilla leader had wanted to air his views to the press, and later in the same war he had enabled him to be the first Western reporter to enter the liberated capital.

So when Terry had called him earlier in the day from some place in Sorak-san and given him the gist of what could be on the cards, he had known it would be worth following up. But in his wildest dreams he had never imagined it would be this good. It had been a hell of a scramble to get the low-light cameras and the directional mikes in place, but the technicians had done a great job as usual and he was receiving every word and every picture on his monitors as clear as crystal. It was dynamite.

Switching to the intercom, he spoke into his mike.

'Jerry, please say you're getting all this.'

Via satellite link from head office in Atlanta came the affirmative answer, preceded by a long whistle of admiration.

'Jesus, Mike. You bet. We're putting it out live now.'

As the world's leading twenty-four-hour news channel, CNN relied on the hottest news items from around the world as and when they happened. Broadcasting live across the globe, Ted Turner's empire had made Atlanta the communications centre of the world.

'Ted'll love you for this.'

Mike eased back in his chair, hands behind his head, a grin spreading from ear to ear.

'Go for it, Dojo. Go for it.'

In the lay-by, Masterson had gone very quiet. Even in the glow of the minibus headlights Terry could see him get visibly paler before his eyes. It had started when one of the CIA operatives had called Felix Carlson back to his limousine to take an urgent call. Felix was glad to get away from the unpleasant scene being enacted in the headlights. He had been pretty pissed off when Masterson had breezed into his office in the first place, arrogantly taking charge, but more particularly he had been uneasy with the whole concept of the operation.

When he came back from the limousine, Felix's jaw was set in concrete, his eyes as hard as ball-bearings. Drawing Eliot and Kwang to one side, he relayed the drift of the grilling he had just received from the director, who had been sitting at home in Washington in front of his television, just in time to see Francis Kwang commit murder, with Eliot Masterson, one of the CIA's high-fliers, an accessory. What was more, Eliot had outlined a completely unauthorized operation to the American public, including the President, whom he had told, obliquely, to go fuck himself: and all on prime-time TV!

After relieving Kwang of his Walther and Masterson of his ID card and passport, Felix detailed four CIA men to escort them back to the limousines, where Lulu, unaware of the turn of events, was getting impatient and wishing they would simply get on with the execution and head back to Seoul.

Leaning on the bonnet of the minibus, Babs and Danny listened to Terry with amazement.

'When I heard that Mike was in Seoul, I made a note of his number. Just before I set fire to Kwang's villa I gave him a ring, and you know Mike: anything for a good scoop.'

But Babs was working himself into a rage. 'You mean you let me believe I was about to die while knowing all the time I was on candid bloody camera?'

'It had to look convincing,' Terry explained. 'You're not the world's greatest actor, Babs.'

Babs swelled with anger. 'Why, you . . .'

Strolling up behind him, Joe Lacorde placed a big friendly paw on Babs's shoulder.

'Babs, baby. No hard feelings, eh?'

With a grace and speed never seen before, Babs spun on his heel with fist flying, laying his CIA drinking partner out cold.

A week later, sitting up in his hospital bed, Alex Leitner was feeling better than he had done for years. That morning the doctors had given him a clean bill of health and to complete his recovery he had told his employers to get lost.

He had been watching the TV on the day of the famous CNN broadcast, his heart monitor bleeping forlornly at the bedside, a cheerless hospital meal untouched on the tray. Moments later, the nurses had come rushing in to find Alex leaning back on his pillows, roaring with laughter. He even tried to send out for a bottle of champagne but the ward sister intercepted his message in time.

His miracle recovery had started that same day when his superiors had rung offering him the job vacated by Eliot Masterson. Deliberating for all of two seconds, Alex had said a polite no thank you and hung up before his mouth ran away with him. Whatever his faults, Masterson had been right about one thing: it was time Alex retired. He'd had enough of jogging in the park when he'd rather be tucking into a hamburger and fries, and he'd done enough arse-licking to wear out a whole yard of tongue. No. From now on he was going to devote himself to his family.

Picking up a copy of *Time*, he turned to the lead article and began to read once more about the intricacies of the North Korean plot and their submission at last to the UN nuclear inspection teams. *Newsweek*, on the other hand, devoted its own lead to the shake-up in the CIA initiated by the President in the wake of the renegade operation.

Pushing through the window blinds, the sun warmed Alex to the core. But the greater warmth was generated by his own expectations of the catch he would land at Chesapeake Bay when he and Stephen went fishing at the weekend.

*   *   *

Burning down the expressway, Babs sped the minibus towards Tonghae. He had been meaning to turn it in and get one of the new red Toyotas with the pop-up headlights, but he and Michelle had decided to hang on to the larger vehicle until after the skiing trip.

Glancing in the rear-view mirror, he smiled at her attempts to get Liang and Little Chiao to speak English. She could hardly speak it herself. But there would be time to take care of that now. In fact, there would be time and money for everything now. Kwang's cheque had been good, even if the man himself was rotting in jail awaiting trial for both murder and treason. In the event that he was released before the end of his life, he would probably find the North Koreans waiting for him, patiently biding their time to exact their own grim retribution.

It was funny how things turned out, Babs thought. Things rarely ended up the way you expected or initially hoped, but somehow one usually found a way of living. And that was what it was all about after all, living. Michelle, himself, the boys. It might not be the family he had dreamed of having, on all those endless lonely, drunken evenings in It'aewan, but it was a family nevertheless. His family.

Sitting up behind the wheel, Babs pulled in his stomach. He would have to be more responsible from now on. With other people depending on him, he owed it to them. He owed it to himself as well. After the sort of life he'd lived, it was a miracle he was still around to make any resolutions at all. But then, looking at his new family in the back of the minibus, Babs realized that life was all about miracles.

With the Sea of Japan and the island of Hokkaido

behind it, the United Airlines jumbo started on the long trans-Pacific haul to Seattle. Sinking still deeper into his first-class seat, Terry checked his watch to see if he would have time to nip upstairs to the bar before the start of the in-flight movie. Deciding he couldn't be bothered, he rang for the hostess and ordered another cognac. On the other side of the spacious cabin, Danny was sleeping, his long legs sprawled across the ample expanse of carpet. There had been a difficult moment at the airport when the security scanner had picked up his tomahawk, but Danny had reluctantly agreed that it could travel in the hold and they had made the flight only minutes before departure.

Terry wasn't sure how long he would spend in Montana, taking up Danny's offer of a hunting trip. A walk in the wilderness seemed about the daftest thing imaginable after what they had been through, but it would be a novel experience to go to sleep at night under the stars and not to have to worry about putting out Claymores, sentry posts or clearing patrols. Perhaps he'd return Danny's hospitality afterwards, but a wet weekend in Swansea probably wouldn't have quite the same appeal, although a Blackfoot Sioux Indian with a real tomahawk would go down a treat at The Bull.

At least Terry would have enough money now to fix the karate dojo. He could even ditch it altogether, although he wouldn't want to disappoint the kids. Either way, he had resolved to give Liz a call when he got back. They could go away somewhere nice and quiet. Maybe Llanberis Pass; there was some great rock climbing there. Terry sighed. Perhaps Paris would be a better idea.

With his cognac in his hand, he gazed lazily out

of the window, watching the billowing roof of white cloud passing beneath. At the front of the cabin the screen flickered into life with a news bulletin before the movie. A reporter was crouching behind a wall somewhere in South America, bullets flying overhead as guerrillas were driven out of the presidential palace that they had stormed earlier in the day. Summing up, the reporter concluded that the people's liberation struggle was likely to go on for many months yet.

Unable to keep his eyes open, Terry drained his glass and leant back, letting the fierce, seductive liquid pull him the last few steps towards sleep. The drone of the engines hummed in his ears, mingling with the closing words of the reporter.

'One thing is for certain, arms and equipment will never be enough. Without proper training the Liberation Front is doomed to a long and difficult struggle.'

Terry pulled off his headphones and settled back. Arms and equipment were never enough. How often would people have to learn the same old lesson? In the end it always came down to the man. The quality of the individual, his training and his will. It had been the case when Alexander the Great crossed into Asia and it would be the same if men ever dodged and dived between the stars. And filing away the name of the war-torn Latin-American republic, Terry allowed himself to sleep.

OTHER TITLES IN SERIES FROM 22 BOOKS

Available now at newsagents and booksellers
or use the order form opposite

All at £4.99 net

22 Books offers an exciting list of titles in these series. All the books are available from:

Little, Brown and Company (UK) Limited,
PO Box 11,
Falmouth,
Cornwall TR10 9EN.

Alternatively you may fax your order to the above address.
Fax number: 0326 376423.

Payments can be made by cheque or postal order (payable to Little, Brown and Company) or by credit card (Visa/Access). Do not send cash or currency. UK customers and BFPO please allow £1.00 for postage and packing for the first book, plus 50p for the second book, plus 30p for each additional book up to a maximum charge of £3.00 (seven books or more). Overseas customers, including customers in Ireland, please allow £2.00 for the first book, plus £1.00 for the second book, plus 50p for each additional book.

NAME (BLOCK LETTERS PLEASE) ....

....

ADDRESS ....

....

....

☐ I enclose my remittance for £_____

☐ I wish to pay by Access/Visa

Card number

☐☐☐☐ ☐☐☐☐ ☐☐☐☐ ☐☐☐☐

Card expiry date

☐☐ ☐☐